The Outcast Oracle

For Carol + Paul –
With many thanks –
Enjoy "Charlie!"

Laury A. Egan

The Outcast Oracle

Laury A. Egan

Humanist Press
Washington, DC

HUMANIST PRESS
1777 T Street NW
Washington, DC, 20009
(202) 238-9088
www.humanistpress.com

Printed book ISBN: 978-0-931779-36-7
Ebook ISBN: 978-0-931779-37-4

Quotations from the King James Bible courtesy of
www.biblegateway.com

Editor: Luis Granados

Cover design by Laury A. Egan and Lisa Zangerl
Cover photograph by Laury A. Egan

Acknowledgments

Heartfelt thanks to poet Karla Linn Merrifield, whose home and environs on Lake Ontario inspired me to write this book. We spent many hours discussing our secularist/naturalist views and our writing, laughing, and dining well, often with the delightful companionship of her husband, Roger Weir.

Luis Granados provided excellent editorial suggestions and welcome enthusiasm; Lisa Zangerl was very helpful in assisting in the text design and formatting; Vicki DeVico provided brilliant PhotoShop magic on the cover. Deepest gratitude to Humanist Press for publishing this book and to the American Humanist Association for their important contributions to free thought and enlightened discourse.

Thanks to Maggie Oberle, who kindly posed for the cover photograph, and to her mother Carol; to my favorite fellow curmudgeons, Pat Barker Cooper and Ann Green, and to dear Dwight Wilson.

And with great appreciation to my parents, Agnes Ricks Egan and Richard Patrick Egan, who wisely encouraged me to think for myself about religion, to follow my own path regardless of where it leads, and to value creative endeavors above all other pursuits.

This book is dedicated to Ruth E. Stagg, with love and gratitude.

The Outcast Oracle

- 1 -

"Charlene Beth Whitestone, you are a darned fool!"

I'm standing in a little clearing surrounded by laurel bushes, shouting at myself and kicking rocks. This is what I do after a bad day at school, and today was nearly a disaster.

Normally, I keep my diary in the secret compartment of my bedroom closet, but I brought it to the school library to transfer short story notes from the diary to my composition book. I was trying to do this without anyone noticing, but one of the girls, Peggy, grabbed the diary, ran over to a crowd of my classmates, and started reading aloud. I jumped to my feet and chased her around the table, finally ripping the book out of her hands. All the kids were heehawing like a bunch of donkeys. My face got hot and I wanted to whack Peggy or else disappear, neither of which I could do because the librarian came when she heard the ruckus. I sat down, feeling miserable and yet incredibly lucky. Lucky because the first entry didn't contain any of our family's secrets.

A little breeze stirs the laurel leaves and brings me back to the sad task at hand. I finger the embossed gold "1958" on the cover and sigh. I don't want to part with my diary because it's the last present my mother gave me, but I must. Gently, I lay the book on the ground and surround it with stones from the creek bed, recalling that I started writing entries in October, two days before my fourteenth birthday. That afternoon I came home from school and my parents had gone. Vanished without a goodbye. Grandpa promised they'd return in the spring like robins, but the robins are bobbing around the green grass and no red Chevy truck is in sight.

It's a toss up if I miss Daddy. He was quick with the belt and heavy on the liquor. Sometimes he could be nice—playing catch or taking me fishing—but he was more likely to get mad if I threw the ball over his head or got my hook snagged. Then big trouble would start. Unless Grandpa or Mama were around to help, he'd hit me until I could escape or his anger got stuck on someone else. I don't know why Mama fell for him—maybe because she likes her liquor, too. Whatever reason, she never married him, though

3

Daddy pretends she did and throws a fit whenever he sees "Whitestone" on my school papers instead of his last name, Cullem.

Mama comes from good stock, educated folk like Grandpa C.B.—that's short for Charles Barrett Whitestone, whom I'm named after. Grandpa has some unusual ways, but he thinks Daddy is a real scoundrel and doesn't understand why Mama left with him last October, especially because she loves me, or so Grandpa says every night before bed. I think she does care, but the love is mixed up with the bad stuff inside her and the need to wander.

Ever since I was little, there would be times when she'd work herself into a lather, talking fast and staying up all night. When these excitements took hold, Mama would disappear for a week or so, spinning all her energy out into the world until she'd find her way home, dead-tired. If one of her spells met up with one of Daddy's drinking bouts, they'd carry on like two wildfires until Mama's heat became too much and she'd get in the truck and fly away. When this happened, Grandpa and I would climb in his car and go to Rochester or Niagara Falls until Daddy sobered up. All in all, I'm not eager to have Daddy return. Mama is a different story.

The diary holds many memories, probably best erased. From now on, I will only write about things I imagine and places that are different from my home of Butztown, New York, which is near Lake Ontario. There's not much to Butztown. A general store, filling station, bank, bar, school, and post office. Most of the people are farmers who grow corn, soybeans, apples, grapes, and raise livestock. Neighbors don't tend to congregate except for school activities and church on Sunday, which is when Grandpa takes center stage.

On the face of things, my grandfather appears to be a man of God—the Right Reverend Whitestone. I don't know why he glued on "Right" in front of "Reverend," but since he says he's always correct about everything, I suppose it's accurate. He has a diploma in a black frame to prove he's a minister or, rather, a fake diploma created in our basement. Because there isn't much competition in the religious market around here—just a small Methodist church serviced by a circuit preacher and a Catholic church in Brockport—Grandpa has lots of customers. He also gets to be tax-free, though Grandpa isn't one to pay taxes in the first place.

Anyhow, on Sundays or when someone dies or a kid needs dunking in holy water—supplied by me from the kitchen sink—

Grandpa holds forth in the "chapel," a large downstairs parlor we expanded on the right side of the house. Eight rows of folding chairs are arranged facing the front of the room, and a couple of Virgin Mary and Jesus paintings are hung around, which Grandpa bought cheap at a Chinese auction. He made the altar cross himself, painted it with gold, saying it was rustic but heartfelt, and winked right after he said this so I knew he was joking. At a busy service, sometimes he has a full house of forty, and sometimes—during hunting season or when the fish are running—the service is mostly attended by women and children. He doesn't care who comes so long as they contribute.

Because I've recorded details of C.B.'s religion business and other shady deals, this is the main reason why I must destroy the diary. I sigh again and spread open the book. After striking a match, I light the gilt-edged pages, puffing on the tiny flame until the fire is licking orange around the white leather and turning the brass lock to a greenish black. The lined pages lift and curl, burning up five months of painful words and heartache. As the smoke swirls through the tree branches, I sit back, relieved that I've done the right thing by Grandpa.

I toss some twigs on the fire, listen to them snap, smell the sweet smoke, and think about my short story. Though I probably won't risk it, I'd love to make one of my characters into a moonshiner because a writer should write about what he or she knows best, and I am fairly knowledgeable about making corn whiskey because it's one of Grandpa's other profitable enterprises. From a little building tucked in a grove of willow trees just off the driveway, we sell the hooch—or rather we're supposed to say my Daddy does in order to protect Grandpa's good name and moral authority.

Last fall, my cousins built the place. It's as big as two times me in one direction and two and a half times me in the other. I actually had to lie down on the grass for the measurements. My cousins Buck and Corey thought this was funny until they realized they also had to dig below ground—my height plus some maneuvering room. Grandpa insisted this had to be done in order to create a hidey-hole for our one-quart Mason jars. After the boys built shelves all around inside the "basement" and placed a ladder so I could get down to the wares, they covered it with boards except for a hatch hidden under a red oriental carpet, upon which we keep a stack of Bibles that Grandpa sells when someone is in need of enlightening. One of my jobs—and I have many—is to get

5

the corn liquor for customers since Daddy's gone and Grandpa isn't so quick on the ladder these days. He's 76 years old and suffering bad from rheumatism. I also have to pay the bills and keep the books, adding up columns of numbers so he knows who owes money. Some of his customers run short of cash when they forget to earn a living because they enjoy the moonshine too much. After a month of credit, if a fellow hasn't paid up, Buck and Corey pay the man a visit.

Grandpa has some legal businesses, too. The corn syrup for the hooch is supplied by Mr. Carter, who leases Grandpa's fields and gives us corn, beans, tomatoes, squash, and a pumpkin or two round Halloween. And Mr. Cossantino rents land on the ridge above the lake for a vineyard. In the autumn, he lets me stomp grapes, which turns my toes purple. Grandpa prefers I stay off our moonshine and keep to Mr. Cossantino's wine or Chivas Regal—Grandpa's drink of choice every night and sometimes before the sermon on Sunday. He says it helps him see God, though I've never seen a trace of God when I take a nip. Once, Grandpa caught me taking a swig before school and told me that was no way to start the day. I did it because I'm often bored, and the liquor slows my brain down. I'm no genius or anything, but the guidance counselor told Grandpa and Mama that I'm very smart. I scored 144 on the IQ test, higher than everyone else by a good measure. Of course, I don't put much stock in those things. I probably do well because I read all the time and because I have to learn five new words every day and use them in one sentence. It's a ton of work, but if I want to be a writer, I need a good vocabulary. Grandpa also doesn't tolerate laziness of any kind, though I notice he lays about most of the day, smoking cigars and scheming, which is what he does best according to him.

Thinking about Grandpa, I realize I'm late to mind the Hooch Shop. I kick the ashes apart and dump some dirt on top, then knock the stones into the stream.

—

"Charlie!"

Through the shed's single window, I see Grandpa ambling down the dirt road toward me, his black cane steadying his side-to-side gait. He's wearing his brown, broad-brimmed fedora, khaki pants, a blue sports jacket, and a white shirt under a blue wool sweater that's fraying at the V-neck where he rests his left hand when he thinks. For Butztown, he's considered well-dressed. Most folks wear jeans or Carhartt pants, sweatshirts over flannel shirts, and yellow leather boots except to church or school.

"What, Grandpa?" I step outside the Hooch Shop.

"Ah, there you are." He sighs and sits in the green metal chair whose orange rust has eaten most of the paint away. The chair doesn't care much for his weight, but it holds him. Grandpa isn't that tall, but he has a big belly that sticks out in front like a shelf. "How's business this fine Friday afternoon, Charlie?"

"Good. Guess the warm weather brings out our customers. Sold four quarts."

"Sixteen dollars."

"No, sir. Fourteen. Dusty Tiebock was short." I feel around in my pocket. "And forty-nine cents. I wrote everything down in the book."

Grandpa C.B. shakes his head and looks at me with sharp eyes through his round spectacles. "Dusty owes us, right?"

"Yes, sir, he does. I told him."

"Best we can do until next week."

I know what this means, and Dusty does, too, because I explained what would happen if he didn't pay up. "Do you want the money?"

"Yes. It isn't prudent to leave it lying about."

I place the cash in his hand, which is all crisscrossed with worry lines—that's what Grandpa calls them. His knobby fingers close around the money.

"Oh," he says, "that reminds me. We're on 'P' today, aren't we?"

"Yes, sir, we are. Prudent, preamble, pontificate, prostitute, and polecat. Those are my words. So let's see. I will begin with a preamble about a prostitute who smelled like a polecat and wasn't prudent about her affections with a minister who liked to pontificate on the purity of love—I threw in another 'P' word as an extra."

"Ha! You're a clever girl!"

I give him a big grin. "I thought you'd like the part about the minister pontificating."

"Indeed," replies Grandpa. "A very useful word around here. If you don't watch out, you may turn into a pontificator yourself."

"I don't think I'm cut out for that."

Grandpa pokes my arm, rises out of the chair, steadies his weight with a wide stance, and pockets the bills and coins. "You never know what you'll be good at until you try. That's sagacious advice, my dear. Who knows, one day you might become an oracle of wisdom." He smiles at this thought and pats me on the shoulder. "Now best keep an eye out."

"I will." I know what I'm keeping an eye out for.

Grandpa shuffles off, singing a hymn or rather several hymns running together. It doesn't matter much because all hymns sound the same. A lot of Lords and Gods and Jesus Christs and Hallelujah this and Alleluia that. A bunch of Amens for punctuation.

After a quick peek down the road in both directions, I go back into the shop and sit at my wooden desk. It came from an old schoolhouse and smells of pencils and dusty books. Initials are carved and inked on its top by pupils who wanted to leave their mark on something. Considering Butztown, this may be the only place their names will ever appear except on their tombstones. The desk has a slot for my pen and pencil, a round hole for an inkwell, and an opening in front where I store the accounts ledger and my composition notebook. To my left, near the window, is a row of books and my well-used Merriam-Webster's. From this shelf, I pull out an ancient copy of *Oliver Twist* that Grandpa said I should read for my edification. I've found this to be true, though looking up all the words I don't know in the dictionary is a lot of work. The book is amazing, however, especially the characters. Sometimes I pretend I'm the Artful Dodger and C.B. is Fagin, though it's a stretch imagining the cornfields of Butztown as foggy London.

I'm reading for a bit, in deep with my new English friends, and don't hear the car coming down the dirt road until a door shuts. I jump and quickly check the window. There stands Billy Shackrack in his blue uniform, staring at me from under the brim of his hat, hands on his hips above his holster and the black belt full of police gizmos.

I raise my hand in a little wave and call out through the open window, "Afternoon, Sheriff."

"Afternoon, Charlie."

He takes this as an invitation to walk around the building. I only have seconds to kick the rug over the hatch and move my chair on top before his big body fills up the narrow door.

"C.B. around?"

"No, sir. Well, I mean, he was awhile ago."

"Writing his Sunday sermon?"

The way he says this doesn't require an answer so I shrug.

Sheriff Shackrack's eyes get all slitty. I can't read what he's thinking, but it crosses my mind that he's looking at me as a woman, although no one has looked at me that way before.

He touches the tip of his black boot to two Bibles on the floor. "Still selling the Good Book?"

"Yes, sir. We sold several today and a pamphlet written by Soren K. Swenson. He's a professor of theology at Southern Minnesota Seminary." I pat a pile of pamphlets written and printed by Grandpa.

Shackrack nods at my ledger so I open it and point to the newest entries. Every purchase of a Mason jar is marked as a sale of a religious pamphlet; two jars equal a Bible; a gallon is a deluxe Bible. When we actually sell a Bible, we list it as the real thing. It's a convoluted system, one I don't explain to the sheriff.

He glances at the book, then laughs, not at me or my neat numbers, but at something else. I don't like the sound of it. He turns and takes a few steps around the tiny space, picking up a jar of raspberry preserves—another one of our lucrative endeavors along with strawberry jam and pickled onions, all canned by yours truly—and then sets it on the shelf. "Well, all right, I guess." He acts like he's going to leave but doesn't. "Your parents ever come back from tending that sick relative?"

I shake my head.

"No loss about your daddy," he says, tossing me a mean wink. Then he takes another slow gander around the room before he heads for the door.

I don't like this comment, although I feel the same way about my father. I let it pass, however, because the less time I'm around the sheriff, the better.

After Shackrack drives off—not to the house to look for Grandpa but through the grove of willow trees toward the road—Harley Garfoyle rushes out of the bushes. He's in a sweat, worried the police car will return.

"Gimme two quarts, will you?" He stands outside the open window and plunks a five and three ones on the windowsill.

"Having a party?"

He removes his red bandana and swipes at the grime and perspiration on his face and neck. "No. Just stocking up."

Harley is one of our best clients, though he's looking more and more like an alkie every day: red nose and splotchy cheeks and a way of holding his eyes in one place too long, as if it hurts to move them around.

I stick the money in my pocket, shove aside the box of Bibles, the chair and rug, and lift up the hatch. As I descend the ladder, I smell the damp earth. It's like being in a coffin underground, a creepy feeling I get upon entering this space I call Worm Heaven.

When I surface with the Mason jars, Harley grins like I'm handing him gold bricks. Some men are like that when they love the liquor too much.

"Thanks, Charlie." He hides the bottles in a paper bag and takes off through the fields.

I sit down by the window, watching in case the sheriff decides to pay another visit.

- 2 -

After the mess I made cooking the trout, which is annoying on account of they have too many bones, I did the dishes and cleaned up. Now I'm in my room working on the assignment Grandpa gave me. He said I'm ready to start learning the sermon-writing business and have to complete three typed pages before bedtime so he can make a decision as to whether they're acceptable for tomorrow's service. I asked him what I should write about, and Grandpa told me anything on the subject of sin is best. People like to feel guilty, and the guiltier they feel, the more they come to our chapel to repent, and the more money they drop on the plate.

So far, I have sin divided into categories. I decide not to mention drinking because that might hurt our hooch business. Telling falsehoods? A jim-dandy! I know a lot about that.

—

"Here you go, Grandpa." I place the pages on the table beside him. "All about lying and twisting the truth."

He folds his newspaper and tucks it between his thigh and the arm of the chair. "Did you give examples?"

"Yes, sir, I did."

"Good girl." He leans forward and plants a kiss on my cheek. I smell scotch on his breath and smoke from his cigar. "I will peruse your literary endeavor immediately."

He removes his spectacles, cleans them slowly with a handkerchief, and then takes my sermon in hand. I settle in the corner of the plaid couch across from him. Before long, Grandpa is chuckling away, shaking his head side to side, as he turns the pages where they're resting on his belly. "First rate," he says, wiping his eye with his finger. "You do take after me!"

I consider this quite a compliment because Grandpa is smart. He attended the University of Pennsylvania and also spent a year at business school.

"Thanks, Grandpa."

"Indeed, Charlie, you shall be on deck tomorrow."

"You mean it's really okay?"

"Absolutely. As written. You have an exquisite gift for hyperbole, my dear."

We'd done *hyperbole* under "H" words, though prior to looking it up, I thought it was some kind of growth on a tree. One of those words that doesn't look or sound like what it is. Grandpa C.B. smiles at me. He also likes to exercise his vocabulary with his flock, as he calls them, because the less they understand what he's saying, the more impressed they'll be. In my sermon, I threw in some multi-syllable words such as prevarication, confabulation, and duplicity, though I spread them around so no one will think I'm being uppity.

—

The next day, Grandpa is in the basement before breakfast, practicing his sermon by tape recording it on the Wollensak. I think he does this because he's in love with his voice, but he says it's no different than an actor working on his performance. After breakfast, we dress for the service. Grandpa wears his black suit and clerical shirt with white collar. I follow him into the chapel decked out in my black velvet dress with the ivory lace collar, white knee-high stockings, and Mary Jane shoes—as gussied as I can get.

People arrive and Grandpa begins sermonizing. After half an hour, he escorts me to the podium. It smells of lemon oil on account of Grandpa polishes the wood twice a month. After some throat-clearing, he says in a round, deep voice, "My friends, this morning you have the ultimate privilege. My granddaughter has seen the light and the light is now within her."

I'm thinking that it's one thing for me to be a liar pontificating about the evils of lying and quite another thing to claim spiritual enlightenment. Perspiration pops out on my forehead as I place my notes in front of me. Everyone is staring at me like I'm the Virgin Mary. I manage a tiny smile, then knit my eyebrows together and gather up all the seriousness I can, reminding myself to talk slowly and pretend my voice is on a rollercoaster.

"Lying is a sin," I begin. "Now most people think a lie is a small thing. Maybe you lie to protect someone's feelings. Telling them they look beautiful when they're a real dog. But then can you imagine some poor soul who keeps being told they're gorgeous when they're not? I ask you: Where will that lead? To vanity for sure! But that's another sin for another sermon."

I pause here to see if everyone is with me. Folks are nodding, so I figure I'm doing fine. "Now what sort of people lie? Weak weasels who choose prevarication over truth. People who want to puff themselves up to look good or to hide something wicked they've done." I open Grandpa's Bible and enjoy the secret humor of what I read next: "From Psalm 101:7: 'He that worketh deceit shall not dwell within my house; he that telleth lies shall not tarry in my sight.'"

I risk a quick glance at Grandpa, who maintains a serious expression even though last night he laughed at this line when he saw it in my sermon. I then throw in a few other passages that Grandpa suggested. These go over big. There's a lot more head-nodding going on, husbands checking with their wives and vice versa. I launch into the nearby areas of deceit, deception, and duplicity—the three "Ds" I call them. When I finish, the silence staggers me with its loudness. I don't know what to do and suddenly feel like a fool. No, worse yet, a lying fool.

"Thank you, Charlene," says Grandpa. He takes my hand, gives it a squeeze. His green eyes, which are the same color as mine, are sparkling. I can see he's trying not to smile so I keep my face straight. The congregation is whispering and looking impressed. When the collection plate goes round, nearly everyone gives double.

—

After the service, Grandpa spoke with Mrs. Croydon, who just lost her sister. He often devotes time to his parishioners if they have family problems or personal concerns.

Later, when he enters the kitchen, Grandpa looks tired, but when he sees me, his expression changes to pride. "Charlie, you are wiser than your years. You did a superb job this morning!" He reaches in his pocket and hands me a twenty-dollar bill. "Put this somewhere safe," he says and walks into the living room to his chair.

By this, Grandpa means in the ground. All around the property he has tin boxes buried, like he's the Alexander Hamilton of squirrels. He believes this is better than storing money in the house because houses can burn or the police can search and find the money. Grandpa has shown me where his tins are located, and I have two boxes hidden near a willow tree containing $142.57. I also have a checking account with $200 in it, which Grandpa started in December after applying for my Social Security card— just in case, he said. I never asked him what he meant, but since my parents left, I don't trust the world like I used to and maybe Grandpa feels the same way. Sometimes I wake up at night and feel the weight of worry like some big boulder lying on my chest. I think about my future and where I'm going, but everything looks pitch black out there in front of me. Grandpa says our lives sort themselves out. This isn't more of his religious talk—he doesn't believe one word of his sermons any more than I do. But I'm not so positive that he's right. I think it sounds kind of lazy to me, trusting in fate. Seems like a smarter plan is to make things happen rather than sitting around in an easy chair waiting for good fortune to come and smack you alongside the head.

After I make lunch, eat, and change clothes, I walk to the willow tree. Its long arms are swaying in the wind like a hula dancer. I stand and take in the smell of spring, which smells green if a color can have a smell. There's a little dampness on the breeze left over from last night's rain. I kneel on the moss, feeling moisture soak into my jeans, and begin digging with my mother's trowel. About six inches down, I see the top of my treasure box, an old Union Leader red tobacco tin with a gold eagle painted on the front. Inside, next to the money, is a photograph of my mother with Grandpa standing next to her, holding my mother's hand. He's wearing a dark suit and looks handsome. Although the photo is in black and white, they both have reddish-gold hair, green eyes, high cheekbones, and narrow faces. My mother is pretty—at least she was before the drink and craziness ate into her. Grandpa says I take after her and not my father, but I don't think I'm in her league or ever will be. All in all, our family doesn't look like we belong in Butztown, except for my Daddy and his people, the Cullems, who are a common bunch. Some years back, all of my father's relatives moved away within two weeks, probably because of some serious trouble they found themselves in. No one knows where they went, which was probably intentional. Daddy is the best of their lot and can be a real sweet-talker when he's sober. Even so, I have never been able to understand what attracted Mama to him, but then again, much of what Mama does is nonsensical.

The Cullems' disappearance might have put the notion in Daddy's head to escape this place. Mama was prone to leaving in general, doing it often but not for long, but I guess this time she decided to stick with my father, although going with him is heading in the wrong direction, wherever that is. She's smarter and better looking than Daddy, which made him jealous when they went into town and men flirted with her even when she didn't encourage them. Daddy has always been quick to pick fights, sometimes even giving her a lick or two, though Mama is likely to give it right back, which she did on a few occasions when he was after me. One time she landed a shovel on his head after he slapped me in the face. Considering their history, I expect they will part ways eventually. All the screaming and yelling I've heard over the last years make for more hating than two people can do and still love each other. My secret hope is that my mother will return, that she'll be sane and done with drinking.

I kiss Mama's picture and wish she were here beside me. Mama could tell a fine yarn and make me laugh when I was sad or fly into a whirl of excitement, sometimes at midnight, insisting we bake a five-layer cake with orange and purple icing or a upside-down cake that's right-side up. And when she was calm in between moods, she'd sit on the porch and sing songs, or we'd make up a play, creating dialogue as we went along. Those were the best moments, but there were other sides to her that were upsetting and strange.

I sigh and feel lonely. Maybe I should try to make friends at school again? The problem is bringing them home, what with Grandpa's ways and the fact that my parents are gone and we have to keep that kind of hush-hush. A few years ago, I invited a girl named Kathy to come fishing. We took a picnic lunch and set off for the lake. Everything was fine until we returned to the house. Right off I could see Mama was working herself into an agitated spell, so I hurried Kathy out the door. I guess she thought I didn't like her after that. A worse disaster happened with Nan and Franny, twins who live on the far side of Butztown. They asked me to their house to listen to records. We had a great time until Daddy arrived and insisted we go get ice cream. He was drunk and drove too fast and scared those girls green. They were the last of my friends.

Feeling depressed, I cover the tin with dirt and scatter some grass and leaves to hide the burial.

Grandpa C.B. says I will be on the sermon docket every other Sunday. So, in addition to my other jobs, I now have to pretend to love the Lord and spread his word. I have lots of words to spread around on the side, too, because I'm working on two stories. Jaylene, the editor of the school literary magazine, promised to publish one if it's any good.

The weather is warming at long last. The goldfinches have turned bright yellow, but there's still no sign of the red Chevy. No letters or postcards or calls from my parents, either. At bedtime, Grandpa doesn't mention my mother any longer, maybe because he doesn't want to upset me, maybe because he doesn't want to upset himself. Week after week, we go on sermonizing, selling liquor from below ground and jars of preserves from above ground. In addition, we have a new enterprise.

Three months ago, on a snowy day, Old Doc Fairchild came for tea. This means he visited in the late afternoon, but we didn't get out the porcelain cups because Grandpa asked him right off if he'd care to partake of something stronger than Tetley's, which of course he did.

Doc is nearing retirement, though some say he should have hung up his stethoscope forty years ago. Some say he never even went to medical school. If he didn't, maybe that's why Grandpa and he get on so well because C.B. never spent a split second at a seminary. Anyhow, they broke out the scotch and got all comfortable, cigars lit, the wood-burning stove crackling. Pretty soon the purpose for the visit became clear. As I secretly listened from the kitchen, they began talking about Dory Blinkenhausen, who is one of Doc's patients. Turns out she has a heart as weak as a butterfly. Doc said she's only 58, looks fit as a fiddle except for being a trifle pale, and has no family.

"I did just what we planned," Doc Fairchild explained. "After I took Dory aside and told her the tragic diagnosis about her heart, she was mightily upset, but by and by she settled down. It was then I recommended she come see you and make her peace with God."

"One and the same thing," Grandpa said, chuckling. "In fact, Dory visited a few days ago."

At first, I hadn't a clue why Grandpa was so pleased. I edged along the Formica counter closer to the living room so I could hear him better.

"I convinced her that the most expeditious way to salvation was to give to my Glory Alleluia Chapel so we could continue our work helping poor souls. Lifting them up from their misery. That sort of thing. She was all set to donate $100 until I explained that a life insurance policy wouldn't cost much—"

"The $10,000 policy?"

"Yes. I told her that I would personally oversee the distribution of funds to those in need and would install a brass plaque on the altar with her name on it so everyone would know of her generosity and remember her name in perpetuity," C.B. replied. "You will be pleased to hear that the insurance application is already in process."

I took a chance and peeked in. Doc Fairchild was rubbing his hands together, saying "Wonderful, C.B." over and over, and bowing his shaggy gray head up and down like it was loose on his neck.

In turn, Grandpa nodded, though he was still concentrating on the scheme at hand. "Doc, have you tidied up Dory's medical files?"

"Why, yes, I have. The most Dory now suffers from is a boil on her posterior. Since I'm likely to get the call from the insurance company to examine her, being the only physician in these parts, and then later will sign her death certificate, we won't have to fret over a thing."

"Excellent!"

I nipped back into the center of the kitchen and clattered dishes before returning to my listening spot. Grandpa sloshed more scotch in their glasses, and once the two were settled again, they began discussing a patient with cancer. Doc Fairchild said he has a hound-dog nose for smelling that dread disease, even though some of his patients can't afford testing or surgery to confirm they have it. As Doc talked about his ailing patient, Gregory Elkhorn, I pictured the cancer making a meal on the insides of the poor man, worms squirming in his guts like some that crawl around in Worm Heaven.

Doc Fairchild finished his medical diagnosis. "And Gregory lost his wife a few years ago and never had children so he has no one expecting to inherit. He's none too bright, either, so he should go along with our plans just fine. I've already recommended that he come see you."

As I grabbed a knife to chop carrots for the stew, it took me a minute to work out their scheme. Finally, I realized that when Dory kicks the bucket, the insurance company will have no suspicion that the recently departed had a tricky ticker. It sounded like their arrangement would only cost Dory a few months of insurance payments because she wasn't long for this world, though knowing the kindness of my grandfather, he probably would offer to cover those. When the insurance company in Hartford paid on the policy, Doc and C.B. would make a substantial sum. I didn't like the whole deal, but I had to admire its cleverness.

Next, the two began discussing Grandpa's idea for a rheumatism potion concocted from moonshine, crushed mint, and a dollop of honey.

"It's more diluted than the usual product, but we can sell it for the same price," C.B. said. "I've been experimenting to find the perfect ratios and am certain the combination is a delectable but medicinal brew."

This seems to be accurate because we are now cranking out Anti-Ache Elixir and Dr. R. J. Riley's Tonic, both made from an identical recipe, and selling them like hotcakes. They're nearly as popular as our hooch, but they're just about the same thing, except the ladies have got it in their heads they don't contain drinking liquor, a misconception Grandpa encourages along with Doc Fairchild, who regularly prescribes both to anyone with a cold, croup, cough, flu, or joint soreness. Since they're so sweet and tasty, the women have developed a serious fondness for them as have a few youngsters.

—

Two nights ago I finished my story about Appleton. I tried to make it sound like a far-off place, changing Lake Ontario to Center Hill Lake, and New York to De Kalb County, Tennessee. I've never been there, but I read up on the area in the *World Book Encyclopedia* Grandpa gave me for Christmas, which he bought cheap because it's missing two volumes and sports a few water stains. After typing the story several times until it was perfect, I decided not to submit it to the high school literary magazine because everyone will know I'm writing about Butztown and may not appreciate some of my characterizations. Instead, I gave Jaylene a story about a boy and his grandfather fishing, and this morning she told me she'll publish it. I'm so excited! Now I'm sure writing is what I'm meant to do. Grandpa agrees, though he says I need to keep up with business and not stray off into my imagination. He says having imagination is a good thing so long as it's applied to making money. He's proud of me even so and intends to buy twenty copies to give away to those who worship with us, which will probably result in them leaving large donations on the plate.

Grandpa has a knack for turning everything into cash, one way or the other. Though he never explained why he brought Mama to Butztown twenty-three years ago when she was a girl—the year my grandmother died from a heart attack—it was probably to create room between him and the law back in Philadelphia, where Grandpa's people are from. One night late, when Daddy was spouting off, I overheard him accuse Grandpa of being a thief like Grandpa's older brother, my Great Uncle Albert. Daddy said they stole thousands of dollars from a local union for which Albert worked as an accountant. Grandpa called Daddy a liar, but Daddy insisted it was the truth. He said that's what happened to Great Uncle Albert—he got caught and beaten to near death. Then both families had to make a run for it, which was a real trial because Albert was a bleeding mess, and my grandmother was weak in the heart. He said the strain of the trip to Butztown likely killed her and definitely killed Great Uncle Albert soon after.

Later, when I asked Mama if the story was true, she told me it wasn't, but she looked away when she said it. I'm inclined to believe Daddy for once, especially because he must have heard the whole thing from Mama one night when her tongue was loose from liquor. I've also noticed Grandpa gets a funny look in his eye whenever we mention his brother or my grandmother. And C.B. takes a real interest in Buck and Corey, the grandsons of Great Uncle Albert, who had to run the farm after their parents died from influenza. They're all the family we have left on Grandpa's side.

Grandpa C.B. is a funny mix of a fellow. Sometimes I think he feels guilty about his behavior, and sometimes he just sails along without a care or concern. It occurs to me that he might be using me like he does members of his congregation, but I get paid for my work, and I am learning all kinds of useful things that he says will put me in good stead when I strike out on my own, which one of these days I'll do. Sooner rather than later, too, since I'm a sophomore in high school, although I'm only fourteen and a year younger than my classmates. Grandpa allows how I'll whiz through high school and get lots of scholarship offers. I'm not so sure about all that, but I'll try my best. Other than giving his opinion on my scholarship chances, Grandpa and I haven't discussed matters of education. In general, he's high on it. When the time comes, I hope he won't fuss about my leaving him.

As I walk home from school, lugging my satchel, I worry about Grandpa. He's acting tired all of a sudden. His color isn't so rosy, and he's coughing whenever he lights up a cigar. He says he's working too hard, but I'm not sure about this because his working too hard mostly involves staring out the window. However, he did get perky when Dory Blinkenhausen dropped dead on Tuesday while she was milking her cow, Norah Lee. That's $5,000 coming our way soon, he says. I'm not very comfortable with all this, but C.B. is now waiting on Gregory Elkhorn, whose stomach is acting up something considerable. Grandpa says it's from the cancer, but that we shouldn't mention the "C" word because no one knows about it except Doc Fairchild, us, and Gregory Elkhorn, whom C.B. told to keep mum or else it will jeopardize the life insurance policy if the company finds out. And if they don't pay, Gregory's attempt to purchase a higher lot in the afterlife will fail, and he'll be handed a pitchfork in the hot place rather than scraping elbows with the angels in heaven. I hope when my time comes I'll have something to trade off for my sins. Not that I believe in all that nonsense, but it doesn't hurt to cover your bets.

After I think about Grandpa, Eli Houk pops into my head. He's a boy in my class whose family moved here from Ithaca last December. He's hardly spoken to me before last week, but he's been hanging around my locker and chatting in the cafeteria ever since. This afternoon, as I was leaving school, he stopped me outside. I thought he wanted a homework assignment, but then he said, "Charlene, would you come to my house for a party on Saturday night?"

I was so surprised, I missed a step. "Really?"

"Yeah," he said and gave me a big smile.

We talked for a few minutes and then parted ways.

In my room, I replay our conversation, remembering how Eli looked. He's pretty cute—dark brown eyes and the smoothest brown hair. He's good in science and math and is kind of funny. He also invited a couple of other kids to the party: Mack, who is going with Laney, and Sven, who hangs out with Maryanne.

I know Grandpa will think I'm too young to be fooling with

boys, yet I want to go in the worst way, and since Grandpa already has a dinner date with Cass Brady—she's a particular friend of his—I don't think it's fair that I can't have a particular friend, too. It's not right, but if Grandpa says I can't attend, then I'll wait till he leaves at 6:30 and make a dash for the Houk's place. I don't know why Eli is interested in me, but then again I don't know much about these things and can't ask Grandpa without him becoming suspicious. The more I think about Eli, however, the more excited I get.

—

"Where's my tie?" Grandpa C.B. is fussing around in his room.

"How should I know?" I reply. I'm too busy planning what I'm going to wear tonight to worry about Grandpa's tie. In fact, I'm flat-out confused whether I should dress up. Not that I have a ton of clothes, but there's a mile between jeans and a skirt, at least to my way of thinking.

A few minutes later, Grandpa steps into the hall, all spruced up in a brown suit and a green-and-gold striped tie clipped to his shirt. His gray hair is slicked back smooth as a duck's feathers. "How do I look?" he asks.

"Fine," I say, kind of offhand, as I follow him downstairs.

"Will you watch television this evening?"

"Maybe," I say, careful to act a little pouty because Grandpa told me yesterday that I couldn't go to Eli's party.

"Charlie, I might be late tonight so don't wait up."

He gives me a hug. I feel guilty about lying to him and know I should have listened to my own sermon on the subject.

"On Monday, after school, do you want to go into Rochester and buy some new clothes?" He studies my blouse, noticing that my wrists are sticking out past the cuffs. "You're growing fast. Why, you're nearly as tall as your mama." He looks away then, as if he hasn't meant to mention her.

"Okay. Sure."

He kisses my forehead and walks to our black Buick Roadmaster, which Cousin Corey washed and polished this morning. Grandpa says he bought a convertible so he can converse with God and have no roof get in the way. I sincerely doubt this was the reason, but I enjoy driving it on the dirt roads near the house. Grandpa won't let me take it on the blacktop until I get my license.

I wait to hear the car's ignition before tearing upstairs and pulling off my clothes. After thinking about it all day, I've decided

21

on my navy skirt and matching sweater. While it's possible everyone will be in jeans and I'll look ridiculous, Maryanne is partial to dresses, so this is probably a safe compromise. After I zip up the skirt, I go into the bathroom and brush my hair about a hundred times until it's shiny, wishing it wasn't so straight, though the gold color is pretty. I wash my face and notice my other flaws, such as a thin nose and a skinny neck, but altogether I must not be put together that poorly if I resemble Mama, who was Homecoming Queen in high school.

I don't know if Eli considers me pretty, but thinking of him, I suddenly recall how his front tooth tilts a little and tucks behind the one next to it. This doesn't make him look bad, just a little less than perfect, and every imperfection helps me feel a little more equal.

At quarter to seven, I'm ready. I take my key from the hook and close the kitchen door. When it shuts, it sounds loud in the still night. Kind of final, too, like I'm leaving one stage of my life behind. I take my bicycle from the shed and set off for Eli's house.

- 4 -

"Hey, Charlene," Eli says as he holds the screen door open for me. He's dressed in jeans and a white button-down shirt, both pressed with care. His brown loafers shine as does his smile.

"Hi, Eli. Thanks for inviting me." I walk into the Houk house and smell chocolate-chip cookies baking and the sweet smoke of hickory from the fire. In the living room, cushioned chairs are gathered round a table, their chintz slipcovers crisp and boxy, edged with dark green piping and printed with chrysanthemums and birds flying around on a yellow background. Oval hook rugs lie on top of wide pine floors. Everything is prim and neat. Not a speck of dust in sight, as compared to our house where every surface has a muted look, except for the chapel, which Grandpa and I keep spotless.

"Let me take your coat," Eli offers.

He's being extra polite. So am I since this dating stuff is breaking new ground. Mrs. Houk steps out of the kitchen and introduces herself. She looks homey like her house. Hair gathered in a bun, blue polka-dot dress, pearls. For a moment, I feel sad that I don't have a mother like Mrs. Houk or a cozy living room.

"Nice to meet you, Charlene," she says. "I'm so glad you could come."

"Thank you, ma'am." No one ever told me they were glad to see me before so I'm not sure what to say. "You have a very pretty house."

Mrs. Houk glances at her son and nods, as if communicating approval of me. "Thank you, Charlene. And by the way, I enjoyed talking with your mother yesterday."

"Er, yes," I reply, regretting my telephone impersonation, "she enjoyed talking with you, too." All my practice orating has given me some accomplishment as an actress, enough to do a passable imitation of my mother. As a rule, I keep it quiet about my parents being gone. Grandpa C.B. says it's best.

After a little more conversing, Eli leads me downstairs to their family room in the basement. Sven and Mack are playing ping-pong, and Laney and Maryanne are throwing darts and giggling.

Both girls are wearing skirts so I made the right choice. A Ricky Nelson record is on the turntable: "Poor Little Fool." My theme song for the evening. There's a big bowl of popcorn, a basket of pretzels, and a plate of cookies on a side table. Red and blue crêpe-paper streamers crisscross the ceiling and dangle from the light fixture along with some loopy chains made of green construction paper. As Grandpa would remark, "festive."

I say "Hi" to everyone. Although I'm taking Advanced English with the junior class as well as eleventh-grade history and French, Laney and Maryanne are in several of my sophomore classes as are the boys, but I've never talked to them much. The girls have always been polite, unlike others at school who pretend I'm invisible. Part of the problem is that I skipped seventh grade, and my new classmates never accepted me as one of them. Even before I was accelerated, however, I had trouble because I'm not naturally a social creature.

When Eli offers me a bottle of Coca-Cola, I'm relieved to have one hand busy. I wish I'd thought to take a swig of C.B.'s scotch before I left, but a Coke will have to do.

Because Eli doesn't want to play doubles with Sven and Mack and the girls are at the dart board, he's stuck with me. I try to convince myself that Eli thinks I'm okay, but shyness has me by the throat and is holding on for dear life.

Eli takes a sip of his soda. "So, Charlene—"

"Hey, you can call me Charlie if you want."

He studies me with his warm brown eyes. Up close, I notice they have lighter flecks in them, like maybe the freckles on his cheeks jumped up into his eyes.

"If it's okay with you, I like Charlene better." He gives me a little smile.

This is the first time a boy has treated me like a girl. "Sure. That's fine."

We're quiet for a few minutes and then he asks, "How'd you like doing that frog dissection on Wednesday?"

"Well, to be honest, I'm not partial to cutting things up."

Eli chuckles. "Girls aren't, I guess. But the teacher held up your frog drawings. And you got the highest grade on the last test. You always do well."

I'm not sure whether to deny this compliment and seem modest or accept it for the truth. This is where having a mother to teach you how to act female would be handy. "Gee, I think you're smarter than me any day."

24

He grins and looks pleased. If this is all it takes to make a boy like me, I'm willing to lay it on thicker than strawberry jam on toast. We sit on two metal folding chairs, watch the ping-pong game, and talk about school. Eventually, Eli sneaks his arm behind me. I feel good.

—

"Do you want to dance?" Eli asks after we play a round of darts.

"Okay."

The other two couples are dancing to "The Purple People Eater," which is the stupidest song I've ever heard. Eli turns off the lights except for one table lamp with a heavy red shade. The room now looks pinkish, even the brown pine paneling. Then he removes the record and puts on Perry Como's "Catch a Falling Star." Before I know what's happening, he takes my hand and leads me to the space behind the ping-pong table. His arms are around me in a flash, and I'm thrown in serious shock because I've never danced with anyone except Grandpa, Cousin Buck, and Daddy. All of them have a fair amount more pudge than Eli, who is hard in his shoulders and chest from working on his family's farm. I wonder if he's ever danced with a girl before. It seems like he knows what he's doing, but he has an older sister who probably showed him the ropes. I move in closer, smelling vanilla cologne on his neck and wondering how close is too close or too far. Eli helps with the decision by tightening his arm around me so we're squeezed together. Do I feel all sharp and bony like he does? My breasts started sprouting last year, but they're not full size yet, not like Mama's. I was embarrassed about growing them at first. Now I think they may be okay.

"You feel real good, Charlene," Eli whispers in my ear.

His breath does a lightning bolt to my knees, and for a minute I don't know what has hit me. "You, too," I murmur.

He takes this as encouragement and presses his hand lower so we're locked together. We move to the music, but I don't hear the words. All I can think about is how wonderful it is to be held. I close my eyes and forget everyone else in the room. I only want to be the girl in Eli's arms.

Just as the song is close to ending, Eli kisses me. His lips are warm and firm. I taste the salt from the pretzels and sugar from the soda. Next thing I know, he's got his tongue inside my mouth, and he's doing a geographical exploration of my molars. I take a peek over his shoulder and see the other couples are similarly engaged. This is a relief because I don't want to be the only girl doing it. No good coming across as easy.

A second later, the overhead lights are switched on. All of us freeze, and when we hear footsteps on the stairs, the three couples fly apart. From the landing, Mrs. Houk leans down to peek into the basement and gives us a suspicious once-over. In the pink light, our faces look guilty as sin. Any idiot could tell what we're doing, but Mrs. Houk just says, "Eli, dear, please leave the light on" and then goes upstairs again.

That interruption breaks things up. We play some games, drink more Coke, but suddenly everyone is shy with each other. Around ten o'clock, Maryanne's father comes to get her, and I decide to play it safe and leave in case Grandpa calls it an early evening with Cass. Eli's father offers to drive me to my house, but I insist I'm fine on my bicycle.

—

Although I hardly remember the ride home or going upstairs, I'm sitting on my bed and thinking about Eli's goodbye kiss while we were standing on his porch. "I really like you, Charlene," he said, and I told him I really liked him. We agreed to meet in the woods near Brown's Lane after school on Monday, though this is a problem because I run the Hooch Shop each afternoon before making dinner and doing homework. However, since Grandpa calls me a conniver, I guess I'll figure out a solution.

Meanwhile, I keep remembering the kisses and the dancing and how Eli looked at me. Even though he's a new student, he's already one of the most popular boys in class, though not number one or anything. It's difficult to believe he likes me, especially because hardly anyone does. Eli explained that's because everyone thinks I'm intimidating. I asked him what he thought, and he said I was just fine. I'm so happy! But I have to keep all this excitement under my hat so Grandpa doesn't catch on.

—

It's Sunday morning and Grandpa just informed me he needs extra help with the service. He's moving around the kitchen like he's walking through a foot of snow. I don't know what's ailing him. Maybe old Cass Brady wore him out last night. I, on the other hand, feel great. My topic—assigned by the Right Reverend Whitestone, who doesn't look so right at the moment—is the perils of taking our Lord's name in vain. Because I do this regularly, I'm once again risking God's wrath. Of course, if I were so worried about God, there would be many habits and behaviors and thoughts I would need to change. And I suspect after Eli and I get together tomorrow, my list of sins will be getting longer. I have to be careful and not behave like my Mama did with Daddy when she was young, just in case the devil is in my genes.

After breakfast, I run upstairs and put on my dress, though I'm sorely tempted to wear my navy blue skirt and sweater so I can feel like I did last night with Eli. As I'm combing my hair, I suddenly remember Grandpa and I are supposed to go to Rochester tomorrow afternoon. Damn!

—

While walking home from school, I dream up a solution. I head to the house, where Grandpa is sitting in his chair reading *The Saturday Evening Post*, chuckling over one of the cartoons. When I come in, he asks if I'm ready to go.

"Oh, I could I suppose," I reply, hunching my shoulders a little.

"Why, Charlie, is there something the matter?" He lays the magazine on his stomach and peers at me over his glasses.

"No, not exactly, but I might be coming down with a cold or something."

This does the trick.

"Well, then, perhaps you better go rest before dinner."

"But we're going to Rochester and then I have to run the store..." I make my voice sound dog-tired.

Grandpa C.B. waves a hand at me. "I'll take care of that and we can go shopping another day. You go to your room."

I don't have to be told twice, though I dawdle and take the stairs as slow as Grandpa does. Once inside my bedroom, I close the door and throw open the window. Lickety-split I'm through it, down the ladder left propped against the siding when Corey lost interest in scraping the paint on the second story. Then I run through the thick cluster of weeds to the shed, where I left my bicycle. In two shakes, I'm flying down the road before Grandpa has left the house.

- 5 -

Across Bertram's Creek, Eli is leaning against a maple tree, smoking a cigarette. I've never seen him smoke before so I figure he's doing it to look older. He's wearing jeans and a pale blue windbreaker. Watching him, I enjoy the idea that a boy's waiting on me. I feel like a real girl and also like a real fake.

When Eli glances my way, he grins and stands up straight. Then he remembers to be cool and his face changes into his normal, every-day expression. He takes a long drag on the cigarette and stubs it out on the ground.

"Hey, Charlene." He gives a little shrug like meeting me by this maple tree is an accident.

"Hi, Eli." I set the kickstand on my bike and walk up to him, once again wondering how close I should be. Are we friends or more?

"I brought this for us to sit on," he says, pointing to a green army blanket.

That decides things. We act like a couple about to have a Sunday picnic and open the blanket, spreading it flat. Eli plops down and settles against the tree, and I do, too, though I try to be dainty about it. From his jacket pocket, he pulls out a silver flask.

"I got this from my father," he tells me, "though he doesn't know I borrowed it." Eli gives me a wink, which reminds me of Grandpa.

I like this feeling that we're together, doing something we shouldn't be doing. I take a swig of whiskey and so does Eli.

"That hits the spot," he says with satisfaction, nodding, like he's an old hand at drinking. "Yes, it does," I agree, taking another sip. The liquor is rougher than Chivas.

"You know, Charlene, you're okay." He circles his arm around my shoulder so our sides are squeezed together.

"Thanks." I try to remember what women do in the movies. Demure, I remind myself. I bring my knees up, keeping them together all lady-like, and turn toward Eli so I can slip my shoulder under his arm. I feel awkward doing this, but I know it's how I'm supposed to act.

28

We talk about school, some kids and teachers, for fifteen minutes or so, drinking all the while. I can tell Eli isn't totally interested in our conversation. Instead, he seems to be waiting to make a move. I'm enjoying the closeness and being with a boy alone for the first time, yet I'm unsure what to do. I don't want Eli to think I'm a kid or inexperienced, even though I am, so I flatter him about his clothes, laugh at his stories, and ask him all kinds of questions to make him feel good. Then I take his hand.

This slips his gears. He brings his lips to mine. Before long, his tongue is busy on the inside of my mouth and mine is working inside his, tasting the whiskey. After a few minutes, he stops and gives us another drink. I suspect he's trying to get me intoxicated, but that isn't so easy because I am an experienced toxicator. This is a dandy word, I think, though it's probably not in the dictionary. I do feel affected by the whiskey, however, or by Eli, whose hands have migrated to my lower neck, poised to make a plunge south as soon as he works up courage. All of a sudden I feel squirmy, with a little panic nipping at my mental edges, warning me to slow down on the liquor and on the fooling around.

"Oh, Charlene, your skin feels so soft," Eli croons. Then he kisses me again. His breaths are coming faster, as if there isn't enough air because our tongues block our throats.

I imitate his kissing, though I try to be more genteel. Next thing I know, I'm lying on my back, and he's staring at me with those beautiful brown eyes with the gold flecks, his cheeks and lips pink from excitement. I notice a beard is starting below his sideburns and above his mouth. The dark hairs haven't quite joined up yet, but they will soon. He's not far off from being a man, I think, before he presses on top of me, his body covering mine. As I realize his intentions, Eli lifts my sweater and blouse. His fingers are warm and give me chills at the same time. On our clothes trip to Rochester, I planned to ask Grandpa if I could buy a bra, which I've been too embarrassed to do even before Mama left. Since I was slow to develop, it wasn't an issue. Now I wish I had one as a kind of roadblock because some part of my mind is yelling at me to watch out. Then again another part is insisting we have way too many clothes on.

Eli moans and calls my name. I figure this is the etiquette so I whisper "Eli...Eli," though the moaning is getting easier to do for real.

After he gives me a passionate kiss, he murmurs in my ear,

"You're amazing." He moves a few inches away and slowly examines my face. "Charlene, will you be my girl?"

I'm thrilled down to my toes. "You mean it?" I clasp my arms around his neck.

He nods. "Yeah." He falls to one side so that I'm afraid and relieved that he's going to stop our adventures. "I didn't know you were so hot."

I didn't know, either. In fact, I didn't have a clue. He reaches for a tall shoot of grass, picks it, and then takes my left hand. Gently, he wraps and knots the grass around my ring finger.

"There," he says, "it's official. We're going together." He gives me a happy grin.

My heart is pounding. "Oh, Eli!" This is all I can get out before he's kissing me again. Everything is fine until his hand edges up my skirt. Suddenly, I'm afraid. Does he assume being his girl is the same as agreeing to go all the way? I grab him so tightly that he has to stop his investigations. I know this is the wrong thing to do, but I'm in a war and need to buy time for the troops to decide whether to beat a retreat or charge forward. Unfortunately, this maneuver backfires as Eli lurches to his knees and tears off his windbreaker and shirt. I stare at his lean chest with the muscles tight across it. He's beautiful, golden in the late afternoon sunlight. When I place my hands on him, he reaches for his pants' zipper.

I shake my head. "Oh, Eli, I can't. I wish I could. I want to. I really want to. But I can't." This comes out in a rush, in one long desperate breath.

"Yes, you can. It's okay. Just this once, Charlene. I mean, you're mine now. You said so. And we need to do it so we belong to each other." His eyebrows are knit together in concern.

We stare at each other for a minute. Then Eli strokes my hair and gathers it behind my neck before kissing me tenderly. We feel connected and natural. What can be wrong with this, I wonder? I want more, but I'm frightened. I think of how Daddy got Mama in the family way when she was a few years older than I am.

"No, Eli, please."

Just then I hear a branch snap behind the tree. A second later, Cousin Corey and Cousin Buck step around the trunk. They grab Eli's legs and arms and lift him into the air. His eyes and mouth open wide with astonishment, and when Eli lands face down on some bushes, he yelps and gathers himself into a ball.

I rush to neaten my clothes, upset that my cousins have seen me with my skirt hitched up. Corey's eyes are glued on my body in a way that is embarrassing.

Buck avoids looking at me. "Charlie, you best be getting home," he says in a low voice. He then notices Corey gawking and punches his brother on the shoulder.

Corey snaps out of his trance and blushes. "Yeah. C.B. sent us out when he found you weren't in your room."

Now I'm in real trouble. "Are you going to say anything to him? I mean, about this?" I ask, scrambling to my feet.

The two look awkward, with their big shoulders and hands. They're more accustomed to wrestling pigs than dealing with a young girl cousin in such a predicament.

"Nah, we won't say nothing to C.B." Buck is keeping an eye on Eli, whose hand is edging over to grab his shirt. "But you best be minding yourself, Charlie. You'll get into big trouble doing this kind of thing. This boy is the type you ought to stay far away from. He'll give you a reputation. Understand?"

I nod and stare at my shoes, feeling like I'm ten years old.

Eli is resting on one knee and trying to slip an arm into his shirt. "I didn't do anything," he mumbles. "Nothing she didn't want."

This makes Corey mad. "You shut up!" He shoves Eli in the chest and sends him sprawling backward. He throws Eli's windbreaker at him, then spots the silver flask and tosses that at Eli, too. "Stay away from Charlie, hear?" Corey squares up and stares at Eli like he'd just as soon tan his hide.

"Come on. Let's go." Buck takes my arm.

As I follow my cousins, I glance at Eli, but he won't look at me.

———

Buck and Corey are silent except to explain how they tailed me by following my bicycle tracks, as if I were an animal they were hunting, and to talk about army boot camp, where they're going in two days. I feel like a jerk and pray they don't tell Grandpa. Because they also seem embarrassed, I don't think they'll mention what happened. When we reach the house, they walk to the log pile to split wood for Grandpa, and I straighten my clothes and run my fingers through my hair. Maybe I'll have a few minutes alone to compose myself before Grandpa knocks on the door.

I step through the weeds, climb the ladder, and hop on the windowsill. My hands disturb the frame's peeling white paint, which presses into my skin. I peer inside my room. The door is open but no one is inside. I sigh with relief, lower my legs to the floor, and grab my comb to re-part my straight hair. Suddenly, I'm desperate for my old, innocent life, which, all in all, was running pretty well. Now, when Charlie has become Charlene, everything is a mess. I look down at the grass ring on my finger and don't want to take it off. It's the first gift a boy has ever given me, and not any boy, but one I like. Will Eli ever speak to me again? I hope so. But what led him to think that giving me a silly grass ring was permission to get fresh? Or did I do something to encourage him? This thought scares me because I have no idea what I did.

I remove the ring and place it in my jewelry case, then change into my jeans, listening for Grandpa's footsteps. All quiet. Maybe Grandpa is getting sluiced on Chivas. He normally has a few drinks before dinner, and it's now 5:10. I peek around the corner of my door and see him sitting in his chair. A glass of scotch is on the table beside him, along with a lit cigar, whose smoke is joining the golden halo of haze around his head.

"Charlie? Please come down here."

Oh, oh. "In a minute, Grandpa," I say, as if I'm in the middle of something. I wait a bit before walking downstairs.

Grandpa C.B. turns his head. He doesn't look so hot. Kind of a mix of pale and red at the same time. "I think we need to talk, don't you?"

I've never heard him use this tone of voice. "Sure." I keep it light and easy, as if I don't have anything to hide. After tossing a log in the Franklin stove, I sit down on the couch across from him, the picture of attentiveness.

He clears his throat and takes a swig of scotch. "You know it's one thing to fib a little now and then, particularly when it doesn't hurt anyone. I may not be a fine role model for you along these lines, Charlie. And for that I apologize."

This takes me by surprise, him apologizing to me. I feel really terrible because the one person in the world whose fine estimation is most important is Grandpa's. His eyes are on me, so I have to answer him. "I know about fibbing versus lying." This sounds nice and neutral. Relief floods over me. Maybe I can squirm out of this scrape without much damage.

"Well, I'm delighted to hear that. Because I would like you to explain whether you were fibbing or lying to me this afternoon when you said you were feeling poorly."

He had me there. A bunch of curse words float through my

mind. "I guess it started out as a fib, sir, and then, with one thing and the other, it might have turned into a lie." I wince a bit because I can't help it.

Grandpa listens to this and sighs. "You're usually such a good girl. I don't understand what's going on." He takes a drag on his cigar, tucks his hand into the V-neck of his sweater, and considers the matter. "Wouldn't have anything to do with a boy, would it?"

I'm shocked by this arrow shot true and clean into my heart. I hang my head because I can't bear to look at him. "Yes, sir, it would, I am sorry to report."

Grandpa places his cigar in the brass ashtray and is silent. Then he leans forward. The chair creaks with his weight. "Is this the very same boy who invited you to the party last Saturday night?"

"The same. Yes, sir."

"And where does he live?"

"The Houks have a farm on Duquale Road. Just moved here a few months ago." I pause for a second, hoping this is enough information, but Grandpa arches his eyebrow, indicating I should continue, so I add, "His name is Eli."

Grandpa eases back in his chair and pours another inch of scotch from his crystal decanter. "I see," he says. "And did you go to the party after I told you that you were too young for such things?"

My chin falls on my chest. "I did. I didn't stay late or anything. But, yes, sir, I went over there for a few hours. Played some darts and ping-pong and had a Coke or two. That's about it. I had a nice time, though, and when Eli asked me to go for a walk this afternoon, well, I wanted to do that. I also wanted to go with you to Rochester. Oh, I don't know..."

Grandpa drinks his scotch. I can't tell if he's mad at me or a tad bit amused. I'm praying it's the latter.

"Charlie, I see now that I've made a grievous error in judgment. I should have realized you're growing up and have some adult feelings. As you know, I went through hell and back with your mother when she was your age. I didn't do a very good job with her, as much as I tried. Your grandmother had passed on, and quite frankly I was unaccustomed to dealing with teenage girls. I guess I was too permissive and unaware. And now I'm bending in the other direction with you. It's because you're like my own child, my only child, and it pains me to think that you're going to leave me one of these days."

"Oh, Grandpa, I'll never leave you! Really I won't!" As soon as I say this, I know it isn't true. Grandpa knows this, but he seems relieved to hear it anyway. "I'm sorry I went off to meet with Eli and that I snuck out when I shouldn't have. It was wrong, and I won't do it again."

Grandpa sniffs and wipes a hand across his eyes. "I will accept your promise, Charlie. But from now on, if you want to visit with a boy, you tell me, okay? We're a team and have a lot riding on the success of our many enterprises. Remember that I'm grooming you to take over for me one of these days. We have to trust one another." He hesitates for a second, his lips press together like they're trying to hold words in. "I love you more than anyone. You are my one great hope in life."

This breaks my heart. I'm getting teary just thinking on how much I love him. "I'll be honest with you from now on, Grandpa. I love you, too."

Grandpa C.B. picks up the decanter and lifts his chin as an invitation. I go get my little glass and he fills it. I take a sip and sit on the floor next to him, my head resting on his knee. He smoothes my hair and I feel better.

"I just want you to be the best person you can be," he whispers, more to himself than to me. "You're my legacy."

I think on this and allow as how he's right. I need to concentrate on the important things and not fritter away my energy on boys—not yet anyway. I have some goals stacked up in my mind that require undivided attention. Still, it felt good to have Eli touch me. I suspect I'll be remembering that for a while, in my spare time, like before I go to sleep at night.

- 6 -

I'm determined to forget about Eli because I'm trying to return to my old Charlie self. Even so, it really hurts that he won't even look at me in class. He acts like I don't exist and seems to be making eyes at Laney now that Mack has moved on to Maryanne after Sven ditched her. I guess that's how it goes, like some kind of chain reaction, except I'm no longer part of it since Eli's interest in me isn't shared by the other kids. Even the two girls aren't friendly, but then again they never were.

I feel pretty low about being dropped into social oblivion yet determined to keep busy writing stories and handling Grandpa's numerous businesses because he doesn't have much vim and vigor these days. Yesterday, after a trip over to old Doc Fairchild's in the morning, Grandpa announced he had written his will and had it scrutinized and made official by Lambeau Hastings, who is an attorney-at-law and one of Grandpa's occasional business partners. I don't like him much because he has a ratty face and darty little black eyes, but Grandpa says the man possesses a nimble mind. Anyway, after Grandpa came home from Lambeau Hastings' office, he showed me a copy of his Last Will and Testament. Everything is left to yours truly. Grandpa says Mama doesn't deserve one brass farthing, though I didn't know what kind of money that was so I looked it up. All this talk and preparations for dying make me uneasy because I don't have anyone else but him, and if he passes on, I don't know what I'll do. I hope Mama comes back soon so I won't have to worry, but I don't have much confidence that I'm on her mind.

———

I'm perusing *Joy of Cooking*, trying to figure out what to do with some venison stew meat that Grandpa procured on one of his forays, when all of a sudden there's an aggressive knock on the front door. Probably whoever is knocking is not someone I want to be at home for. I close the cookbook and walk to the window to take a peek through the blinds.

To my unhappy surprise, Sheriff Billy Shackrack is standing

there, his big police hat in his hand. I open the door, say hello, and shove my fists in my jeans' pockets but don't open the screen. I don't want him in the house and I know Grandpa doesn't.

"Charlie, where's C.B.?" he asks in that loud, deep voice of his.

I shrug. "I don't know, sir."

"His car's in the driveway."

"Yes, indeed it is. But he's not in the house. Could be somewhere along the lake fishing—he likes to do that some afternoons—or it's possible he's visiting Mr. Carter or Mr. Cossantino. Sometimes they swing by on their tractors and take him to inspect property, asking Grandpa's advice about this and that. Or he might be down by the creek. Why, there's no telling where Grandpa C.B. is, Sheriff." I pause because I'm rattling on faster than the freight train that runs through Rochester late evenings. I glance up at Shackrack but can't make out his expression because he's standing in shadow. I suspect he's not buying my lying. "I'll tell Grandpa you stopped by and were asking after him."

I start to close the door, but the policeman isn't one to be put off. He grabs the screen door, and before I know what's happening, he's standing in the living room, filling it up with his official presence. The screen door snaps shut with a loud smack.

"I'll wait," he says, and without asking permission, Sheriff Shackrack crosses the room and sits in Grandpa C.B.'s personal chair, something no one has ever done.

"Well, okay, then," I reply. "I was just fixing to make stew, so if you'll excuse me—"

"Hold it, Charlie. I don't want you running off and warning C.B. that I'm here."

This is precisely what I have in mind. "Can't I just throw some things in the pot?" I ask. "Everything is already chopped."

The policeman locks eyes with me. "Okay," he says, "but don't get any funny ideas."

I don't mention that I'm full of ideas, not one of them containing an answer to my problem about how to tip off C.B. I hope he can hear what's going on from the basement and doesn't pop up all of a sudden. As I walk into the kitchen, I mull over how to warn him, and when I'm out of the sheriff's sight, I grab a can of potatoes, open the downstairs door, and toss it onto the easy chair near the foot of the steps. If Grandpa sees this weird behavior, he'll get the drift something is peculiar upstairs, if he hasn't already heard the sheriff's voice.

I return to the cutting board, gather up the meat, and place it in a pot with carrots, onions, and celery. There's no time to brown the venison, so I pour a hefty tot of burgundy over it and turn on the burner. Then I return to the living room and sit on the couch, wishing I had thought to take a slug of wine on the sly while I had the opportunity.

Shackrack is making himself comfortable, messing with Grandpa's pillow and his cigar humidor, which he checks out, sniffing one of the expensive imported stogies Grandpa favors. For a minute, I worry that he's going to steal one, but he doesn't. I don't like the policeman touching things or sitting in Grandpa's place like he was in charge, but I'm powerless to protest. And what's making me more anxious is the reason for the surprise visit. I wonder what mischief is afoot and heartily hope Grandpa knows the law is presiding over his living room.

We hang out for a bit, the sheriff and I. We look at each other, but then our eyes slip away fast, or at least mine do. His stay on me longer, giving me the kind of glance I don't like except maybe from Eli, about whom I am determined not to think.

Nearly a half hour later, after two trips to stir the stew, I'm sitting on the couch and fidgeting with my shoelace, twisting it around my finger one way and then the other. I'm thinking we're losing business since I'm not in the Hooch Shop, but if I had been there when the Sheriff arrived, I might have been caught. I don't know what the rules are about kids my age selling moonshine, but I figure I wouldn't get any awards as a model citizen despite my fine grades and many academic achievements.

"So, Sheriff," I begin, "I'm kind of curious. What do you want Grandpa for?"

He stares at me like I have some nerve, which I do. "It's about his Anti-Ache Elixir, the one he's selling."

"Mmm, yes, sir."

"The Rowbottom boy took some and fell down the stairs into the cellar."

"Sammy?" I ask. "Why, he's so dumb he probably forgot he opened the door."

Sheriff Shackrack isn't amused. "He's in the hospital."

"Oh, I'm very sorry to hear that." I could care less about that fool, Sammy Rowbottom, but I can see where this is leading. "Well, now, that's too bad. He must have taken too much medicine," I explain. "It's serious stuff. At least that's what the manufacturer told Grandpa, and I know for a fact Grandpa always warns folks about following the directions. Trouble is it tastes good and so people don't always drink the amount they're supposed to. I can't see how that's Grandpa's fault, however. Just between us," I add, nodding toward the sheriff.

He takes all this information in and sorts it through his policeman's brain. Then he asks who the manufacturer is.

"Let me see. I believe it's General Medicinal Drug Laboratory and Pharmaceutical Company in Little Mountain, Montana. Yes, sir, I remember their invoice. Do you want me to get it?" I'm hoping he doesn't because the invoice is from an imaginary company, printed on a letterhead Grandpa produced on the Vandercook Press he hides in the basement behind boxes of Bibles. I always thought Grandpa was being overly careful making up these fake bills and cards, but he says it's sensible to be fastidious about details, and now I allow as how he's correct.

Shackrack mulls over this information. "You're sure C.B. didn't make this stuff?"

"Absolutely, Sheriff," I reply. "So I can't see how he's done anything wrong. And, besides, I believe we're out of the Elixir. Only Doc Fairchild has any left."

The policeman scrutinizes my face for a hint of dishonesty, but I studied with the best. Finally, he grabs his hat and stands up. "Well, Charlie," he sighs, "I can't hang around here all day. When your grandfather comes home, you tell him not to sell any more Anti-Ache Elixir or else I'll charge him with peddling dangerous drugs. The only person allowed to sell these products is a medical doctor or a pharmacy."

"I'll tell him, but just so you know, I've taken this medicine myself and it worked miracles. It's all about how much you take," I remind him, my brow raised and serious. "Of course it's not as good as the medicine Doc Fairchild gave me…that Dr. R. J. Riley's Tonic…" I drift off here, wondering if Shackrack realizes the two potions are one and the same.

"I don't imagine it is since Dr. Fairchild is a reputable physician and takes care what he gives people."

I stifle a snort and maintain a concerned expression on my face.

"Now you tell C.B. I'm keeping an eye on his activities, you hear?" The sheriff puts on his hat, strides across the floor in half as many steps as I'd take, and goes out the door. The screen slaps behind him.

I watch the sheriff march down the drive. His patrol car must be hidden around the bend in the road beyond the Hooch Shop, which, thankfully, is locked. I slide the bolt on the front door, and as I walk into the kitchen, C.B. cracks open the door to the basement.

"Is he gone?"

"Yes, sir, he is."

Grandpa heaves a big sigh. "That was a close call."

"It was," I agree. "Did you hear everything?"

"I did indeed. Good thinking about the invoice, Charlie." He comes over and gives me a hug. "Brilliant, in fact."

I grin at him. "I suppose we'll have to stop selling the Elixir, right?"

He nods. "Too bad. We had a fine business purveying both products."

"I could mention the Tonic is still available. To special clients. And keep it underground just in case."

Grandpa C.B. winks at me and agrees, heads into the living room, grunts with displeasure. "And he had the effrontery to sit in my chair!" He picks up his embroidered cushion, gives it a punch, and replaces it. Then he straightens the lace armrest covers and the one on the back of the chair. "He has no respect," Grandpa murmurs under his breath, as he sits down, still out of sorts and kind of harrumphing a lot.

I pour him some scotch to soothe his ruffled mood.

"Thank you kindly," he says, wiggling into the familiar confines of his chair. "Now, let's hear your vocabulary lesson."

"Yes, sir. I'm all set." I sit across from him. "Fabulate, fathom, fealty, feign, and facetious."

"All right. And your sentence?"

I give him a smile. "The clerk feigned to fabulate a facetious story about showing fealty to his boss, which his boss could not fathom on account of he knew the clerk didn't like him."

"First rate!" chuckles Grandpa.

—

Dinner is late because of the inopportune visit from the law. I'm just about to set the table when I hear a sharp rap on the front door. I rush into the living room. Grandpa has heard the knock and is already out of his chair, crossing the living room to the coat closet. As he opens the closet door, there is a louder bang.

"Charlie...the cigar," he whispers.

I run over to his ashtray and grab the stogie, setting it in my mouth and clenching my teeth. Grandpa closes the closet door behind him and begins fooling with the false panel that hides some of our finest corn whiskey. If C.B. sucks in, he can just fit in the enclosed space. I wait until he's quiet, though it's hard to hear over the noisy rapping. Finally, I head over to the front door and unlock it. Lo and behold the sheriff is standing there, looking cocky, holding the screen door ajar with his big black boot.

I take a puff from the cigar and exhale a cloud of smoke. The policeman enters the house without a word, though he looks askance at the cigar and stares at the Chivas Regal in the glass. As nonchalantly as I can, considering my hands are shaking, I walk over to Grandpa's table and take a sip of scotch.

"Okay. Enough fooling around, Charlie. Where is he?" Shackrack asks.

"Not here yet."

Just then Deputy Gary Rees steps in from the kitchen, whose door I must have forgotten to lock. Rees is a skinny, pimply-faced man who looks like he should be in high school, which it took him two extra years to complete on account of his brainpower needed ample time to muster its full potential.

Shackrack shakes his head, indicating that their little trick of coming from two directions hasn't worked. "Check the house," he orders his deputy.

As Rees walks toward the chapel, I take another drag on the cigar. "You know maybe I've been watching too many TV shows like *Perry Mason*, but don't you need a search warrant to come in here?" I make this sound easy, but I'm scared.

Sheriff Shackrack rests his hand on the knob of the coat closet door, which he's about to open. He glowers at me. "Not if I have a reason to search a place."

"Really? I could've sworn you do. Well, then," I say, taking another inhale from the cigar, "I'll keep what you said in mind."

"What do you mean?" The policeman looks madder than a bear whose honey hive has been pilfered.

I shrug. "Just what I said."

"You're as ornery as your grandfather."

I treat him to a small smile.

He scowls and considers the situation a minute. Then he shouts at his deputy, "Come back here, Gary."

I give the sheriff another smile, one without a trace of smugness.

He lets out a long breath. "You ought not to be drinking and smoking at your age. That's illegal."

"Grandpa allows me both...just before dinner. He says there's no harm in it so long as I stay in the house and don't get drunk."

Shackrack is looking me over, his attitude switching gears. "Well, you ought not to do either. Pretty girl like you...you should behave better."

I can't see how being pretty has anything to do with behaving, and I'm not positive that his flattery is honest anyhow, so I don't reply.

"You know, if you dressed up, put on some make-up and all," he says, "you'd be a real looker."

His words come as a surprise. I can't understand how this new Charlene, brought to life by Eli's attentions, is now looked upon as female fair game. This is a new danger to reckon with, one which is downright worrisome, especially because Shackrack has moved closer. Prickles are running down my neck, but I figure the best defense is a good offense. "You know, Sheriff," I begin, "while we're watching how we behave, you might watch yourself."

"What?" Shackrack's eyes widen in astonishment. He then places his hands on his belt and stares down at me like a big eagle on a lowly mouse. "What are you accusing me of?"

"Oh, well," I stare off into the clouds of cigar smoke. "I think you know. It wouldn't look good if I reported that you and Deputy Rees were fooling with me while Grandpa was gone." I sound bold as brass, but inside I've got a serious amount of fearfulness congregating.

Deputy Rees returns. He stares at Shackrack and imitates the sheriff's pose with hands on hips. They both stare at me like they've swallowed a large dose of consternation.

The sheriff clears his aggravation from his throat. "We've done no such thing."

"Mmm," I reply, letting the sound drift between us.

Sheriff Shackrack turns to his deputy and asks if he's seen any traces of C.B. Deputy Rees reports that Grandpa wasn't in the kitchen—obviously since Rees came in that way—nor in the bathroom, dining room, or chapel, which constitutes all the rooms on the ground floor, at least those that are visible.

"Do you want I should go upstairs?" Rees asks. Syntax isn't his strong suit.

"No. Guess not." Shackrack glares at me and beckons Rees to follow him out the door. All he says to me as he leaves is that he'll be back one of these days.

- 7 -

Gregory Elkhorn, the man insured for $10,000, has succumbed to his cancer. While I feel sorry for Mr. Elkhorn, I'm also unhappy about how we're profiting from the poor man's death. Grandpa said an extra nice sermon on his behalf, extolling the man's virtues and explaining how he gave generously to the Glory Alleluia Chapel, although Grandpa implied it was through donations rather than mentioning an insurance policy. We did a goodly haul that Sunday, allowing as how everyone felt guilty because they hadn't laid down much money on behalf of the sick and needy, who, of course, happen to be us. Grandpa capitalized on the situation by fabricating a story about a guy named Andy who worked in a paper factory and was burned to a crisp in a huge whoosh of a fire. He said the man couldn't work anymore because he didn't have any hands left. Then he explained how Andy had six itty-bitty kids who were standing in the shadow of Death's Door. Andy's wife, Eleanor, had perished from TB after a long illness, but she had been a fine Christian woman before God nipped off with her. Anyhow, after Grandpa suggested everyone should help Andy and the children, the ladies reached for their handkerchiefs, and the men pulled out their wallets while I'm trying not to laugh over the thought that popped into my head: The Story of Handless Andy.

Grandpa says the check from the insurance company will come in by and by, and then we'll move more money into cash holdings, which means into the boxes set out around the property. Some invoices will be paid for services rendered by such as W. M. Lawson, who has never seen a day on this earth, and goods purchased, such as from the G & C Bible Publishing Company or All Saints' Church Apparel, Candle, and Supplies, Incorporated, neither of which exists except for the post-office boxes Grandpa rents in several towns. He takes the checks and cashes them, using phony bank accounts. Keeping track of these transactions is partly my job. I maintain a listing and fake receipts of our official church expenses while Grandpa handles the financial disguises in order to waylay nosy IRS fellows or the police.

While we're busy with these plans, I keep thinking about Eli though I don't want to. These last two days I've caught him staring at me in class when he thinks I won't see him. Does he still have a sweet spot for me? He's been acting frosty ever since that afternoon a few weeks ago, but now he seems interested again. I still have feelings for him, even if he was wrong to act the way he did. Maybe boys can't help themselves when they like a girl. After all, I didn't do such a fine job pulling on the reins myself.

—

"Charlie, where's the pot of glue?" C.B. calls up from the basement.

"I'll bring it down." We're scraping off Anti-Ache Elixir labels and replacing them with Dr. R. J. Riley's Tonic labels. This is a lot of work, but Grandpa says we would be fools to circulate more of the Elixir because Shackrack told us to stop.

"Let's offer the Tonic for a quarter less than Doc is selling his," Grandpa says.

Doc Fairchild insists on a 55 percent cut for whatever he distributes because the police are snooping around. This doesn't strike us as fair because we are the manufacturing agents, but when Grandpa sells the bottles directly to our customers, our profit is nearly 80 percent, so the more product we move ourselves, the better.

We finish cleaning all traces of our monkey business and load up the trunk of the Buick, which I brought round to the side door so we can accomplish the transfer in private. It's still early morning with only a pink glow seeping through the bright green new leaves. I hate being up at this hour as does Grandpa, but he says the early bird won't get caught by the worm. Then he chuckles, imagining Sheriff Shackrack as a crawly critter.

"Come on, let's get this to Ye Olde Hooch Shop," Grandpa tells me. "Then I'll take you to school."

—

After the final bell rings, I place my English, history, and geometry textbooks into my satchel, thinking that I need to replace their brown paper covers because they're looking scruffy. And, in a weak moment, I had drawn a few E.H. initials on the inside flaps, which I don't want anyone to see. Next, I tuck in my history report with the big red "A+" marked on top. The piece is about the role of Fort Ticonderoga, Ethan Allen, and the Green Mountain Boys during the Revolutionary War. I feel pretty good about it, though I often receive grades like this. I'm the only kid in class who always types papers, which gives me an edge.

As I leave school and head home, I'm thinking that all in all it wasn't a bad day. Then I see Eli standing by the basketball court. I stroll down the sidewalk as if he's not there and continue off the school lot. Over my shoulder, I catch him walking behind me. Has he heard my cousins are in the army and knows they aren't around to protect me? I pick up speed, cross the street, and cut through the cornfield like I always do and he doesn't, because he lives in the other direction, but Eli is still following me. Now I'm confused as to what action to take so I slip through the rows of cornstalks. These should have been cleared last fall except Harley Garfoyle is a lazy cuss and way too fond of our moonshine. A breeze stirs and makes the corn clack and scrape. The shadows cast by the afternoon sun send tiger stripes across my path, which is knobbed with nubs of corn. I'm getting nervous and walk faster. Eli does, too.

"Charlene, wait!" he yells.

I stop. Curiosity is one of my downfalls.

Eli rushes up. He's carting four books under his left arm. His red plaid shirt is pulled to one side, caught on what he's carrying. He gives me his crooked-tooth smile and looks embarrassed.

"Hey," he says.

"Hi." My heart is pounding like a big old timpani drum.

"Mind if I walk with you awhile?"

"No, I guess not."

I turn and start down the row. Eli comes alongside of me, which is difficult because the space between the corn rows isn't big enough for both of us to walk easily. He lets me go ahead but stays close, his shoulder bumping mine. We're silent, uncomfortable, unsure what to say.

"Charlene," he begins, "you know I still like you."

I swallow hard. "Yeah?" I look at him. "Well, I guess I still like you."

Eli steps in front of me. "Really?"

I nod. We walk to the end of the cornfield and enter the woods.

"Do you want to sit for a spell?" he asks.

I'm supposed to be at the store in twenty minutes, but I agree. He leads me to a knoll above the creek. It's a little damp so Eli piles some brown leaves and we sit on them. A bunch of blue-purple violets are growing between clumps of emerald moss nearby, and the water from the stream smells cold and clean. As I'm taking all this in, Eli stares at me, perhaps working on a speech. Finally, he lays a hand on my elbow.

"I want to apologize for my behavior. I should've been more respectful, especially considering how I feel about you."

I'm wondering about his feelings for Laney. Eli has been all flirty with her, passing notes back and forth during class and leaning against her locker afterward. I've also heard rumors that Laney was putting out for Mack, but they got into an argument, and she told him to take a hike. That's when I think Eli moved in, maybe expecting he'd get lucky with her. Perhaps she refused to put out for him, and he got mad and decided to try me again.

"I accept your apology," I reply, though I am not sure where this will lead.

He gives my arm a squeeze. "You're the best, Charlene!"

I don't respond to his enthusiasm because suspicion is clouding my mind. He doesn't seem to notice my lack of participation, however, and goes on about how great I am, how pretty, cute, smart, well, you name it. I take his words in and think they're a bunch of junk. At long last, he gets to the point.

"I'm so glad we're talking again." He looks down at his black high-top sneakers and rubs at one white rubber toe. "You know the May Day Dance is coming up at school. Would you go with me? That is, I mean, if you don't already have a date."

My suspicion burns away like thin morning fog. Eli grins, hopeful, and yet worried that I'll turn him down. The fact that he isn't sure whether I'll accept flips the switch.

"Sure, Eli, I'd like to go with you." I give him a smile.

He rocks back and forth with excitement then leans over and kisses me on the cheek. For a second, I think it's going to be a real kiss, so when it lands away from my mouth, I'm disappointed. On impulse, I place my hand in his. He rubs my fingers, playing his through mine, and before long I really, really want him to kiss me.

"Like I said a few minutes ago, I need to be respectful of you." He twists the side of his mouth in a half smile. "You know, maybe we should get to know each other better."

I'm upset with this direction and relieved at the same time. Why is everything to do with boys like this? One part one thing and one part another thing, like oil and water, so I never know which is which or what to do. "That's fine," I reply.

"Okay, let's see. If you want to know about me...well...I plan to be a farmer when I grow up. I guess I'm already a farmer because I work for my father most afternoons and weekends. I want to buy a couple more acres of land and add a soybean field. Increase the size of our orchard. Maybe buy a new John Deere tractor. My father and I have been discussing my role when I graduate high school—"

"You mean you're not going to college?"

He shakes his head. "What's the point? Maybe I'll take some winter courses in agriculture, but there's work to do, a farm to be run, responsibilities." As he says this, Eli stares at the ground, flicking over a dead poplar leaf, and furrowing a finger in the dirt to create a little track, like he's farming in miniature. "How about you?" He covers the track with the leaf.

"Oh, I don't know," I reply. "If we can afford it, I hope to study English."

"Really?" Eli glances at me, his eyes unfocus, and then he returns to his construction, adding twigs and pebbles and leaves.

"Yeah. I want to be a writer more than anything."

"More than anything?" he asks in a voice that has a tinge of hurt in it.

"Did I say something wrong?"

He removes his hand from mine so he has two to work on the project beside him. "No, of course not." He shrugs. "I think it's great you want to be a writer, but that means you won't stick around here. You'll head off to some fancy school and meet all kinds of new people. Beatniks and Commies and other odd folks. You'll turn into someone else, Charlene."

I can see that Eli doesn't understand anything about me and probably isn't very interested. Boys are less likely to be keen on a girl's dreams than a girl is about a boy's, but even so, I suspect most of my classmates would agree with Eli's attitude about college and my career plans. I shiver as that old loner feeling drops its chilly shroud over my shoulders.

I pick a violet and twirl it between my fingers, giving myself a flower present since I've lost Eli's hand. "I may go off to school, but we have a few years before that. And who knows what can happen in between? I might fall down dead or another girl could come along and catch your eye. Anyway, even if we have different goals, we can still like each other, right?"

"I guess so. But I was kind of imagining us together. You know…with a house of our own…nice big porch and a tree swing for the kids—"

"Kids? Hold on! I don't want any kids!"

Eli looks up, surprised. "What do you mean? Every girl wants a family. Three children at least. To help with the farm and the house and all. That's just the way it is, Charlene." There's a trace of anger sloshing around with his astonishment.

I reach for his hand, but his fingers feel cold. "Well, maybe one..."

He shakes his head sadly. "And what if he gets sick or is a weak child. Then what?"

I sigh, frustrated. "Well, then, I guess we'd have another, wouldn't we? But right now, can't we just hang out and have a good time?"

Eli leans away a fraction, ponders what I said, and manages a faint smile. Suddenly, I feel so desperate to win his good opinion that I consider having five kids by him next week, even if the little voice of mine is warning that this boy is all wrong.

"Yeah," he says at last. "You're right. We should enjoy each other." His hand lies still in my palm like a dead weight.

I feel like I have to win him over, though I don't understand why. What's wrong with me wanting a college education, a career without children? I'm fine with him being a farmer so why can't I follow my life's calling? I have to bite down on the unfairness and admire him so he'll like me and we can go to the May Dance together.

"I think you'll make a great farmer," I enthuse. "You're so good at everything. I bet your handy with all that machinery, too." While I'm laying it on, he's sneaking quick glimpses of me, his face brightening out of its overcast. I go on in this vein for some time until Eli moves closer; his left hand leaves mine and circles under my arm.

"So you think being a farmer's wife would be fine with you?" he asks.

I shrug and then laugh.

He chuckles. "Okay, okay. But you have to understand. I have all these ideas for the farm and want everything to be just as I imagine. You know how that is...I can't help but dream."

"That's the way it should be," I agree, though my dreams have never featured a farm with cows and chickens and soybeans.

Now Eli is grinning, happy with the prospect of fitting me into his perfect fantasy. He paints pictures of our life down to the Christmas stockings on the mantelpiece—seven of them. Clearly he's forgotten what I said about children, but I don't interrupt because he's holding me and the togetherness feels good. When he finally stops talking, he looks at me like he's never seen me before. Then he leans over, kisses me, and whispers sweet things in my ear.

We go on like this, squirming around on the moss until I feel the damp piercing through my skirt. This awareness brings me back to Grandpa and my responsibilities. I stop kissing Eli.

"I'm sorry, but I have to get home. I have chores to do."

He ignores what I said and embraces me again, tighter, and kisses me so hard I think my teeth will break. His body is hot with excitement, his cheeks flushed.

"I have to go, Eli."

"Oh, Charlene…" he's panting a little, like he's been running a race. "Not yet!" He moves in for another deep kiss. "Please stay a few more minutes."

I'm having trouble breathing myself. He notices this and presses against me. "Come on, we're so good together. We should just…I mean, oh, darn it…I want you so much!"

"I want you, too," I reply, wishing immediately that I hadn't admitted it.

"Really?" He grins at me. "Oh, Charlene, don't worry! I'll get us some protection."

Now I'm in deep. I shake my head, feeling the pressure from him and also the pressure from inside me. I disentangle my arms from his and stand. Eli joins me and tries for another hug.

I pull away. "Eli, if I don't go home, I'll be in trouble."

"Okay, I guess. But it isn't fair to do this to a fellow. It hurts being frustrated."

I had no idea this was the case and said so.

"Yeah, it can be real uncomfortable," he adds, "but next time I'll be prepared."

- 8 -

I'm sitting in the Hooch Shop, writing at my desk. I just sold some Dr. R. J. Riley's Tonic to Mick Galloway, who has the reddest hair and face I've ever seen. The tonic is for his wife, or so he says in his thick Irish brogue. He also bought a bottle of moonshine for himself. I guess the Galloways will be doing a few merry jigs tonight.

Anyhow, I'm on duty turning a buck, but all I can think about is Eli and what to do about him. I hope Grandpa lets me attend the dance, yet if I go, will Eli have expectations afterward? Does he think we'll sneak off around back of the schoolhouse and do it in the woods? I don't remember what I said to him exactly, though I suspect he was more encouraged than I meant for him to be. I wish I had a girlfriend to discuss this with. Someone who would help me out, especially at the dance. The only girl who talks to me—Jaylene—isn't interested in boys, just politics and causes that no one here in Butztown gives a hang about. I should be nicer to her, but she gets riled about everything and rushes off, tilting at windmills like Don Quixote.

Tonight, I'll ask Grandpa about the dance. If he says yes, maybe he'll offer to buy me a new dress.

I unlock the kitchen door and immediately see the note on the table. "Out grocery shopping—C.B." Translated, this means Grandpa is in the shanty we use for making moonshine. It's hidden in the woods uphill from the back of the house. When I was about six years old, Corey, Buck, and Grandpa moved parts of a falling-down hut and re-built it over an old root cellar in which they'd set up an underground copper still vented to the outside by a stovepipe that we raise only during the distilling process. Then they dug a side tunnel entrance to the still and covered it with branches. The building on top is weaving in the wind, but it disguises a solid enterprise beneath its shambles.

The track to the shanty runs about a quarter mile up from our barn and turns to woods and high weeds and grass that disguise the still's location. When the time comes for transporting the summer and autumn batches—about eighty quarts each—my cousins borrow Mr. Carter's mule, load a wagon with hay and empty Mason jars, and haul everything to an area below the still. They carry the jars inside, fill them with product, hide them in the wagon, and ease it to the barn. From there, we hide jars in a secret compartment behind the coat closet in the living room and in a space between floor joists in the chapel hidden by the altar. As needed, we sneak product to the Hooch Shop. The summer batch usually lasts until Christmas, when we close. In March, we open again, selling whatever is left and then bringing the autumn moonshine down later in the spring, which we will do soon.

It's getting close to dark. Yesterday, Grandpa announced it was time to check his extra-fine whiskey that's been aging in six oak barrels. I assume he won't be home until late since he often enjoys his product too much. Because he's probably eaten, I root around in the icebox for some fried chicken Grandpa cooked last night. All the while I do this, I'm wondering how Grandpa and I are going to bring down the autumn batch without Buck and Corey, who are away in Fort Sill learning how to be soldiers. They should have no difficulty with shooting because both boys can plug a chipmunk on the nose from fifty feet, but I'm not sure their independent minds will fit in with military ways.

Thinking about my cousins reminds me of how they treated Eli and the last conversation we had. It left me feeling that I'm on a different highway than everyone else. It's bad enough to be creative and smart, but damn it all if being a girl doesn't tip the scales into serious unfairness. If I were a boy, Eli would respect my ambition to attend college. This inequality is all wrong, but if I want to be an item with Eli, I suppose it's up to me to bend and fit in.

—

A racket wakes me. My Baby Ben clock says 12:39 a.m. I'm sure it's Grandpa C.B. staggering into the kitchen after too many samples of his handiwork. I slip into my bathrobe and go downstairs. The light is on and Grandpa is tilting against the counter at an unstable angle.

"Grandpa? Are you all right?"

He salutes but misses his forehead. "Tip top, my dear. We have some fine, fine product to sell to our eager clients." He's slurring his words and has a happy look plastered on his face. Or maybe it's a happy plastered look. Either way, Grandpa is not nearly sober.

"Hungry?"

"No." He waves his arm in the air but that unbalances him so he has to take a quick step in my direction. Then he has to compensate for that, and in two more steps, I'm holding him upright, or doing my best.

"Grandpa, I think we should go sit on the couch."

"Capital idea!"

Placing his arm over my shoulder, I steer him into the living room and escort him to the sofa, where he attempts to sit on the edge but sprawls backward onto its length. I lift his feet up and cover him with a quilt. In two shakes, he's snoring like an elephant with a serious sinus condition. I turn off the lights and head upstairs. Grandpa isn't usually this bad except during distilling time, but even so he does enjoy his liquor. Then again, so do I, which I need to watch because Mama and Daddy had their problems with it. As I return to bed, I giggle at the thought of me coming in drunk and Eli having to tuck me in. Although the picture is amusing, men don't take care of women like women take care of men.

—

The next afternoon, Eli walks me home. We kiss some and go through the same squirming by the creek only this time we sit on pine needles he's gathered in a mound under a tall tree. Luckily, he wasn't able to purchase protection, so I have an excuse to restrict our activities. I also tell him that I need to ask Grandpa about the dance and must go home. I don't really want to leave, but the sensible part of my brain is at the helm. Or maybe I'm just too worried about what to say to Grandpa.

As I'm walking toward the house, the sunlight is angling on the roof, creating small triangular black shadows below the dormer windows. I notice how run-down the place is, with weeds growing around the porch and much of the white siding half-scraped. The only area my cousins painted and fixed was the addition and entrance to the chapel, where they built an overhanging roof on top of two impressive Doric columns scrounged from an old hotel. Everything is painted bright white except the ceiling underneath, which is a pale sky blue. Grandpa called this touch of color "uplifting." I wanted to paint some clouds there, but Grandpa allowed as how not one of us had sufficient talent for such an artistic endeavor. Other than this side section of the house, the rest is a disorganized sprawl of buildings tacked together and some standing alone as needs dictated over the last century.

While I am resolving to finish the house painting on my own, Grandpa staggers out of the barn with the wagon. It's piled high with hay, and he's got both hands on the wagon's yoke and is leaning forward and pulling. The wheels are moving slowly, but then Grandpa suddenly stops and bends over. Seeing this, I drop my satchel on the ground and run toward him.

"Grandpa! Are you okay?"

Perspiration is soaking through his white shirt. The back of his neck is scarlet. He straightens slightly and looks at me. Although his face is contorted with pain, he makes an effort to hide it. "Yes, I'm fine," he replies, though his voice sounds husky and weak.

"Where's Mr. Carter's mule?"

"Sick," he says, still trying to catch his breath.

"You should have waited for me, Grandpa."

He raises his arm a few inches and stares at his watch. I'm forty minutes late, and though he doesn't say so, the message is clear. I've let him down.

"I'm sorry," I whisper.

Grandpa removes his handkerchief from a back pocket and swipes at his face. "We need to get this wagon up to the still, Charlie. I never tried to do it without the boys."

"I'll help you. But maybe you should rest for a bit."

He nods. "Yes, I think I might."

I walk him over to our log-splitting stump. He doesn't look good.

"You need to go to the hospital or something?"

"No, I just over-exerted myself a little, that's all."

"Well, okay," I reply, though I doubt he was at the exertion long enough to cause this reaction. He doesn't look like he wants to talk about it, however, so I stare at the wagon and the hill and realize that it's very unlikely that one old, over-exerted man and myself can push and pull this wagon to the still. Then I have a bright idea.

"Grandpa, how about if we do the transfer using the Buick?"

He looks at me, surprised. "We've never done that before, Charlie, because it would look suspicious if we got caught with the car up there."

We usually throw an axe and a few logs in the wagon to give the impression we're cutting firewood. "I could say I was learning to drive. Kids practice in funny places."

"I suppose you're right, but that's a lot of lifting for you."

"I can do it." I'm not sure I want to leave him to get the car keys, but Grandpa flips his hand at me to scat. I grab my satchel and go into the house. A few minutes later, I drive the Roadmaster around to where he's sitting. I've driven the car all around the property, with and without Grandpa.

"Now get in and I'll take you to the house so you can rest." I beam with pride as I help him to the passenger seat, but I wipe off the smile when I see how wobbly he is. It's kind of like last night though now he's cold sober. "You sure we shouldn't go to the hospital?"

He shakes his head and I close the door. After I take my place behind the wheel, I glance at him and see that his eyes are closed. Should I take him to the hospital even though he doesn't want to go? When I have to half-carry him to his chair, I'm even more worried. But once he's caught his breath, Grandpa tells me to get going.

—

It's dark by the time I load eighty full Mason jars onto the floor of the Buick, the seats, and in the trunk, using newspapers to keep the glass from breaking and a blanket to cover the jars inside the car. I'm sweating like crazy because I had to make twenty trips to the still with the empty jars brought from the wagon via the Buick, fill them each with product, and another twenty return trips to the car, carrying only four jars at a time for fear of dropping them.

I stretch my back and get in the car, turn on the ignition, and realize I can't use the headlights. This will make the drive down difficult. I set off in first gear, carefully inching toward the house, scared that I'll slip into a ditch or the Mason jars will break from all the bumps. Finally, after a few sickening lurches, I pull alongside the kitchen door and check to see if the law has nosed out our enterprise. Satisfied that all is quiet, I sneak the moonshine inside.

Grandpa is slumped in his chair by the table, asleep, looking like he's been in a prize fight and lost after thirteen rounds. He wakes when I come in.

"Oh, Charlie, let me help you." He starts to rise.

"No, you just rest awhile," I say, as I go to the closet and remove the hidden panel.

After stowing half the jars, I return to the living room and ask Grandpa if he wants some water.

"A little of the usual," he replies, meaning scotch.

"Well, all right, but are you feeling up to it?"

C.B. gives me a sour look. "Medicinal" is all he says.

I fetch Grandpa his drink and continue distributing Mason jars in the closet. When every possible cubbyhole is crammed, I decide the rest of the hooch can stay in the Buick's trunk until tomorrow, because I can't move the heavy altar without Grandpa. I walk into the kitchen, wash my face and hands, and open a cold Coke. Then I begin boiling rice, frying two fat sirloin steaks, and heating canned succotash.

When we're sitting at the table, Grandpa doesn't inquire as to what happened at school or what my new vocabulary words are. This is how I know for a fact he's ailing because these conversational topics are constants in our lives.

"Do you want me to call Doc Fairchild?" I ask, though that quack is almost the last person I'd trust in medical matters.

"No, thanks, Charlie. I'm fine. Just overdid it a little. Not as young as I used to be."

Guilt is rolling around my stomach like a fiery lump of coal. If I hadn't been fooling with Eli, I would have been there for Grandpa. Now I don't know what to do about the dance. I hate to ask Grandpa if I can go, especially when he's feeling poorly. He needs me around to take care of him, and I need to be sure he's okay, because if something happens to him, I'll be left without anyone and would be sent into foster care. And that scares me a lot. Even if someone reports that my parents are gone, Grandpa says social workers might investigate his character and means of employment, which might pass muster, but it's also possible that his activities are known in certain quarters. Last fall, rumors about his moonshine attracted the attention of a federal revenuer, who luckily didn't find the still or any hooch.

I bulldoze some kernels of corn to the side of my plate, thinking on this and also about how much I want to attend the dance with Eli. If I tell him I can't go, he'll find another girl. I don't understand why he's even interested in me. Sometimes I think he picked me because I'd be grateful and willing to do whatever he wants, but whenever I see him and he gives me that private smile, I get fluttery and feel warm all over. Oh, I am so confused!

If this is what it's like being a grown-up, I don't like it. I can see this balancing one thing against another leads to trouble. Maybe that's why Mama is the way she is. Maybe the world just got too much for her. Right now, it seems as if I have to decide whether to lose Eli or risk hurting Grandpa C.B.

If Grandpa looks better by dinner tomorrow night, I'll ask his permission.

—

After I return from school, we shift Mason jars to the space under the altar. Then, I cook pork chops and baked beans because this is one of Grandpa's favorite meals.

"How are you feeling?" I ask him, kind of casual, while we're eating dinner.

He glances at me. "Oh, I'm fit as a fiddle," he replies, taking a bite of meat.

Grandpa appears to be in fine spirits, with improved color. I chew away and try to stoke up some courage. Finally, I take a swallow of milk and clear my throat. "Grandpa? There's something I have to ask you."

Grandpa pauses, a knife in one hand and a fork in the other. "What is it, Charlie?"

"You know how we talked about me being too young for boys? And that you didn't want me thinking about them yet?"

He nods.

"Well, I seem to be thinking about them a lot."

Grandpa is quiet, staring at me. "Especially that young man who asked you to the party?"

"Yes, sir. Him most of all."

"I see."

"Anyhow, Eli has asked me to go to the May Day Dance next Saturday. It's at school."

"And you wish to attend?" He lowers his eyes and eats some beans.

"I do. Yes, sir."

Grandpa sighs. "I see you are determined to go—"

"Not determined. No, sir, but I'd like your permission."

He wipes his mouth with the napkin. "All right, Charlie."

"All right I can go? Really?" I'm so thrilled I almost choke.

He hesitates and seems a little sad, like he's remembering something long ago. Then he snaps out of it. "Yes. And tomorrow, shall we drive to Rochester to buy you some new clothes and a dress for the dance?"

I leap from my chair and run around the table to kiss him. He laughs and hugs me tight.

- 9 -

"Are you sure this is okay?" I ask Grandpa. We're in Sibley's Department Store. I've just walked out from the dressing room in a pale blue gauze dress with a scooped neck and a full skirt that cascades below my knees. It's decorated with white and pink flowers and a scatter of rhinestones and looks lighter than air. I'm also sporting a new bra underneath and feel strange all got up like this.

Grandpa C.B. examines me from head to toe. When he twirls his fingers, I turn so he can check the back. As I do, I catch myself in the full-length mirror and am stunned by my grown-up appearance.

"The dress is a color your mother liked to wear," he says, his eyes soft with memory.

"But, Grandpa, it's $14.99," I whisper.

He shrugs. "What's money when my granddaughter is attending her first dance? Besides, you look beautiful. Prettier than your mother, though very much like her."

I don't believe that I'm prettier than my mother, but I give him a squeeze, careful not to muss the dress. "Thank you, Grandpa."

After Grandpa pays the cashier, we place the packages in the Buick. I now have three new pairs of shoes—black patent leather with low heels for the dance, brown loafers for school, and a pair of white Keds. Also three bras, a white cardigan sweater, underwear, knee socks, a green skirt, shorts, a pair of jeans, and three button-down blouses. Grandpa says these might only last a few months considering how fast I'm growing. Because I've been making do since Mama left, I'm overwhelmed with all of these purchases.

The Buick's convertible top is down—the first day it's been warm enough. During the hour-drive home, we're in high spirits. Grandpa is laughing about his new "gifting game."

"I need for you to make up four names for me, Charlie. You know the sort."

I do. Lived in, comfortable, with character. Names to remember but unusual ones that no one in the county would have.

"This is good practice for you—creating fictitious names," he says.

I allow how this is true because I want to follow the writing trade. "And then what?"

"This is called a Pyramid Game. The last time I did one was when you were a baby." He smiles, remembering. "It goes like this. Imagine a pyramid standing on its point. I'm the point. Above me are four people—all fakes. These fake people give me $5 apiece—this is pretend—and then I find four real people to give each of the fakes $5 and also $5 to me. These sixteen people might be members of a church group, for example. At a meeting, they hand me money and put $5 in envelopes to the four fakes, who I explain I'm representing because they're at work."

"And these envelopes go to the post office boxes you're renting under different names. Like you do with W. M. Lawson."

"A very useful fellow," Grandpa gives me a mischievous grin.

"Okay," I say, calculating sums in my head. "So these sixteen people give you $5 each for a total of $80 and another $5 to the four fakes, or $80."

"Ah, you're quick! At this tier, I've made $160. Now, these sixteen must find four new people each, sixty-four total, who give the fake four people $5 each and the real sixteen people $5 each. This means the fake four receives another $320. Since the group of sixty-four gives the tier below them $5 per person, each member of the original sixteen tier receives twice what they sent to the folks below them, all of whom are me, in one guise or another. And I make $480."

"And the first tier of real people expands the pyramid, which they'll do otherwise they lose the money they sent to the tier below them."

"You have it, Charlie. Unfortunately, this design falls apart eventually. Some people may earn money or break even; others might lose money. However the initial church group usually makes a profit as promised so I can honestly say the plan will work for them." He gives me a sly look. "And because I'm present only at the first meeting and we use mail thereafter, with the transactions in cash, there is little evidence. I use the name Reverend Xavier Kay to prevent anyone from finding me later. Precautions, Charlie!" He winks.

I return his wink. He has a fondness for the name "Xavier" because it sounds so much like "Savior."

"I've made appointments with the bingo committees of three

churches for tomorrow and Saturday. Now, most folks are partial to gambling, which churches encourage when it suits their purposes of making money. And nothing appeals to people more than gambling under the guise of doing good works, especially when they can line their pockets. I explain they can donate a quarter of their return to their church—or all of it—as I will do with whatever proceeds I receive. When I dangle the real hook, that they can double their investments or more, their eyes glisten with greed. I'll wear my collar, of course, and carry a Bible." He chuckles at his own cleverness, which never ceases to amuse him.

I do more calculations. "So with three groups you could earn $1,440?" I whistle in amazement.

"Yes, but we have to be careful. It's a federal crime to use the mail for something like this."

I sit there with the wind streaming through my hair, stunned at this brilliant scheme but troubled by the possibility of people losing money. And it's worrisome to think that if the government catches Grandpa at this gifting game, he could go to jail.

—

"Hi, Charlene."

I turn and see Eli holding a handful of violets surrounded by a paper doily. He's blushing and grinning as he stands in front of my hall locker.

"Happy May Day," he whispers.

I can tell he wants to kiss me, but he can't in school. "Oh, Eli! No one has ever given me flowers before."

This pleases him. "Well, tomorrow night you might get something else," he says, "when I come by your house." He stares at his shoe, then glances at me with his tucked-up grin.

I realize he's going to buy me a corsage, which is why he asked the color of my dress yesterday. I give him a big smile. We shuffle around a little, bumping against each other just to make contact. "I'm looking forward to the dance, aren't you?"

"Yeah." He tries to sound casual, but his eyes are twinkling. "See you after school?"

"I better not today. I have chores to do or I can't go tomorrow."

"Okay, but I'll miss my kiss."

—

After I get home and change clothes, I go to the coat closet and load my satchel with filled Mason jars and carry them to the

Hooch Shop. Fridays are always the busiest for us and today is no exception, especially since it's May Day. Regular as clockwork, Dusty Tiebock runs across the field at 3:30, glides into the shop like a ghost, and buys a quart and pays all the money he owes us, which I note in the ledger. Garrison Klemm arrives a few minutes later from the other direction because he lives near the lake. He takes two jars and a bottle of Dr. R. J. Riley's Tonic for his wife. As he leaves, Lorna Hartnette bicycles down the track with red saddlebags flopping on both sides of the back wheel. She ties her long gray hair in a ponytail and favors rolling the cuffs of her jeans to flash her skinny ankles and knotting the ends of her blouse so that an expanse of belly shows. She says this is Hollywood style, though I cannot attest to the accuracy of this statement. Lorna probably thinks she looks fetching and hopes to get lucky one of these days, allowing as how she is now single and on the troll for an eligible gentleman. Her husband, Mr. Roy Hartnette, took off some years ago before these fashion alterations occurred. Seems like he knew things were heading downhill with Lorna and decided to hightail it while he had a bit of handsomeness left.

Lorna squints at me, doing drinking math in her head: how many people she's expecting multiplied by how much each will imbibe. "Two quarts will probably do us fine, Charlie."

After I hand over the bottles, she stuffs them into the bicycle's saddlebags and explains she's holding a May Day shindig. Lorna and her kith and kin are big on celebrating every holiday you can imagine and some they make up as an excuse to drink.

This is how it goes for two hours. I'm up and down the ladder with hardly a break. Seems like everyone in Butztown has a serious case of spring fever. Truth be told, so do I. All I can think about is tomorrow night and the dance. I try to read some Dickens in order to steady my mind, but I can't follow his long sentences. Eventually, the business calms down and I see Grandpa driving in, dust flying behind the Buick. He nods at me as he passes, looking high and mighty and regal. I figure he's had a fine day pyramiding.

—

Now that I'm alone and the house is quiet, I can sit a spell and think about Eli. As much as I like him, I worry that he wants to go all the way. During our last afternoon together, he implied he would buy rubbers, but I heard they break sometimes and the poor girl gets stuck with a baby. This idea frightens the hell out of me. I never want to have kids under any circumstances.

I also worry about my reputation at school. Boys like to brag, and I doubt Eli would keep his crowing to himself. You'd think he would because how we feel about each other is private, but rumors about fast girls get started somewhere, mostly by the boys themselves, who need to establish their Romeo reputations. Of course, if I say no to Eli, then he'll probably get mad and go off with another girl. I surely wish this birds-and-bees situation wasn't happening. I don't feel ready to deal with babies or rubbers. Grandpa would call this a quandary and so it is.

As upset about this as I am, Eli looked so proud when he gave me the violets. I wanted to hug him. It was hard not to go off after school to our special place, but we'll have a wonderful time tomorrow. I don't think I'll sleep a wink tonight on account of the dance.

—

I'm pacing back and forth in the living room even though my patent leather shoes pinch, and my new starched petticoat feels itchy. Mostly I can't wait for Eli and his father to come. I hope they'll arrive soon before I get any hotter.

Grandpa is watching me with a far-away smile on his face. He tells me I look several years older than I am, beautiful, pretty, all kinds of things. I think he means what he says, even though he's scrutinizing last week's issue of *Life* magazine, the one with Marilyn Monroe on the cover nibbling her diamond earring. There seems to be a huge gulf between me wearing my little string of pearls and old Marilyn swanking around with her pouty lipstick smile and blond puffed-up hair. I never want to be that kind of girl, but the comparison isn't helping my confidence.

Grandpa catches me staring at the cover, glances at it, and closes the magazine. Then he lifts out of his chair and goes upstairs, returning with a pair of short white gloves. "Here," he says, "every lady needs these."

My Mama's gloves. I slide them on my fingers thinking the last hands inside were hers. A wave of sadness floods over me as I smell the palms and catch the scent of Prince Matchabelli perfume, which she wore on special occasions, as I do, too, tonight, having dabbed some behind my ears from the bottle in her room. For a minute, tears well up, but I grit my teeth and force them away. This is no night to cry.

When Eli arrives, I watch him stroll along the front walk to the door. Grandpa C.B. lets him in and shakes his hand while I stand there, staring at Eli, who is dressed in a navy suit and gold bowtie. His brown hair is freshly cut and perfectly combed, and he's just as handsome as any Prince Charming I've ever seen. Even though my legs are a little wobbly, I manage to cross the floor. Suddenly, I don't care if my toes hurt being shoved into pointy shoes.

"Good evening, Charlene," Eli says.

I have an urge to laugh at how formal he is, but the occasion has infected me, too. "Good evening," I reply, trying my best not to grin.

We hang out for a moment, our eyes glittering at each other. Then Eli remembers the corsage in his hand. It's in a clear plastic box steamed up by the pink carnation and fern inside.

"This is for you." As Eli begins to give me the box, he laughs nervously. "Oh, sorry." With shaking fingers, he opens the container. Grandpa, sensing Eli's nervousness, takes the box so that Eli is free to pin the corsage on my dress, which he does without sticking me.

"Be home by 11:00, okay?" Grandpa says. "Or a few minutes after." He gives me a wink.

—

The gymnasium is decorated with shimmery yellow and white streamers. Pink filters on the lights give a romantic glow so that we almost forget the bleachers and the fact we're standing on the basketball floor, whose lines are obscured by sweet-smelling sawdust spread to protect the hardwood. The school also must have kidnapped an entire florist shop because a jungle of green plants has been arranged to enclose an area for dancing. I take in these transformations and imagine I'm in some far-off place rather than Butztown High School. It is also a real pleasure to observe the expressions of my classmates as they see Eli and me together. I feel so proud to be on his arm.

I place my purse on a cafeteria table, and Eli helps me remove my white sweater, which he hangs over a folding chair.

"Do you want to dance?" he asks.

"Sure."

"I learned the box step this week. From my sister. It's pretty simple."

Unlike at his house, he takes my gloved hands and holds me with plenty of space between us. Here, we're being scrutinized by teachers and parents, who are making a great show of manning the punch bowls, yet their eyes are glued on us in case we exhibit any frisky behavior. I let Eli guide me around the imaginary square, one stride forward, turn, and so on until I can't help laughing.

For a second, Eli gives me a startled glance, then he smiles and draws me closer. "That's enough of that," he says, and begins his own pattern, hinting at the direction by squeezes of his hand on mine and pressure on my back.

I like this much better. We're not exactly Ginger Rogers and Fred Astaire, but the little bumps and missteps make us keenly aware of each other as we try to mesh our bodies together.

—

Eli and I keep to ourselves, dancing, drinking punch, staring into each other's eyes. The sort of behavior that seems to last for hours or seconds, like time is all twisted up. Finally, although I hate to break the mood, I have to go to the girls' room. I take my purse so I can add more lipstick, and Eli walks me through the open double doors and down the hall.

Inside the bathroom, as I pass the mirrors, I catch a glimpse of Mama. I freeze and she quickly disappears into me—a flushed kid wearing a blue dress and a pink carnation held on by a pearl stickpin. This vision makes me wonder where my mother is, what she's doing, and if it's possible she's coming through the mirror to let me know she's thinking of me. I remove her gloves, press them to my face, and place them in my purse because they're too precious to wear.

When I step into the hall, Eli isn't there. I figure he went to the boys' room. I stand across the way, by the window. The stars are impossible to see because of the outside spotlights, but I know they're there because I can feel their magic. Just as I'm thinking this is the best night of my life, I hear laughter from inside the boys' room, and then Eli, Slick Rick Doorman, and Booky Bartell emerge, looking like they've done something they shouldn't have.

Rick's nickname fits. His black hair is greased back with Brylcreem, and he's swanking around in a pale blue blazer like he's Elvis. I can tell he's spent time studying the King because he's got the same slack-mouthed expression and kind of lounges against walls as if he's too bored to stand up. In contrast to Rick, who is skinny and flat-assed, Bobby Bartell, who everyone calls "Booky," is a solid slab. Stupid, too, hence his ironic nickname. Neither of these boys is in my classes, and neither has ever glanced at me once. I didn't realize they were friends of Eli's. In fact, though I'd

62

noticed earlier that Rick was glued to Sharon Chestler during a slow dance, I hadn't seen Booky until now.

"Hey, there she is," Eli says, not to me, but to Booky.

"Jesus Christ!" Booky exclaims. "That's your date?"

Rick and Booky stop like they're a yoked team of horses.

"Yeah. What's the matter?" Eli asks.

Booky steps closer to me. I smell alcohol and know some drinking has just occurred. A quick peek at Eli's red face confirms this.

"You're the moonshiner's granddaughter." Booky looks at me like I'm filth.

"Come on! You're crazy," Eli says.

Booky Bartell shakes his head. "Yeah, she is. My pop just told me it was C. B. Whitestone who gave my cousin Sammy that tonic. The stuff was so full of poison that he got sick as a dog and fell down the stairs. Broke a bunch of ribs and his collarbone. Nearly died."

Eli gives Booky a shove. "You've got this all wrong. Charlene's granddad is a minister."

"Oh, no, he ain't. Not by a stretch," Slick Rick puts in. "He's a con man of the first order. My uncle says so."

"And who's your uncle, Rick? Some dumb jerk?" Eli retorts.

Rick juts his chin, and though his body hasn't begun to fill out, I suddenly see the resemblance before he announces Sheriff Shackrack is his uncle.

Even though C.B.'s clients are discreet because they don't want to lose their cheap source of hooch, I often wondered how folks know how to find us. No one at school has ever breathed a word that Grandpa's various business activities are known, but his reputation might be one reason I've been shunned.

Eli glances in my direction. Although he's hopping mad at Slick and Booky, I can see he needs reassurance that my grandfather is none of the things the boys said. I should lie and protest, but I'm too upset to think.

When I don't utter a word, Eli takes me by the arm. "Charlie?"

I notice "Charlene" has disappeared like Cinderella's carriage after midnight. My happiness evaporates and misery floods in. Unable to answer, I shake my head and run down the hall and outside into the cornfields. Tears fly out of my eyes and I can scarcely see.

- 10 -

I crash through weeds and bushes, tears streaming down my face. When I stop, doubled over and out of breath, I listen to be sure Eli isn't chasing after me and am relieved to hear silence. I don't want him to see me crying, but I'm also hurt that he doesn't care enough to follow me. He probably went off with Slick Rick and that idiot Booky to finish the liquor, trading stories about yours truly that would make me furious. Then again, Eli might have stood up for my honor or waited to hear my side of things if I'd stuck around and been braver.

I clench my fists and feel like pounding on something. I don't know if I'm angry or sad. One thing's for sure, it makes me sick hearing Booky and Rick talk about C.B. like he was scum. He's a good man, and even though his scams hurt poor folk and he takes advantage of weaknesses like religion, gambling, and whiskey, he also visits sick parishioners and gives counsel to those in need.

"Why do you have to do these things, Grandpa?" I shout, banging a fist on a poplar tree. "Why?" I slump against the trunk and stare at the moonlight through the new green leaves, unsure if I'm more upset with Eli and his friends or Grandpa. The cool wind on my face makes my tears feel like tiny ice crystals. I wipe at my cheeks yet can't stop crying. "Oh, everything is ruined!" I think about Eli and how happy I was. My first boyfriend, my first dance!

"What's wrong with me that no one likes me?" I ask the moon, but all the moon does is stare back. I strip a piece of bark from a stick. "What a stupid fool you are, Charlie, thinking Eli liked you! If he cares so damned much, why didn't he come after you? Huh? Why does it always have to be like this?" I shout. "You'll never have a boyfriend! You're a loser!"

As more tears fall, all I can think about is how I'm not like other kids, that I was born with something missing. I stare into the cavernous hole that is my life. I have no friends and am an outcast—always doomed to exist outside of everything and everyone. Then I remember how I felt at Eli's house. It was wonderful to be with a normal family, in their cozy living room, with a mother who made cookies and wasn't crazy. If I were Eli's girl-friend, I could go over there after school and do my homework at the kitchen table, have fun, and be a regular girl. Now, none of that will ever happen.

I lean against the tree and listen, but Eli isn't coming. I wish we could have this out here, alone, rather than in school, where things will be even more difficult once Slick Rick and Booky spread tales about what happened at the dance. I picture Rick licking his greasy chops over how I ran off, and this makes my blood boil. I should have held my ground and lied.

As for Grandpa and Eli, I try too hard to be the perfect girl they want. I'm C.B.'s cleaner, log-chopper, cook, accountant, drink-fetcher, and seller of hooch and Bibles—whatever he requires. I'm fed up with all this and need to stand up for myself, to find out who Charlene Beth Whitestone is and what I want.

I swipe my arm against my face and shiver since I left my new white sweater at school, and the night dampness has settled over the woods. Truth be told, I'm afraid to go home and admit to Grandpa what happened. What can I say to him?

—

"Charlie?" Grandpa calls when he hears me at the side door.

"Yes, sir?"

He walks into the kitchen as I let myself in. The clock says it's only 9:40. No time to be coming home from a dance and arriving on foot rather than by car, alone, with red eyes.

"What happened?" He crosses the room and places both hands on my shoulders.

This makes me feel like gravity has returned to my body. I press against his wool sweater. "Oh, Grandpa!" My voice is choked and tears start again.

He steers me into the living room and onto the couch, holding me so that I'm even more disgusted with myself for not standing up to Booky and Slick. He hands me his pale blue handkerchief. I blow my nose and wipe my face.

"I know you're thinking that Eli got fresh or something," I begin, "but he didn't. We were having a great time, dancing and talking. Oh, Grandpa, everything was so nice!" I describe the decorations and how pretty the gym looked. I'm also desperate to confide how I felt being included and fitting in, but I don't.

"So what did he do?" he asks, frowning.

"It's sort of complicated." I'm beating the mental bushes, desperate to find a path out of this treacherous jungle. "See it's like this...I mean..."

"Did someone say something about your parents?"

I stifle a sigh of relief, then nod. "Yes, sir. Some boys joined up with Eli, and they got to telling him that Daddy's a no-account drunk and Mama is crazy."

"I see."

I can hear the sorrow in those two little words, but nevertheless I'm on safer ground. "One of them was Sheriff Shackrack's nephew."

"Rotten lowlifes," Grandpa mutters. "Don't pay any attention to them."

I agree with him about Booky and Slick Rick being rotten.

Grandpa lets out a long breath. I hear a funny rattle in his chest that sounds like he inhaled fluid into his lungs. "Charlie, your mother is a fine woman," he says, after a cough, "but she suffers from troubles. One of these days soon, she'll smarten up and come home. You can count on that."

I don't believe him—about Mama returning. I want to ask if I've inherited some of Mama's emotional problems, but the words won't come out. Though Grandpa and I spend a lot of time exercising our vocabularies, neither of us is good at discussing how we feel.

"And your young man, Eli...how did he behave when these boys started in?"

"I don't know, Grandpa. I was so surprised and upset that I took off and left him standing there. I know that was foolish, but that's what I did."

"Well, sometimes we don't always know what to do in certain situations. Your young man will come round once you've had a chance to explain. If he cares about you, that is, and I'm sure he does."

"But what can I tell him about Mama?"

Grandpa is silent, then he rubs his chin. "I wouldn't say anything about her except that she's off visiting relatives. Tell him she has a sister who is doing poorly. In South Dakota. And that she's absolutely fine."

This is our usual story, one that we've spread for months whenever we need to account for Mama's lengthy absence. "All right, Grandpa. I'll do that."

—

I'm due to give the sermon. However, Grandpa says it's okay to skip today's service. Before the congregation arrives, I walk to the place where Eli and I sat and kissed. I'm hoping he'll mosey by, but all I've seen is a group of deer passing through the bushes, their ears alert and their noses twitching.

I am so confused and sad. I try to separate my interest in Eli from my wish to have friends, even though the two seem glued together. I liked being hugged and kissed, visiting his house for the party. I also liked attending the dance with my classmates, but I don't seem able to twist myself into the kind of girl Eli wants or the kids at school will like. I know this, yet I wish Eli would come back.

From my pocket, I take out a pen and notebook and start to write about how I feel. This doesn't work so I rip out the pages and crumble them. I try composing a poem, but the words are a jumbled mess like my mind. Frustrated, I pick up a stone and hurl it into the stream, wishing I could grow up and be done with all this confusion. Then, suddenly, another stone skips in the water. I whirl around and see Eli standing a few feet away. He holds my white sweater and is wearing neat khakis and a yellow shirt that glows in the late morning sun. He's probably fresh from Sunday service. The Houks attend the Catholic church in Brockport.

"Hey," he says, coming nearer, hesitation in his step and on his face. "I thought you might be here."

I don't know what to say so I wait, hope warming my heart and scaring me at the same time. Eli closes the space between us and offers my sweater. "You forgot this."

"Thanks." The fact that he brought my sweater makes me feel great. It means he was searching for me.

"Can we talk?"

I nod and he sits beside me, resting his arms on his knees and staring at his shoes.

"I figure we have some things to say to each other," he says.

"Yeah, I guess so."

Eli sighs. "After you ran off, Rick and Booky told me a bunch of things about your grandfather. They also told me your parents are gone." He peeks at me uncertainly. "I thought my mother talked to yours? Before the party."

"Well, no, she didn't. You see, Grandpa decided some time ago it would be best if we didn't let on about my parents being away. I don't know why he doesn't want people to know, but my family is kind of private. Mama and Daddy are with my aunt. She's very sick."

"Oh," he says, "sorry to hear that."

"Yeah. My aunt has a heart condition. No one knows how long it will be before she dies." I start to add the bit about South Dakota, but Grandpa always says to keep stories as short as possible. "So when your mother called, I didn't mean to be dishonest. It just popped into my head to pretend I was my mother."

Eli frowns and shakes his head. "So you lied to my mom?"

I rub my neck. "I suppose. It was more of a fib than anything. I didn't mean any harm."

"Sounds like you and your grandfather do a fair amount of fibbing."

I don't like this, even if it's the truth. "Only when circumstances force us." Since I didn't mean to agree with him, I add, "I can't properly explain about my family, Eli. We're not like yours, though I wish we were. Grandpa has been taking good care of me. In fact, he's as good a grandfather as ever lived."

"One who sells moonshine?" Eli's lips compress into a tight line.

"Well, my goodness!" I reply, anger getting the better of me. "What's wrong with that? No one is forcing people to buy the stuff!"

"No, maybe not, but he's certainly encouraging folks in their bad habits. If they didn't have such a cheap supplier, they'd be better off. Rick says—"

"I don't want to hear what that stupid Slick Rick says! Anybody who slinks around like he's Elvis Presley is just plain cheap. And his uncle the sheriff is even worse!"

"Hey, easy! I didn't mean to get you all riled up, Charlene." He lays a hand on my shoulder as he says this.

I shrug his hand away. "Well, I am riled up plenty! I don't see why everyone criticizes my family. They're doing the best they can. Making fine corn whiskey is a talent," I say, staring hard at Eli. "Besides, if you could get your hands on a jar of his moonshine, I bet you wouldn't complain! You'd pour some in your silver flask and think you were sitting pretty."

Eli backs up like I'd swiped at him. "Hold on there—"

"And furthermore my grandfather takes pleasure in his work just like your daddy likes to drive his tractor up and down your fields a million times a day."

"Now don't you go and talk about him!"

"Why not?" This is going in the wrong direction, but I can't stop. "I just want you to show the same respect for my grandfather as you would for your own." My hands are balled into fists, as if I'm ready to punch my way out of the argument. I release them and try to calm down, but it's a long way to get there.

We glare at each other and move a few inches apart.

"Charlene, I had no idea you possess such a mean temper," he says, tucking in his chin.

"Well, you're mighty smug, aren't you, Eli? Sounds like you think my family isn't as good as yours."

He bolts to his feet. "Look here, I came all this way to return your sweater and to patch things up between us. I had a great time at the May Day dance until you ran off without explaining—"

"Why the hell should I explain anything to anybody?"

"Don't you swear at me, Charlene!"

"I will if I want to!"

"If you can't behave like a young lady, well, you can go fight with another boy 'cause I don't want anything to do with you ever again!"

"Like a young lady? And of course you acted like a fine gentleman? Letting those jerks insult me the way they did. I didn't hear one peep out of you!"

"They were only telling the God's honest truth!" Eli retorts. "And from how you're behaving, I think the situation with your family is far worse than they said. I won't mention any of this to anybody, but we're through." With this, he glowers at me, turns, and stomps off.

I want to run after him, but I have too many insults boomeranging around in my brain. I stand there frozen, breathing hard, itching to beat the hell out of something. I grab a dead branch and whack it against a tree. The impact reverberates through my hands to my arms, sending a warning for me to stop. I drop the branch and realize I'm shaking with anger, which scares me almost as much as what I'm angry about. I don't like these feelings because they remind me of my father and how he flies into rages.

"Oh, hell!" I kick some dirt. "Please don't make me like Daddy!" Tears squeeze into my eyes, and I collapse on the ground. "Please!"

Suddenly, I feel overwhelmed by my family: my loony mother, my abusive father, and Grandpa, who loves me but has made me a partner in his illegal activities. I don't want to be like any of them. "It isn't fair!" I shout, as I press both hands against my head to stifle my internal tirade. I always thought the reason the kids at school kept their distance was because they didn't like me, but it could be because of my family's reputation. And the worst part is I don't know which it is. My only chance to find out was with Eli, and now he'll go off with some other girl who'll be thrilled to live on a farm and have a dozen babies and a porch and soybeans and a husband who drives a bright green tractor up and down the fields all day.

The futility of my situation makes me feel trapped. I can't escape who my parents are or who Grandpa is, and I'm too young to take off on my own. I wipe my face with my fingers. Well, I don't have to go along with Grandpa! I don't have to be his hooch-seller, sermon-writer, cook, and all-around servant! I'm not some dumb little kid he can con into doing whatever he wants!

I dry my face with my shirttail and picture Grandpa C.B. sitting in his chair with a tot of Chivas, fussing because I'm not home to prepare his Sunday supper. I jump to my feet. "I won't!" I promise myself.

- 11 -

When I reach the driveway, I slow down to catch my breath. It's 2:30, way past when we usually have Sunday supper. I walk quickly around the house to the kitchen door, but as I touch the door knob, I hesitate, worried that losing my temper at Grandpa may create a situation far worse than the one I'm already in. Even so, something has to be done.

The kitchen is in shadow except for a shaft of sunlight falling across the yellow-and-white gingham tablecloth. Next to the glass salt and pepper shakers are my green checkbook, two envelopes, Grandpa's brown fedora, and his black fountain pen. All of this strikes me as odd because my checkbook was in my bureau, Grandpa always keeps his pen in his inside breast pocket, and, if he's inside the house, he hangs his hat on the stand by the front door. I lay my sweater on the counter and walk into the living room. Grandpa is sitting in his chair, wearing his dark gray suit, a glass of scotch beside him. When I come into the room, he gives me a small smile.

"Ah, there you are, Charlie," he says in a quiet voice.

I stand opposite him, determined to have my say. "Grandpa, I can't go on like this."

He raises his eyebrows.

"No, I can't. Last night I told you Eli and his friends were talking about Mama and Daddy. Well, they were also talking about you. About the moonshine business and your scams and schemes. I'm not positive, but I think the reason no one will be friends with me at school is because they don't want to get mixed up with a family who breaks the law." I study Grandpa's face, which is strangely still. "I don't care so much about the whiskey. The pyramiding and insurance stuff and selling fake medicine to people who think it's going to make them feel better…that's not okay with me. If you want to do these things, you'll have to count me out."

We stare at each other for a minute. When Grandpa starts to reply, I hold up my hands. "No, sir, I've made up my mind. I'm really upset about all this." I begin to pace back and forth in front of him. "I'll continue to sell the whiskey until Buck and Corey come home, but I won't write any more of those lying sermons or pretend I love the Lord. No more of that. And I wish you'd quit selling insurance policies to poor people who are dying." As I talk, I keep crossing the floor, working myself up. Then I face Grandpa. "I think it's pretty horrible that you've involved me with all this stuff. You did the same thing to Mama and look what happened to her."

Grandpa's chin falls on his chest. After a long sigh that ends in a cough, he raises his head. "You're right, Charlie. I haven't acted properly towards you. I apologize."

This surprises me. I sit on the sofa, though I'm almost too agitated to stay still.

"I've always taken the easy way around things rather than buckle down at a job," he says. "I could have been a businessman or a lawyer...anything I wanted, but for some reason, I loved nothing better than to outsmart people. To use their gullibility against them. I suppose I believed they were getting what they deserved, but mostly it was a big game to make myself feel clever and to turn a fast buck." He lights a cigar, takes a puff, and stares over my head like he's seeing ghosts. Then he sighs and looks at me. "After I married your grandmother, I made a serious mistake. She was a good woman who loved me, just like you're a good girl who loves me. Because of my selfish behavior, taking chances that I shouldn't have, I subjected her to so much worry that the blessed woman's heart gave out. This left your mother in my care. And as you said, I didn't do right by her, either. I should have been a better father to Eileen." He stops to sip his drink, then lays his head against the lace pinned to his chair. "I've fouled up my life, your mother's life, and now yours."

I'm alarmed by this outpouring of remorse. I've never heard Grandpa talk this way. Suddenly, I want to tell him everything is fine, but I can't switch emotional gears fast enough.

He takes a deep breath, exhales, winces, and closes his eyes like something pains him.

I sit in silence, unsure what's happening. Time seems suspended. "Grandpa?"

He opens his eyes and squints, as if he can't see me. "Charlie, I want to tell you something else, something I should have told you before. A month ago, one day when you were in school, your Daddy called. He was in a bar in Arkansas. I don't know what town, just that he'd landed there when his money ran out. Anyhow, he was drunk and mad because your mother left him. He wanted to know if she was here. I told him she wasn't. I asked if he had a job, and he said he was working in a tavern. Someone started shouting at him and he hung up. That's all I've heard from him. I've heard nothing from your mother. The only good news is that he's far away from here, and she's not with him or at least wasn't then."

"Why didn't you tell me this before?" I demand.

He shakes his head. "I don't know. I guess I didn't want to upset you or lead you to believe your mother was on her way home."

"Well, you know what I think? I think you're happy Mama's gone so you can have me all to yourself...to do the things she wouldn't do for you anymore. I remember how mad she was last year when you tried to make her sell fake pieces of Sputnik."

Despite his somber mood, he chuckles. "That was a good one. The existing remnants from a Russian satellite that fell to Earth. Some scrap metal I melted with a Bunsen burner."

"Yeah, but instead of doing the scamming yourself, you asked her to do it." Grandpa is silent, so I continue, "All you were interested in was your little con. You didn't care about her at all. You never considered what our neighbors would think or what they'd tell their children about our family." This comes out nastier than I intend, and I regret it immediately.

"Charlie, you're right. I didn't think about any of that," he whispers. "I'm sorry you feel this way about me. Very sorry." He stubs out the cigar and lays back as if this small activity tires him. "Oh, and I thought we were getting along fine."

This slows me down. As his green eyes study me through his glasses, I notice how depressed he looks. "Well—"

He shakes his head to silence me. "No, Charlie, what you said is fair. I can't make it up to you or bring your mother home. The best I can do is this." He reaches into the breast pocket of his suit and pulls out a thick packet of bills. "You may not want this money, but it's yours. I've also deposited a thousand dollars in your checking account and another thousand in your mother's in case she returns. The rest is here and around the property. You know where."

I stare at the stack of hundred-dollar bills. I've never seen so much cash. "Oh, my god! Grandpa, what's the matter?"

He closes his eyes again, and I'm even more scared. "I just want everything in order."

I come to my feet, quickly crossing the room, and kneel in front of him. "Are you okay?"

"Yes, of course." He chucks me under the chin and smiles. "And I certainly understand how you feel about helping me out. I appreciate your offer to keep selling our whiskey, though, since I can't manage the ladder very well. Maybe we won't do any more distilling next fall. After this last batch is sold, perhaps we'll close up shop. Let's see how it goes."

He's being so nice that I feel miserable about what I've said to him. "I'm sorry, Grandpa." Although I intend to say more, I'm caught between my guilt over not helping him and my guilt for helping him.

"No need to apologize. You do what makes you comfortable, Charlie, and I'll be grateful." He rests a heavy hand on my shoulder, as if his arm is weak. "Now, I need to move the Buick under the shed. It looks like rain."

"I'll do it."

"No, that's all right. Why don't you start supper?"

Even though a few minutes ago I was determined not to be his cook any longer, suddenly I don't mind. In fact, I'm willing to do just about anything for Grandpa.

"And here," he says, handing me the money.

I take it and come to my feet. He stands and uncrooks his back, grabs his cane, and starts off toward the kitchen, his gait slow and unsteady. As he does so, I notice his gray hair is kicked up over his white collar, ruffled from sitting so long against the chair. For some reason, this makes him appear very old and fragile. I want to rush after Grandpa to neaten his hair, but I'm too astonished by the tenderness I feel for him and too overcome by his gift.

He puts on his brown hat and jams his keys in his pocket. Then he opens the door and steps outside, holding onto the door frame with his left hand as he eases down to the slate paving stone below. When the door closes, I stare at the money, tempted to count the bills, but I go into the kitchen, slide the cover off the bread drawer, and place the roll inside, realizing it's probably from the insurance payouts made to Grandpa's church.

Although I'm upset and worried, I open the icebox to see what I can cook for dinner and decide on frozen fish sticks and a salad. And because the weather is turning foul, cream of mushroom soup. The first drops of rain slash the side of the house as I walk into the pantry, affix the can to the wall opener, and crank until the lid pops up. I toss the top in the garbage, and am spooning the soup into a saucepan, when the Buick's horn sounds—one long, continuous blast, not Grandpa's usual cheery two or three toots. Instantly, I drop the can on the counter and rush out the door. A sudden squall has blown off the lake, whipping the trees to a twitchy frenzy and sending intense rain against my face so that I'm almost blinded. My clothes are soaked in seconds as I run around the back of the house. The Roadmaster is half in the shed, the rear window dotted with raindrops, and the brake lights lit. At first, I worry Grandpa has had an accident, but there's nothing to hit except the wall of the shed, and the car is four feet from it. Then the horn stops and the brake lights go off. I freeze. Perhaps the engine stalled? I keep walking toward the Buick until I see something large and dark fall to the right inside the car. Frightened, I hurry past the dividing wall and grasp the car's door handle. Through the window, I see Grandpa slumped across the front seat, his glasses awry on his nose, and his brown hat upside down on the floor, its white silk lining gleaming in the silvery light.

"Grandpa!" I throw open the door, but he doesn't respond. I push his shoulder and his left hand slides off the bottom of the steering wheel. His fingers don't move, and the big purple veins on the top of his hand have gone flat and pale.

I run to the passenger's door and open it. Grandpa's gaze is fixed, unwavering. Panic squeezes my chest so hard I can't breathe. I sit on the far edge of the seat, terrified to touch him. His stillness astonishes me, but I force myself to take his pulse. There isn't one. I try the other wrist, but there's no beat there. Tears begin to tumble down my cheeks.

"Oh, Grandpa," I sob. "No! You can't be dead. You can't!" I repeat this several times as if my words could revive him. "This is all my fault! I did this!" I rock forward and back, holding myself and replaying my angry condemnation of his activities, of him. How ungrateful and hateful I must have sounded! How hurtful I was! As I think this, I realize I have inflicted the ultimate pain on another person. Self-disgust and shame are heaped on grief, producing a fiery mountain of emotion. "I killed you!" I wail over and over. My words reverberate within the car, bouncing off the windshield and windows until the loudness hurts my ears, and I drop my voice to an urgent whisper. "Forgive me, Grandpa. I didn't mean what I said. I didn't!"

The weak evening light fades from the sky. I plead with him to offer his blue handkerchief so I can wipe my tears. If he will, I promise never to sass him or give him a cross word or argument.

I'll never fuss about cooking or tending the Hooch Shop or helping him print fake invoices and labels. If he wants to pyramid all of Rochester, that's fine with me.

I turn off the ignition and step out of the car, hoping the rain will erase his death, that I'll go into the house and find him sitting snug in his big tweed easy chair, sipping scotch, smoking his cigar, and reading the newspaper. Energized by another spurt of pain, I begin running in haphazard circles, faster and faster, between the car and the house, trying to outdistance the terrible hurt, almost oblivious to the thunder rumbling overhead.

When I can run no more, I stop, panting, return to the Buick, and sit beside Grandpa. He hasn't looked well for a long time. He must have known he was dying. All the preparations about money and the will, the insurance scams so I'd have a large amount of cash, point to it. Doc Fairchild probably told Grandpa his heart was bad and to settle his affairs. I sensed all this—the tiredness, wheezing, and coughing—and selfishly ignored it. All I worried about was stupid Eli and how no one liked me at school. My ranting at Grandpa was the final shock. I press my white shirt-tail against my eyes and admit the unbearable truth again, swallowing the awareness into the depths of my being: I killed my grandfather.

I feel like a pike has impaled me. I should be bleeding, losing my life's blood as punishment for what I've done. I lift my head and shriek with anguish, then feel ashamed for disturbing Grandpa's peace. Glancing at his face, I see how pale it is and become even more upset. How am I going to manage without him? What will I do? I think on how we kept my parents' desertion more or less a secret, of how Grandpa was worried the state would come and take me away from him. He once read me a newspaper article about Lucy Bee Eggers, a teenage girl beaten to death in an orphanage outside of Rochester. He said if something happened to him and my parents weren't around, that I should never go to the authorities, that they couldn't be trusted, but he never told me what I should do, how I'm supposed to manage until my parents return. Most people would call Sheriff Shackrack or Doc Fairchild. I'm too frightened.

"Oh, please come back, Mama," I whisper, "please." But like my other wishes, this one falls on the deaf ears of the universe. Maybe I should call Eli? No, he would tell his parents, if he would talk to me at all, and they'd report me to the school or the police, and I'd be begging for scraps at the workhouse like Oliver Twist.

My neighbors might help, yet most likely they'd do the same thing.

A big clap of thunder makes me jump. I stare at Grandpa and realize I can't leave him in the car, that I have to deal with his body. The thought of digging a grave and placing him in it without a coffin is too awful, but I don't have enough wood to build a coffin.

I mull this over until the answer comes to me. I walk to the workbench and grab a long-handled shovel, sledge hammer, heavy metal wedge, and rake. These I place in the car. Then I steel myself into touching Grandpa's hand, startled at how cold it is. I pull him across the seat to the passenger's side, close the door, and come round the car in order to push his legs away from the pedals. When I have enough space, I sit behind the wheel, turn the key in the Buick's ignition, and back the car out of the shed.

- 12 -

I keep the headlights off because I don't want anyone to see the car driving up the hill—not that anyone will be around on a stormy late afternoon in this wooded section of our property. The windshield wipers do their best to clear the glass, but they don't work on my tears, which are falling steadily. I catch myself murmuring all kinds of things as I creep along, avoiding rocks and bushes and runoff streams. At the big curve near the steepest part of the incline, the Buick slips sideways in the damp earth. I give the car some gas, risking a spin-out, and pray the rear tires grab. They do, though it's awful to think of all that mud on Grandpa's beautiful whitewalls. About two hundred feet from the still, I stop the car, set the emergency brake, and carry the tools to the hidden entrance beneath the shed, moving the brush aside to reveal the short tunnel built like a mine shaft into the underground foundation. I leave the sledge, shovel, and wedge, then go inside to light the kerosene lantern on the workbench. Removing the canvas covering the moonshine equipment, I walk back with it to the Roadmaster and place it beside the passenger's door. Although the storm has moved off over the lake, the rain continues.

I feel weak and shaky and chilled all through. As I contemplate moving Grandpa, I tell myself I'm strong, but Grandpa weighs twice my weight, maybe three times. It takes enormous effort to haul him out of the car by grabbing his belt and lifting him until his body lies on the cloth. It's upsetting to treat his body so disrespectfully, but he would understand, or so I keep repeating out loud. After closing the door, I take a deep breath and grasp the tarp with both hands. The muddy soil helps, yet I'm only able to slide him a few feet at a time before I have to straighten and rest before pulling again.

It takes a long while to drag Grandpa to his final resting place besides the copper moonshine equipment. When I finish, my body is quivering from effort and cold. I hunch over to extract his wallet from his pants, and from his breast pocket, I remove his neatly folded handkerchief and press it against my face. Then I slip off his gold watch and stuff all three items in my front skirt pockets. I leave the wide gold wedding band on his finger since he has never taken it off.

Because Grandpa didn't believe in what it represents, I remove his white clerical collar. After straightening his damp suit jacket, he still looks unnatural, perhaps because I've never seen him lying on the ground before or because of the eerie light from the lantern that haloes his head and shoulders. I consider lifting him up onto the workbench, thinking, idiotically, he'd be more comfortable there, but he's too heavy.

"Oh, Grandpa, you deserve a nice funeral and a fancy coffin and lots of folks paying their last respects. I'm so sorry for this, for everything." I touch his cheek but withdraw my fingers because his skin feels so strange. Then I fold my hands together and squeeze my eyes shut, imagining his body floating upward in a bright blue sky with white pillowy clouds supporting his head and carrying him beyond a pink sunset. I don't believe in God or heaven—nor does Grandpa—but our spirits go somewhere, and this is the most beautiful scene I can envision.

A few minutes later, I cover Grandpa with the canvas. I look around at all the Mason jars, distilling paraphernalia, the folding chair where he sat while the moonshine was percolating, and realize my instinct is right. Best to close the still with Grandpa inside. If Buck and Corey want to start moonshining again, they can deal with what they find. Though I feel guilty, I carry the remaining jars of moonshine and the six heavy kegs of aged whiskey to the car, wrapping the hooch in the newspaper left behind from the last trip. This haul will fetch a decent price, and at some time in the future, I will need the money.

I return to the still to take a last look. In the flickering light, I whisper, "I love you, Grandpa...and I always, always will." Then I take a few steps away from the small workroom, leaving the lantern burning so he won't be in the dark, and insert the splitting wedge behind a support joist and tap it in tight. I swing the sledgehammer and slam the wedge hard. Dirt falls on my head and over the still as I jump out of the way. After several more strikes, the wood collapses and soil and ceiling planks cascade into the opening. I repeat this with the other primary supports until I'm coughing from the dust and caked with earth. Using the shovel, I dig away at the sides of the entrance to seal the tunnel, heap loose brush on top, and step back, letting the rain wash over me. I walk down to the Buick and retrieve the rake in order to frizz the meadow grass crushed by the tarp and tires. It won't take

long for the weeds to grow and cover everything, particularly because it's spring.

—

The house frightens me with its silence. Like it knows I killed
Grandpa. The only noises are the whir of the icebox and the
drumming rain on the roof and windows. I strip off my filthy
blouse, skirt, and knee socks, and wash my face and arms in the
sink, drying off with a tea towel. Standing there in my underwear,
all of a sudden the kitchen feels enormous, like I've lost a ton of
weight and have shrunk to midget size. The cobwebs hanging
from the painted yellow beams move in a draft, back and forth, so
that I feel dizzy. I pull my eyes away and spy the fish sticks. The
thought of food makes me nauseous so I throw them in the garbage. On unsteady legs, I walk into the living room and notice the
gold light emitted by Grandpa's lamp, as if his spirit was shining
around his chair. I add scotch to his glass, mixing it with the little
he left before going outside, and drink this in a long gulp, pouring a refill before sitting in his chair and covering myself with
the green-and-blue blanket Mama crocheted for his seventieth
birthday.

—

Sometime before dawn, I wake, aching in every muscle. My Timex has stopped because I forgot to wind it, so I check Grandpa's
watch that I placed on his table last night: 5:18 a.m. I pull the blanket around me and listen to the wind howling off Lake Ontario,
thinking of Grandpa dead and lying covered by canvas. Tears fill
my eyes and I shiver with cold.

Although I don't want to move, I force myself to go upstairs
and put on jeans, a red Cornell sweatshirt, and my Minnetonka
deerskin moccasins, which my grandfather bought me. Even
though some of the beads in the Thunderbird design are missing,
I love the shoes, now even more. I stare at them and slump on my
bed, sobbing.

The sun is up when I finally go downstairs. The icebox is
nearly empty, but I decide to fry the last strips of bacon and two
eggs even though I'm not hungry. As I do this, I recall Grandpa
hadn't gone to the store on Friday, probably because he was ailing. A fresh stab of guilt hits me. If I'd only paid attention to him, I
might have insisted we go to the hospital, and Grandpa would be
there right now, sweet-talking the nurses and carrying on.

As I eat breakfast, I open the envelope on the table. Inside, is a letter to Mama in which Grandpa wrote he loved her and asked her to take good care of me. His tender words tear at my heart. Will my mother ever read them, I wonder? The larger packet, addressed to me, contains bank statements for four of his fake people, including W. M. Lawson. In each account, Grandpa left a dollar, thus removing all the cash so I wouldn't have to worry about withdrawing money. Within a folded sheet of paper are post office keys, each tagged for identification. These boxes will require checking because his pyramiding money will be arriving over the next weeks. Another paper shows a hand-drawn treasure map with each of his tins indicated by an X. Although Grandpa made me memorize these locations, I scrutinize the map and then destroy it. Next I find his will, leaving me the house and contents, and a new life insurance policy for $5,000, with me listed as his beneficiary. These documents pose a real problem because I can't trot over to Lambeau Hastings, attorney-at-law, and announce C. B. Whitestone has passed on. This news would bring an avalanche of trouble because there would be no way to hide Grandpa's death from school and the authorities if the lawyer applied for the life insurance money and legally dealt with Grandpa's will. Furthermore, since I can't produce Grandpa's body to prove he's dead, the life insurance company wouldn't pay out anyway.

I scratch my head over what to do. I could take the lawyer into my confidence, but he's a slippery fellow and might hold out for some of my insurance money. After all, it doesn't take a genius to know Grandpa was too old and sick to be insured except through some crooked business with Doc Fairchild, which the lawyer would surmise. It's also possible that Lambeau Hastings might have been privy to some of Grandpa's deals and knows money is tucked away, though I'm sure Grandpa didn't mention the tin boxes. I think on this quandary, weighing the value of the insurance versus the danger of being carted off to an orphanage, and decide I'd rather stay in my own house and take my chances. At some point, when I'm older or Mama comes home, if I'm not found out before, I'll make up a story that Grandpa went fishing and drowned, his body lost in Lake Ontario. It might take longer to settle his affairs then, but so be it.

After I wash dishes and scour the mud off my sneakers, I go to the bread drawer, remove the stack of bills, and count to $7,800. This, plus the $155.39 in Grandpa's wallet and what is deposited in my checking account and Mama's, is probably half of the insurance payments, the other half already given to Doc Fairchild. All in all, I'm sitting on a heap of cash, enough to pay my way until college and then most of my tuition. I go upstairs to Grandpa's desk and remove his checkbook, flipping through his stubs to the last entry: $989.53. This should cover the household bills for quite a while. And forging his signature is a snap because of the light box in the basement that allows me to trace his handwriting, which I've already been doing for Mama's signature on my report cards and Grandpa's on checks to pay household expenses. C.B. told me once it would be good practice. Now I know for what.

I sit back in Grandpa's desk chair and am astounded with the intricacy of his planning.

—

After calling the school to report that Charlene Whitestone is battling a powerful flu bug, I get Mama's trowel, stick my feet in my rubber boots, place the stack of cash in a brown grocery bag, and head outside. The weather has cleared, leaving the tree trunks black and the green leaves twinkling with morning sunlight. Puddles reflect a pale blue sky and now and then fat drops fall on my head, startling me. As I walk along, I almost forget that Grandpa is dead, but when I remember, my heart aches and bewilderment fills me, as it does when I try to imagine the concept of infinity. Death kind of feels like the same thing—impossible to grasp.

I come to his first hiding place near a fallen oak tree. Termites swarm around the rotten trunk, and a narrow-faced cardinal looks down on me from his perch in a nearby maple as I shove the trowel in the soft dirt. Under different circumstances, this would be fun, kind of like a giant Easter egg hunt, but I'm fighting down the rising panic in my throat, worried about exposing myself to the new pain of uncovering his treasures.

My initial search was off by two feet. When I finally lift up a yellow and black Russian Imperial Cookie box, I smile in spite of my sadness, thinking that Grandpa must have discovered this along with his Sputnik remains. The box has been in the ground for a long time and contains $385 and eight silver dollars from the 1880s and 1890s wrapped in chamois cloth. I stuff everything in the paper bag, fill the hole, and with the cookie box under my arm, go to three other burials and find more old coins. In the last spot, I discover a domed-top tool kit with a buckle latch. This has been recently removed because the weeds haven't grown over the surface. The box contains six stacks of hundred-dollar bills—$20,000. Was this the money from the insurance scams, including Doc Fairchild's half?

I sit down on the grass to gather my wits and figure out what to do. If I ride my bike over to Doc Fairchild's and give him his part of the insurance money, he'll wonder where Grandpa is and why I look so upset—in my condition my acting skills aren't up to par. I mull on this and decide to wait for Doc Fairchild to come by for "afternoon tea" or to inquire about the loot, at which point I can tell him Grandpa is "visiting sick relatives" or "away on business." When he realizes Grandpa is permanently gone, I can play ignorant or an alternative would be to say the insurance company is refusing to pay and is sending an investigator. That would scare him out of his red suspenders. One thing is for sure: he can't report me to Sheriff Shackrack, and Doc isn't exactly robust so physical threats aren't likely. As a side benefit, I might be able to force Doc to cover for Grandpa's absence, saying he's in the hospital or some such fabrication.

I'm relieved to have this range of potential solutions. As Grandpa always says, I'm a clever girl. With this determined, I set off for the other burial locations.

—

By the time I finish digging, I've amassed $21,890 in paper money, sixty silver dollars, and assorted other coins from the 1800s. I calculate my net worth at over $30,000, though the coins are worth far more than their face value. Add in the $5,000 life insurance policy left to me, the pyramiding cash yet to come in, future sales of our products, the money in my own checking account, and I am sitting on a fortune.

Stunned, I rock back on my heels and contemplate this curious state of affairs. If Mama and Daddy return, could they claim the money? As provided in Grandpa's will, I have a legal right to it even though most of it is from illegal or questionable sources. I wouldn't trust Daddy not to come after it, but it's unlikely he knows what a large amount is involved or that it's buried. Grandpa told me he'd never mentioned to either of them where he kept his cash, though Mama might have witnessed Grandpa digging one of his first holes. Once her craziness became worse, however, Grandpa enlisted me as his helper and moved locations of the tins because Daddy was snooping around. My father was allowed to run the Hooch Shop and pocket cash from the sales because there was no way to stop him and because it suited Grandpa to blame Daddy as a moral regenerate who sold the stuff. Otherwise, Grandpa told him nothing.

I decide it's sensible to keep things hidden. And in case someone knows about Grandpa's burial spots, I set off to my willow tree and dig two new holes for the cookie box and the domed tin, inserting all but $150, which I'll keep for household expenses along with the money in Grandpa's wallet and checking account. If Daddy shows up, he'll search the house and outbuildings for cash, grill me with questions, throw a tantrum, and wallop me a few times before driving away with all the moonshine whiskey he can carry. Mama won't hit me, but she might take what she can find and go off again. At least she'll have some money in her checking account, enough to satisfy her for a while. As for giving her some of Grandpa's holdings, I'll wait to see if Good Mama or Bad Mama shows up.

I glance at the sun and pledge that I will carry on alone for as long as I am able. Grandpa would have wished for me to do that. Then I return to the house and select my vocabulary words, though I've decided not to worry with alphabetical order. I write: rabid, recumbent, remunerate, renal, and requiem. "The furrier remunerated the farmer for the recumbent body of a rabid raccoon who died of renal failure and then sang a requiem before removing the pelt." A bit convoluted, but he would have liked this one.

- 13 -

I skip school on Tuesday because I'm still in a bad way. Between bouts of crying and being afraid, I'm in no condition to pretend life is normal. A flu bug of any consequence will knock a body out for several days, so this excuse should be good through Wednesday. In the meantime, I clean the house and plan how to survive alone.

Right now, I'm sitting in the kitchen, tuckered out, drinking a Coke, wondering what to do next, when I hear a little rap on the living room window. At first I think maybe it's a bird, but then I hear it again. I sneak into the living room and raise one of the blind slats. Harley Garfoyle is standing there, his head swirling around in all directions. Jesus! I forgot the Hooch Shop!

I rush out of the kitchen door and around the side of the house, key in hand. "Sorry," I cry as I approach Harley.

"Well, that's okay, Miss Charlie. I oughtn't to be here on a Tuesday, but we got some friends visiting, and, well, I thought maybe I should be hospitable."

I walk toward the outbuilding with Harley tacked to my heels. He's nervous and full of jitters, worried that Sheriff Shackrack will come nosing around.

"How many jars do you want?" I ask.

"Oh, let's see, one might do, but two would be mighty fine." He has a gleam in his eye, lit by the internal wick of alcoholism.

I unlock the door, leaving Harley outside because he hasn't had a bath for a coon's age, and all the sweating he does makes for a powerful odor. After moving the Bibles and Oriental rug, I shove aside the hatch and descend the ladder. Being underground feels even creepier than usual because I'm imagining Grandpa lying in that sealed room. My mind starts to conjure how hot and airless it is in there and what might be crawling on him, and my shoulders scrunch in horror. Quickly, I grab two Mason jars, place them in the cloth bag I use to carry them, and climb the ladder.

"Harley, now I know this may be a hardship for you, but next week the price is going up to $4.50 each."

He frowns at this news, stacking his forehead wrinkles one on top of the other. "Oh, well," he says, "I guess your rates haven't changed for several years."

"No, they haven't," I agree. "Lord knows I tried to talk C.B. out of it, but he was adamant."

Harley squeezes his eyes and nods. "Okay, I reckon that's still a fair enough price."

"Costs more in the store," I remind him.

"And store-bought ain't as fine as your product," he says, grinning.

"No, it isn't. And by the way, we'll be selling some aged whiskey once I find some containers...I mean, once Grandpa does."

Harley's eyes light up. That old alcoholic flame again. "Whitestone's Finest? Golly, I'd be interested in some of that. Why'nt I bring some quart bottles over next week?"

I agree to $7.50 a quart, which is high, but this is blue-ribbon sipping liquor. "That's fifty cents off if you bring your own bottle. Eight dollars otherwise," I explain. "And it won't last long. Might be the final year we offer it."

Harley gathers up his hooch and scampers off. I sit behind my desk and try to read *Oliver Twist*, but all I can think is that I'm doing the very thing I told Grandpa I wouldn't, even raising the prices to make more money. This makes me kind of sick, but closing the shop would be suspicious. Besides, once I sell out our supplies, I'll have little or no income except for the rentals from Mr. Cossantino and Mr. Carter, which only pay the electricity, phone, and oil bills with a bit over. The matter of Sunday chapel and the religion business is another can of worms, one I don't have to open until later in the week.

—

It's the last period in the day. So far, I've avoided Eli and he's avoided me. I'm sitting in my junior English class, trying not to catch Mrs. Kimbell's eye because I want to keep a low profile. When Mrs. Kimbell asks a question, I keep my hand down.

Mrs. Kimbell is in her sixties, with salt-and-pepper hair pulled back and gathered with a tortoiseshell barrette. Sometimes she seems like a grandmotherly type, but she can also be lively and enthusiastic when she's excited about a poem or a story. Since last fall, I've received the highest grades in her class, with many long comments written in the margin.

As the bell rings, Mrs. Kimbell stops me on the way out the door.

"Charlene, I understand you've had the flu." Her gray eyes shine with concern behind her silver-rimmed glasses.

"Yes, ma'am. I've been very sick."

"Perhaps you shouldn't have come to school today. You don't look well."

"It was a toss-up," I explain. "I almost stayed home."

Mrs. Kimbell is silent, examining me a little too close for comfort. Suddenly, I have an overpowering urge to fall into her arms and cry. Tears form in my eyes, but as desperate as I am for sympathy and someone to talk with, I'm more frightened by what would happen if I did.

"Maybe you should go to the nurse?" she suggests, taking my arm.

The contact with another human being is a shock. I stand there, fighting to smile, but her silky dress, printed with a mess of purple and pink flowers, looks like a tropical haven.

My silence worries her, so Mrs. Kimbell leads me to a desk and sits me down. She takes a chair across from me. "Shall I call your mother?"

I smell the scent of gardenias, as if the flowers on her dress are alive. "No, that's all right. Mama's not home. I'm fine, just a little shaky from being sick." I can't meet her eyes because my prevarication skills are at a low ebb, and the magnetic pull toward her bosom is powerful. Instead, I stare at her black, thick-heeled shoes, trying to fight off the desire to tell the truth and beg her to take me home. She'd make chicken soup and put me to bed like a real mother would. This thought is too much. Tears begin to fall.

"Charlene? What's the matter?" She places her hand on my shoulder.

I shake my head and swipe at the telltale tears. "Oh, it's a family thing," I say at last.

Mrs. Kimbell tucks in her chin, surprised at the switch between my illness and my family.

"I really can't talk about it," I add, though I want to talk about it in the worst way.

"I see." She's quiet for a moment, then says, "You know I taught your mother many years ago."

I glance at her, astonished. "You did?"

"Eileen was very talented. Like you."

"Really?"

"Yes. She only wrote a few stories for class—not as many or as good as yours. But she might have become a fine writer if..."

"If?"

Mrs. Kimbell smiles. "Well, your mother had some problems."

"Even then?" This slips out despite how careful I'm trying to be.

She nods. "I haven't seen her for years. She didn't come to the parent-teacher meetings last fall, did she?"

"No, as I recall she was busy." I sneak another peek at Mrs. Kimbell. She looks kind of sad. "I'm sure she would have come but—"

"I understand." Mrs. Kimbell removes her hand from my shoulder. "It's not my place to talk about Eileen, especially about such things as her mental condition."

My curiosity quickly replaces my sorrow. This is the first time I've heard an opinion about my mother except from Grandpa, and he never said much. "I know Mama has something wrong. I wish you'd explain what you mean. I won't tell anyone what you say. I promise."

She presses her lips together, as if trying to keep the words in.

"Please?" I ask.

"Well, let's just say your mother suffered from an uneven temperament. Sometimes she would be on the top of the world, talking loudly in class so I'd have to send her to the principal, or then she would be so quiet that I couldn't get her to talk at all. And her attendance was very irregular, though she always had an excuse." Mrs. Kimbell observes me carefully. "Eileen also had a peculiar way with the truth."

"Kind of like me?" I say, meaning my story about being sick with the flu.

Mrs. Kimbell smiles. "Kind of like you, yes, but not at all like you otherwise."

I sigh with relief, hearing that I'm not crazy like my mother, though I also realize what Mrs. Kimbell is saying—that she's aware that I make things up. "I know I fib a little now and then," I admit, "and I'm sorry. It's just that sometimes it's easier to do that than explain what's going on at home." I'm tempted to keep talking, to pour out the whole sad story of my miserable existence. I force myself to stop.

"Is your mother okay?" Mrs. Kimbell asks.

"Yes, ma'am, she is." I'm not happy that I'm at the lying business again, but I don't know what else to do. I stare at my teacher and feel a gulf open up between us, a gulf I've created, or rather one my family has. Suddenly, I despair that I will ever connect with anyone, even Mama if she returns, since she's too disconnected within herself to reach out to me. "Everything will be fine. Really. Now, I have to get home."

Mrs. Kimbell rises but seems as reluctant to end our conversation as I am. "All right, but if you want to talk, I'm always here. And if you need help, you can also speak to Mrs. Roche."

Mrs. Roche is the guidance counselor. She's nice but the last person I can trust. "Thank you, Mrs. Kimbell." I say, reaching for my book bag.

—

On the way home, I keep my composure for fear that Eli will suddenly appear. By the time I reach my driveway, however, all the hurting pours out of me. Instead of changing my clothes, I run to the lake, sobbing. There, I sit on a boulder and listen to the swish of waves against sand and stone, the sharp cry of a seagull. Over and over, I replay the scene with Mrs. Kimbell. How I wanted her to rescue me! I'm sure she sensed this, but I didn't give her an opportunity to help. This is what I must do—keep everyone at a distance and shut myself away.

- 14 -

That night, I venture into Grandpa's room for the first time since his death. I confess I'm a bit scared his ghost might be roaming around or having a good snore on the bed like Grandpa used to do, but the room is quiet, as if it died along with him. I go to the closet and smell the odor of cigar smoke, hair oil, and aftershave cologne on his jackets. In his dresser drawer, all his socks are neatly balled up into little fists of black, brown, and blue, with a stack to be mended by someone who has the patience. All of a sudden, I wonder if his girlfriend Cass darned his socks and realize I have to tell her some story. I lay down on Grandpa's corduroy green bedspread, holding his pillow tight, pretending it's Grandpa. If I close my eyes, I can almost convince myself he's here, but as good as my imagination is, it isn't good enough. Nor can I stop the tears.

"Damn!" I sit up and reach for one of Grandpa's handkerchiefs, though I really don't want to use them. I want to keep his things like they are for when Mama returns. I switch off the light and head to the typewriter in my room. After fitting a sheet of Grandpa's stationery in the roller, I write Cass a letter from Grandpa explaining about a new girlfriend named Janet. I try to let Cass down easy, mentioning how pretty and smart Cass is, but that sometimes men can't explain their behavior and must count on the goodness and sense of women to understand. I figure this letter sounds loving but firm, and though it will bring Cass heartache, she'd have more heartache knowing Grandpa has passed on. After I finish the letter and type the address on the envelope, I take it to the light box in the basement and trace C.B.'s signature using his fountain pen.

—

On Saturday morning, rain is sliding down the windows like the house is weeping. I sleep late, desperate to erase the present with dreams. After clinging to the last flimsy edge of one, I imagine the smell of bacon wafting up from the kitchen or that I hear Grandpa cursing because his flapjacks are sticking to the skillet.

Finally, the day must be faced. I trudge downstairs, pop bread in the toaster, brew some coffee, then take stock of the pantry's contents: a few cans of peas, beans, chili, stew, and Chef Boyardee ravioli. I decide to drive the Buick to a distant grocery store. Because it's raining, if I dress in Mama's clothes and high-collared coat, no one will recognize me through the fogged-up windows, though I plan to avoid town.

After breakfast, I slip into one of my mother's dresses, dab powder on my face, apply liner and mascara like Mama showed me, and add red lipstick. I look at least five years older—old enough to drive a car. On the way out the door, I grab Mama's rain hat and coat.

I've never taken the Buick on the road so I'm nervous, what with having to drive faster than I ever have and on the same street as other automobiles going with me and against me. Add in that I don't have a license and I'm tarted up like a showgirl floozy, and, my goodness, no wonder I'm a wreck! I start the ignition and take off down the drive, past the grove of willows, my hands tight on the wheel. The wind is whipping back the cottonwoods and giving the windshield wipers a workout. At the main road, I swallow hard and make a left turn onto the blacktop. I press on the accelerator and feel the car surge forward. Pretty soon, I'm doing forty miles per hour, and though I have to watch to stay to the right of the center line, I'm kind of enjoying myself, sitting high and pretty in Grandpa's fine car.

At the store, I buy a ton of canned goods, Coke, coffee, bread, eggs, and Swanson TV dinners. Since chicken is on sale, I get packages of drumsticks and breasts and also some hamburger to stock the freezer. I spend a lot of money, but I don't want to take the chance of driving on the road often. At the cash register, the lady gives me a long stare. I smile and say "good morning" like I'm Mrs. Susie Housewife on a grocery run. Afterwards, I tank up the car, hit post offices to pick up pyramid envelopes, each holding five dollars, and then head for home, sad that my adventure is at an end. I pull the Buick around by the kitchen door and unload everything quick as I can. Then I contemplate what I'll do about tomorrow's church service.

—

The next morning I'm up early to wash my hair and put on my velvet dress. At 8:45, I open the chapel and watch as the cars roll down the driveway and park at all angles on the grass and dirt.

As people enter, I shake hands with each member of the congregation like Grandpa always did. Finally, I close the double doors, take myself over to the pulpit, and read from the Bible, trying to keep my voice from quavering. After this, I welcome everyone.

"Good day to you all," I say. "You may be wondering where Reverend Whitestone is this morning."

A few people nod, but no one seems perturbed that he's not present. I suppose this is because they're used to me and my twice-a-month sermons.

"Well," I continue, " Dr. Fairchild has asked him to rest for a few weeks on account of Grandpa's heart is weak."

Some of the women frown with concern so I quickly add, "But he'll be up in no time. He's asked me to carry on the service for him, if that's okay with everyone."

This seems to go over fine. I give a speech about the dangers of good people working themselves to a frazzle and how all of us need to pitch in and help those who give so much to the community. I urge everyone to volunteer for the PTA and school bazaar and also to give money to save the starving children of West Virginia, who were left without fathers after a coal mining accident killed seventeen men. I make this nonsense up and feel ashamed of myself, but when the plate is piled with cash, my guilt fades.

Mamie Croydon is sitting in the front row, a slim, wispy brown feather springing from her tiny dark hat. Unsure what else to say, I ask her to close by leading the congregation in a few hymns, which she does with feverish pleasure, her face turning pink with godly feeling, her neck wattles shaking like an old rooster, and the feather whipping like a metronome. Since I can't sing worth beans and can't tell one hymn from another, I request that she take charge of music for the next few weeks. Mrs. Croydon is delighted and assures me it is the least she can do. After the service, people offer to bring casseroles or fried chicken for Grandpa. I tell them he's not up for visitors on strict orders from Doc Fairchild.

All in all, I skate through the morning without a hitch and figure I have several weeks of grace before I have to concoct another story.

On Thursday, Harley Garfoyle buys three quarts of aged whiskey and so does Lorna Hartnette. I give Mr. Cossantino a discount on two quarts so I can empty one keg. Then I read a sad letter from Grandpa's girlfriend, Cass, in which she writes that she's moving to Ithaca where her brother's family is. She says she's shocked and hurt by his news and now has no reason to stay in Butztown.

Although it's tempting to reply, it would be cruel to prolong her unhappiness.

—

School is finally over, which is a mixed blessing. I won't have to forge signatures on any report cards, but then again I won't be able to talk with Mrs. Kimbell. She's been reading my stories, marking up where my sentences get carried away with themselves and where commas have sprouted like weeds in the wrong places. She says I'm a born writer and has been encouraging Jaylene to publish my work in the school magazine. My third story just appeared in the spring issue. Mrs. Kimbell has also mailed two entries, one to a contest for high school students, and the other as a submission to a literary journal that accepts work from teenagers. If I win the contest, I'll receive a hundred dollars and publication. We also talked about where I might go to college, and she recommended Cavendish Falls College, where her younger sister is a professor in the creative writing department. Mrs. Kimbell said the tuition is very expensive, but I reassured her we could afford the school. She promised to speak with her sister about me.

So, all of a sudden, after the regularity of classes and the connection to Mrs. Kimbell, I'm on my own except for my hooch customers, although they scoot away fast in case Sheriff Shackrack is cruising around. And speaking of him, he's been absent from the premises ever since his last visit just before Grandpa died. For this I am truly thankful, but I'm also careful. I lock all the doors even when I'm home and wait until late at night before moving product from the house to the shop.

On July Fourth, I pick a bucket of raspberries for preserves. Afterward, because the day is fine, I make a peanut butter sandwich and set off for Lake Ontario to fish. By and by, there's a tug on the line and the fight begins. When I finally reel the fish in, I have a whopper brown trout. I'm pleased as punch, particularly when I put him on the weight scale and see he's eleven pounds. In the kitchen, I lay out newspaper on the table, remove his innards like Grandpa showed me, follow the cookbook's instructions, and slip my prize in the oven. To celebrate, I pour a quarter glass of scotch, which I've been doing now and then, as if Grandpa were sitting in his chair and holding forth on the day's events. It's early for drinking, but Grandpa could invent any excuse to break drinking rules, and, after all, it is our nation's birthday.

The trout is a welcome change from chicken, hamburger, and frozen dinners. I wish Mama or Grandpa were sitting at the table, or even Eli, who, despite my resolve to forget about him, pops into my thoughts whenever I'm feeling lonely. I imagine Eli and I together, side by side, the kitchen golden with candlelight, and my beautiful fish on a silver platter. He'd praise my cooking, and we'd stare into each other's eyes like we did at the May Day dance. Then I recall our argument, how we want different kinds of lives, and begin to clean the dishes, disgusted with myself for fantasizing about a boy who isn't right for me.

"Stupid fool," I mutter, as I dry my hands on a tea towel. "Pull yourself together, Charlie!" I walk into the living room, still talking aloud and wondering what to do next and figuring I'll be doing a lot of wondering over the summer. Since I ate early and it's only 4:30, I have a long evening ahead.

As I'm about to turn on the television, someone knocks on the front door. I jump up to peer through the blinds. Old Doc Fairchild.

I consider not answering, but he says, "Charlie, I know you're in there."

Because I have to face him sometime, I open the door. He enters, glancing around the room, eyes sharp.

"Come for afternoon tea?" I ask him.

"Why, yes. I'd be pleased to partake," he says, his hat in hand.

"The usual?" I'm running low on Chivas and hate to give him any, but I want Doc to be in a jolly mood and to addle his brain a mite. After he nods, I pour him a hefty tot and go get a Coke for myself. When I return, Doc is sitting in the chair we use for company. He lifts his glass and takes a long swallow before asking where C.B. is.

"Grandpa isn't here."

"Oh? I heard he was ailing. Heart trouble."

"Mmm. He did have some chest pains the other day."

"Why didn't he call me?" the doctor asks.

I remember the story I told the congregation and realize one of them must have said something to Doc. "Well, he didn't call on account of he felt better."

"He did, did he?" Doc tips scotch into his mouth. "Then how come I heard he was too sick to give the sermon? And that I told him to stay in bed for several weeks?"

I'm cursing myself for lack of preparation. "Well, Doc, it's like this. Grandpa was in Rochester and took sick so he went to the hospital there. They checked him out and said he was suffering from…exhaustion, yes, indeed! And that his heart wasn't quite right. Told him to take to his bed until the middle of July or thereabouts and then come back for another appointment." I sip my soda, thinking furiously. "And the reason I said you had diagnosed him…"

Doc hangs on this last sentence with a fierce look in his eye, like he knows I'm lying.

"Well, I told them that so they'd understand how serious Grandpa's condition was…is. I mean, coming from a respected medical doctor like yourself that carries more weight in the community than from some dumb doctor in a Rochester hospital." Seeing Fairchild's glass is empty, I rush to refill it.

"I see," Doc says. "I'm sure you're correct that people hold me in high esteem, but I'd like to see C.B. to check his condition. After all, he's my patient."

"Of course. I'll give him the message when he gets back."

"Gets back? And when would that be?"

"Oh, I'm not sure. He didn't say."

Doc raises a craggy eyebrow. "He's not acting like his heart is troubling him."

"No, you're right, but you know how Grandpa is. He aims to carry on when he can. And like I said, he's feeling better today. Why, he even went fishing this morning. Caught a big trout. In fact, we ate it a little while ago, just before Grandpa left." The smell of fish has permeated the living room, assisting my fabrication.

"Well, I told him to be careful." Doc is tempted to say more but realizes he shouldn't divulge confidential medical information about Grandpa. He finishes his drink, eyeing the Chivas bottle. When I don't offer more, he stands and puts on his hat.

"By the way, has he received any correspondence from a life insurance company?"

"No, sir. Not that he's mentioned." I give him an angelic look and escort him to the door. "We'll see you soon," I call after him, hoping that I never see him again.

- 15 -

Life goes on. Days pass slowly and nights are nearly endless. It's kind of like living on a deserted island with a lot of hooch bottles to keep me company. Too bad I can't send a message to Mama in one, but she's probably far away from the waters of Lake Ontario.

Over and over I wonder why everyone's left me. I know Grandpa didn't intend to, but Mama and Daddy don't have bad hearts as an excuse, except of course maybe they do. I don't like to consider their lack of love because it hurts so much. Mama has a crowd of things in her mind, so many things that she can't stick on any one thing for long, even if that one thing is me. Truth be told, sometimes I'm angry at her, but as Grandpa always said, she can't help the way she is. Daddy is another matter altogether. I'm better off without him even if I have to go to an orphanage. Though I don't believe in evil or any of those other religious words, Daddy is not a good man. And if he came home by himself? That's pretty scary to imagine.

Sometimes I sit by the lake and think on my classmates, who have families and friends, and feel like I'm being punished, though I have no idea for what. I try to be positive, imagining this experience will make me grow up faster and be more independent. All in all, I can't wait to be an adult because right now I'm about as miserable as a kid can be.

When I get into one of my troughs of depression, I'm tempted to take a swig or two of Grandpa's scotch, but after Doc Fairchild's visit, I've stopped in case Doc comes round again and expects a drink. He'd guess something was fishy if there wasn't any Chivas Regal on account of Grandpa being a religious admirer of that particular liquor. So, I've been partaking of Grandpa's aged whiskey on weekends or when I'm feeling low. Unfortunately, this alcoholic remedy isn't helpful and usually makes me feel worse.

I've also been trying to eat properly, although it's a lot of work to cook for myself and keep groceries in the house. Mr. Carter, who rents land from us, brought corn and tomatoes and promises squash and zucchini soon. I thanked him and explained that Grandpa wouldn't need corn syrup because he was ending his moonshine business. Mr. Carter was surprised so I explained that with Corey and Buck away and Grandpa getting on in years, distilling was a lot of work. It was tempting to tell him the truth, but I kept thinking about the consequences of honesty and decided honesty was dangerous. After that, we had a nice chat and he left.

It pains me to be so deceitful yet look what happened after I told Grandpa the truth about my feelings: he keeled over dead. So I keep quiet and live like a hermit. Except for a few casseroles brought by parishioners, I'm eating a lot of canned chili and TV dinners. The weight scale says I've lost five pounds, though when I measured myself on the door frame, I've grown another inch. How I can do both at the same time is beyond me, but I figure that's what teenagers do—grow in funny ways.

Mr. Charles Dickens and I have become better acquainted. I'm now reading *Great Expectations* and can identify with that poor kid, Pip. And though sometimes I get Dickens' style twisted in my head so I start to write like him, I've completed several stories, experimenting with using first person and then re-writing the same story in third person to see the difference, an exercise Mrs. Kimbell suggested. I wish she could read them. I considered riding to her house on my bike and checked her address in the phone book, but I was too worried that some darned fool thing would come shooting out of my mouth or I'd start sobbing the minute I saw her. Sometimes late at night, I imagine Mrs. Kimbell giving me a big hug and making everything all right, though that's too tall an order for her or anyone else except maybe Mama, if she returned with her mind settled.

Other than that, no one has been around except at last Sunday's service. Several folks inquired about Grandpa and asked when he planned to return. I explained he was feeling better but was away seeing a specialist. My excuses will run out soon or one of the lies will trip me up, but I'll continue services for as long as I can. Because there was plenty of money on the collection plate, and Grandpa always said he gauged the success of his sermon by that, I imagine I can hang on for a bit. In preparation for this "specialist" story, I move the Buick up in the woods so no one will see it. After I do this, I write a check on Grandpa's account made out to C. B. Whitestone for $180, endorse it using the light box, and ride my bike to the bank, where I go to our favorite teller, Mrs. Noonan. Because I often bring checks to her so Grandpa doesn't have to leave the car, she gives me the cash without batting an eyelash.

—

I cross off July 16th on our Currier & Ives wall calendar. Every morning, after I'm dressed and the breakfast dishes are done, I mark the day. Each one feels like a tiny accomplishment of survival. The next item on my agenda is another cashed check, this one for $140. I figure one every few weeks won't be too suspicious.

After riding into the woods and hiding this money with the $180 from the previous check, I return to the house for a few hours of writing before my afternoon duty selling moonshine. As I sit at the typewriter, I suddenly hear a man cursing like he's trying to keep a lid on his temper. I rush to the living room window and see a dark blue Ford truck parked by the Hooch Shop. A man wearing jeans, a black-and-white shirt, and a tan cowboy hat is banging on the shed door and throwing his shoulder against it.

Without thinking, I rush outside and down the stairs. "Hey!"

Seeing me on the porch, the man stops his assault. As I hurry across the driveway, he places his hands on his narrow hips, like he's on home turf, though from his fancy black boots, white shirt with a black yoke embroidered with red roses, and his Roy Rogers' hat, I suspect his home turf is somewhere out West. His eyes are large and pale, hovering between green and blue.

"Hello, there," he says. His voice is kind of lazy, like he has all the time in the world to get his words out. He doesn't sound quite like a cowboy, but the only cowboys I've heard are fake ones on television.

"Who are you?" I ask, acting bold. "And what do you think you're doing?"

He pushes back the brim of his hat, allowing a lock of blond hair to fall on his forehead. The guy is just about perfect except his lips are full and soft, kind of girlish.

"My name's Blake William Cody." He gives me the once-over, then a slow smile lights his eyes.

Despite my anger over his door-pounding, I'm dazzled. As I stare at this man, with his blond, wavy hair falling to his collar, I consider his name. "Any relationship to Buffalo Bill?"

"Well, I don't usually advertise it, but you're absolutely correct. He was my great grandfather."

I don't know whether to be impressed or suspicious. I can't

work out why anyone would announce he's Blake William Cody and in the same breath insist he doesn't brag on his pedigree. I also can't calculate the generational math, either, though I suppose it's possible that this man—who is about thirty years old—could be Cody's great grandson.

"And I imagine you must be Charlene Whitestone, Eileen's daughter," he says.

My heart, which has been beating hard because I was scared and then because of his handsomeness, stops dead at the mention of my mother. "What? Is Mama here?"

Blake shakes his head. "No, but I expect she's on her way."

"Really?" I'm so excited I can hardly keep from jumping up and down.

"Yeah, Eileen should be coming on the train or bus. Least that's what she told me."

I can't believe the news after all these months of waiting. "When?"

"Why, I reckon she'll be here any day now."

His vagueness bothers me. "Is Daddy coming with her?"

"No, I run him off a few months back." He lodges his thumbs on his black belt, which is buckled with a big silver steer's head and horns. "I know he's your daddy and all, but from what I saw, Eileen's better without him."

I'm tempted to join in this disloyalty, but I know better than to say anything against my father, even if he's nowhere around. However, I'm surprised Blake had the nerve to scrap with Daddy, on account of Blake, who is well-built but only a hand taller than I am, is a pretty boy compared to my father. I figure this story about running Daddy out of town is just Western talk and that cowboys tend to brag. I'm also surprised that Blake knows so much about my mother's schedule. This starts me wondering about Blake and Mama.

"Are you and Mama friends?"

He shrugs and smiles. "You might say that."

I want to ask more but decide to find out the purpose of his visit. "Well, if you know Mama so well, how come you were banging on the shop door instead of coming to the house and introducing yourself?"

"Oh, gosh, I'm sorry," he says in a confidential whisper, as if someone might hear. "See, it's like this. I heard tell your Grandpa's a moonshiner. Your Mama said he keeps the bottles in a shed." Blake scrapes his fingers against his chin, which is smooth

99

shaven. "Guess after my long drive I was a little thirsty. Sorry about the ruckus and all. Didn't mean to be so rough."

I stare at this cowboy-god and accept his apology, though it doesn't sit right. Finally, I gather up some nerve. "So, are you Mama's boyfriend?"

He laughs and takes a step toward me, resting a hand on my shoulder. "Yeah. I suppose you could call me that."

I notice five pearl snap buttons marching up his cuffs with another set sewn vertically down the front. On either side of the shirt, little smiley-pockets grin at me. I covet this shirt in the worst way. I covet him, too, and feel my face redden.

"Though if I'd known she had a daughter pretty as you," he says, giving me another grin, "why, my goodness, if I'd known that, shoot, I might have waited for the younger version."

He's probably joshing me or maybe this is how cowboys behave, although I don't recall Gene Autry or the Lone Ranger acting so flirty.

Blake laughs because I'm nervous. Then, to my surprise, he hugs me. His chest is hard and his arms are strong. I don't know whether to enjoy the moment or push him away.

He draws apart as if he regrets doing so. "Now, since we're almost related, why don't you think of me as Cousin Blake? And because we're practically relatives and I'm sure we're going to be pals, how about a little of your Grandpa's whiskey?" His hand cups my shoulder. "By the way, where is your grandfather?"

I snap out of my dream world. "Grandpa?"

"Yeah. Your mama said he was a preacher." He gives me a wink. "And a real character."

"Oh, absolutely."

"Probably runs in the family," he teases.

"Yes, it does." I want to get off the subject of C.B. and hooch. "Where are you staying?"

He walks a few feet to his truck's fender and pats the Ford like a trusty horse. "Right here, unless you have an extra bed. In that case, I would be much obliged to sleep on something softer than the front seat." He walks back toward me. "I don't want to put you or your grandfather to any trouble, however."

I ponder this and can't help frowning. He sees this and runs a finger on my forehead. I recoil from his touch because it's too familiar by far.

"Now, no need to fret, Charlene. I understand I'm a stranger who just dropped out of the blue yonder. I'm fine sleeping out here."

"No, it's just that…" My brain stalls. Truth be told, I'm worried this cowboy might have some tricky ideas about bunk arrangements. "I mean, sure. I guess it's okay if you use Mama's room." I really don't want him in there and suddenly think of her jewelry. "I'll need a few minutes to straighten it up."

Blake nods and gives me a smile. "I'll pull together some things while you do that," he says. "And you ask your grandfather if it's okay."

Anticipating that comment, I've turned my back on him and am heading toward the house, feeling like I've swallowed rocks.

—

After I remove Mama's jewelry and stash it behind the false panel in my closet, I return and fluff up Mama's bed. I fight down a wave of disquiet that this stranger is going to sleep in her room. For some reason, I never think of it as belonging to both my parents, though they slept in it together. I hadn't considered this before, but it is Daddy's room, too, even if the house belongs to Grandpa and now, in fact, to me. I consider how mad Daddy would be if he found Blake sleeping in his bed and shudder with fear. On the other hand, Mama will be home soon and can sort things out. This thought makes me happier than I've been in months. I smooth the bedspread and imagine her sitting there, telling me about her adventures down south. When she's in the right mood, Mama can spin incredible stories. Of course, she could come home and be crazier than when she left, in which case, without Grandpa to keep things even, I'll have to handle Mama, something I've never had to do by myself. As excited as I am to have her return, my situation might get even more complicated.

I hear Blake open the screen door and enter the living room, his high-heeled boots thunking on the wood floor. I poke my head out and tell him I'll be down in a minute. He raises a hand to signal that I should take my time. Under his arm is a rifle in a tan buckskin case, which is partly concealed by a buckskin jacket decorated with fringe and colored beads. The sight of the gun makes me really anxious. Suddenly, I have a hankering for Sheriff Shackrack to drop by on one of his unexpected visits.

I delay as long as I can before walking downstairs. Blake's Stetson is hung on the hat rack and the rifle is tucked in the corner, covered with his jacket. A giant army duffle bag is by the stairs. It looks to me like old Blake is planning a lengthy visit. I wonder if he intends to get a job or whether Mama told him that Grandpa has money, because from what I can see, unless Blake hires out to a Wild West show, he's too fancy for farm work, which is about all that's available in Butztown.

Blake gives me a smile. "Now you wouldn't have any of your Grandpa's whiskey or maybe some scotch, would you?" He eyes the Chivas Regal on the bar.

He seems very keen to have a drink. "Sorry, but I can't let you have any of the Chivas. Grandpa is very particular who he gives it to." I walk into the kitchen, open the cupboard, and take out a bottle of red wine that's been open for a month or two. It doesn't look appealing, but I figure since we haven't had lunch yet, it's best to start Blake on light stuff. I pour a glass and bring it to him. He's sitting on the sofa, his legs crossed, showing off his fine boots, and glancing around the room as if he likes the look of the place.

"Why, thank you, Charlene," he says as he accepts the glass.

"You're welcome. And you can call me Charlie if you want."

Blake nods. "Okay, Charlie it is." He sips the wine and the lines around his eyes scrunch as he makes a face. "Oh, my, this has been around for the longest while."

"Sorry. You can have some whiskey with lunch…unless you'd rather have a soda." I'm hoping he won't start drinking this early because I don't know how he'll behave if he gets liquored up.

"That's okay," he replies, forcing another swallow of wine. "Now, Charlie, I don't believe you told me where your Grandpa is."

"Ah, no, I didn't. Well, Grandpa has been having a little heart trouble so he's off to Syracuse to visit a doctor."

"Oh, I see. Sorry to hear that. When do you expect him home?"

I'm trying to figure out whether I should call Mr. Cossantino or Mr. Carter to come rescue me from my visitor. But then I'd have to explain about Grandpa's absence and a whole mess of things. Although I'm suspicious about Blake, I decide to see what his game is and wait for Mama.

"Grandpa will be back soon," I explain. "Now, if you want some lunch, I'm making egg salad sandwiches."

"That would be mighty fine."

—

Blake is quiet while he eats two sandwiches and finishes the bottle of wine. Afterward, he says he wants to take a nap, so I show him the room and watch as he carries his stuff upstairs, including the rifle. I want to ask him about it, but I don't. In fact, I'm trying to act like it's an everyday occurrence to have a cowboy with a rifle come to stay.

After I hear Blake snoring, I run outside and check his truck. Inside the glove compartment is his registration. It lists the owner as Blakewell James Benko of Eudora, Arkansas. "Blake William Cody indeed," I mutter, returning the registration. In the truck's cab, there's a dirty pillow, navy blue blanket, some empty beer cans and food wrappers, a pair of brown and gold alligator boots with silver tips on the pointed toes, and a stack of road maps held together with a pink rubber band. I close the door and check the rear of the truck. Wrapped in a tarp are a new pick-axe and long-handled shovel, a black footlocker, and more beer cans. Mighty curious, I think. Tools, a fake name, and the lie about being related to Buffalo Bill Cody. A cold shiver shoots down my neck. Something isn't right by a long shot. What did Mama tell this guy about Grandpa and our business? She knows about the the still, Worm Heaven, and some of what Grandpa was getting up to with his schemes, but she's unaware of the secret compartment in my closet, which Grandpa and I built on the sly. If Mama does know about any of Grandpa's hidey-holes, it's unlikely she would tell a stranger unless she'd been drinking and thought Blake was serious about her. If she did know about the burials, however, this would explain why Blake has tools because he doesn't look like he's done much shoveling or pick-axing.

Now, to be fair, using a fake name and pretending to be related to Buffalo Bill Cody is no worse than being a sermonizer and saying you're a child of God when you're a devout heathen. On this score, Blake and I are sort of even in the lying category. I worry what his game is, however, and have a hunch he's up to serious no good.

I walk to Ye Olde Hooch Shop, take a quick check out the window, then uncover the hatch and descend into the damp earthen space below. I carry two bottles of regular whiskey up to the main room. After smoothing out the carpet and restoring the stack of Bibles on the floor, I bring the moonshine to the kitchen, hiding the jars in two separate places. Blake is still snoring upstairs, so I clean the dishes and then sit down to consider my predicament. Something is nagging at my consciousness. I close my eyes until it comes to me. If Blake says Mama is coming on the train or bus, why didn't she hitch a ride with him?

- 16 -

As I'm trying to decide what to prepare for dinner—whether to treat Blake like a guest or a fox in the hen house—he saunters down the stairs, his cowboy boots giving fair warning of his arrival in the kitchen.

"Howdy," he says.

I start to say "howdy" back and get hold of myself. "Hi."

"Had me some great shut-eye. Yes, indeed." He yawns and stretches, then pulls a chair away from the table and sits. "What've you been up to?"

"Oh, not much." I turn to open a cabinet. I feel his eyes on my back and turn quickly to face him. Sure enough, he's staring. "Are peas okay?"

Blake gives me a smile with those soft lips of his. His light-colored eyes are twinkling like I've said something amusing. "Peas are fine. I promise to eat my vegetables." He chuckles and tips the chair back, using his knee against the table to steady himself.

"Best not do that," I tell him. "Grandpa doesn't like it."

He wipes the smile away and sits up straight. "Sorry. Guess I'm not used to living so high on the hog."

I can't decipher if he's annoyed or fine with me correcting his behavior. I know Grandpa would have told him the same thing, and because this is my house, I figure I'll say what I please, and if old Blake doesn't care for it, he can leave. I place the peas in a saucepan on the stove, while watching my visitor out of the corner of my eye.

"So, how did you and Mama meet?" I try to sound mildly interested whereas in fact I am mightily interested.

"That's a long story." He rubs his mouth. "Say, I'd be happy to tell it, but maybe I could try some of your Grandpa's whiskey? I've heard it's the best moonshine ever made."

As I'm listening to him, his voice sounds more Southern than Western. If he's from Arkansas, this makes sense. Then I remember that Grandpa said Daddy called from a bar in Arkansas. What if Blake heard tales about Grandpa's money from Daddy, got ideas, and headed north? Like Mama, Daddy can be talkative when he's overindulging.

I pour Blake some whiskey. "Ice?"

"Yeah, a few cubes."

I hand him the drink and watch how interested he is in it, how he rushes the alcohol to his mouth. The two shots are gone in a flash, and he holds out the glass for a refill. I give it to him. "Now, about Mama," I remind him.

"Oh, yeah. We met one night in a little bar in Hot Springs. Hit it off right away. You know how those things are." Blake looks at me and shrugs. "Well, maybe you don't. Unless you have a boy-friend or something."

"As a matter of fact I do."

He smiles and takes a last swallow of hooch. "This is fine stuff," he says, eyeing the bottle. Without asking, he pours another drink, setting the Mason jar by his right hand.

"So was Mama all right?" I place hamburger patties in a skillet.

"Oh, she was better than okay. A little high-wired, if you know what I mean." He stares at the ceiling with a happy expression on his face.

It doesn't take much imagination to figure out why Blake is pleased with himself. I'm sure he and Mama had a fling, which isn't a surprise because Mama has loose ways when she's in her fast moods. I now align Blake with Mama, though he said he met Daddy, too.

"So when did she say she's coming home?"

He takes a sip. "Any day now. Why, she could call tonight or…tomorrow. Could be the next day, but I doubt it. She was ea-ger to see you, Charlie. That's what she told me. She said, 'Blake, I miss my little girl something terrible.'"

This doesn't sound like Mama so much as Blake pretending to talk like her. My distrustful nature is on high alert again, par-ticularly because Blake is sneaking glances in my direction when-ever I'm busy cooking. While cutting a tomato, I inquire as to why Mama didn't come with him. I don't look at Blake when I ask because I don't want to tip him off about my suspicions.

"She needed to make a stop in Baltimore or maybe it was Washington. I don't rightly remember. One of those places. Said she'd take the train or the bus. That's all I know."

This is pretty phony, but I let it pass. Blake is pouring another drink as I flip the hamburgers. "I see. And was Daddy there when you and Mama met each other?"

"Yeah. I think they'd broke up by then and were just hanging out at the same watering hole. Didn't even know your daddy was there until I got to talking to Eileen. After a little bit, your daddy came over and expressed his displeasure about my presence, so to speak." He cups his hand over his fist. "Had to pop him one." Blake shook his head. "I didn't want to fight him, understand, but he hit Eileen—not hard—but hard enough that I couldn't sit by and see a gal being hurt."

I can't imagine Blake popping Daddy one without getting demolished. The whole scene as described doesn't feel right. Mama knows better than to flirt when Daddy's around, and if they were on the outs, she wouldn't hang around any bar where Daddy was drinking. "What kind of work do you do?" I ask him, to change the subject.

"A little of this and a little of that." He narrows his eyes at me like he's caught a whiff of my suspiciousness. "Some ranching out in Colorado and Wyoming. Did a cattle drive or two. Tough life." Thinking of this makes him thirsty. He drinks some more.

I don't know if Blake is an expert liar or telling the truth. Even if his truck is a mess, he appears too fussy about his clothes to get them dirty. Try as I might, I can't picture him riding days on end without a hot shower.

"So why exactly are you here?" I set plates of food on the table and sit at C.B.'s place.

"Why, thank you, Charlie." He lays a napkin in his lap and gives me a smile. "Do you say grace or something?"

I almost choke on my Coke. "No, absolutely not. Grandpa saves religion for the service."

Blake picks up his fork and gives me a sly wink. "Well, I say amen to that."

I realize he's avoided answering my question so I repeat it.

He chews on a piece of hamburger like it was a fine steak that requires his full attention. Then he says, "I suppose I came to see you, Charlie. Just to see if you were as pretty as your Mama said. And here I find you're even prettier. Mighty smart, too."

—

After dinner, I sneak a tot of whiskey because I can't handle Blake's tall tales about the old West and his various cowboy escapades, all of which sound as true as the hogwash I utter on Sundays to the congregation. It occurs to me that Blake knows I don't believe him, but he's just so enraptured with his lying that he can't stop, like he's showing off—one addicted deceiver to another.

We go into the living room. I stake out Grandpa's chair because I don't want Blake sitting in it. He sprawls on the couch, the liquor working on him so that he's getting careless with how he sits. He lays an arm across the back of the sofa and squints a little, as if I'm hard to see.

"You know, Charlie," he says in his slow voice, "I wish you didn't have a boyfriend 'cause you sure are beautiful."

I'm wishing my boyfriend was sitting next to me, though Blake is a fine sight to look upon. "Thanks," I reply, "but I don't think Eli would like you flirting with me."

"Oh, Eli is it? Well, gosh darn, I suppose if I had me a good-looking gal like you, I'd be jealous of every cowboy that so much as looked in your direction."

"And besides, you and I aren't exactly the same age." I say this to chide him a little, but somehow it sounds like I'm making nervous excuses or, worse yet, flirting.

"No, I suppose we're not. Tell me again…how old are you?"

"Fourteen. I'll be fifteen in October."

"I see," he says. "Well, you are a young filly, then, aren't you?"

This cowboy talk is wearing thin. Plus Blake seems to have forgotten how he and Mama are supposed to be involved with each other. I point this out, but he just laughs.

"See it's like this, sometimes I can't help myself, sugar," he says, patting his chest. "You might call me a lady's man. Love women. Yeah, absolutely love 'em."

Blake goes on for a bit, though I see he's getting drifty from all the hooch. He's still giving me the eye, however, which is making me fret.

"Well, I guess I'm off to bed," I say, trying to appear calm.

"So early? Why don't you have a drink with your Cousin Blake?"

"No, thanks." I come to my feet. "You know where your room is. Just turn off the light, will you?" I cross the living room to the staircase.

He yawns and adjusts the sofa pillow under his head. "Okay, I will."

I rush upstairs and lock the door, which won't do much good if Blake is determined to break in. As much as I don't like leaving him to roam around the house, I feel safer in my room. I get into bed fully dressed, in case I have to make a fast exit out the window. Downstairs, I hear him rumbling around, which surprises me because Blake seemed drunk enough to pass out. I worry about what he can find, but everything of value is hidden on account of Grandpa was worried about raids from the police or the revenuers. And all of the cash is in the ground or in my closet and pocket.

I think over what Blake said about my parents and have an uneasy feeling that Mama or Daddy told him something about Grandpa's money so that Blake took off with gold-digging fever. The more I listened to him this evening, the more I didn't buy that malarkey about Mama coming, unless she was the one who blabbed, realized later what she'd done, and is returning to put matters right. However, Mama has no notion Grandpa is dead and probably thinks C.B. can handle Blake. Most likely, there is no rescue on the horizon.

I hear Blake's boots on the stairs and hold my breath. He tries my doorknob, finds that it's locked, and staggers down the hall. In a few minutes, the springs on Mama's bed creak and there are two clunks as he takes off his boots.

—

I jump awake. The house is silent but something woke me. Early light is filtering through my curtains along with summer heat. I listen and decide it's too quiet. No snoring, cowboy boots thunking, kitchen or bathroom noises. Curiosity has a bite on me so I unlock the door and look around. Down the hall, the door to Mama's room is closed, but my senses tell me no one is inside. I creep along to Grandpa's room and notice the desk drawer is ajar. Then I walk to the window and glance out. On the edge of the trees, I see Blake with his tools. He's heading toward one of Grandpa's first treasure spots, one that hasn't been in use since Mama left.

"Well, well," I say to myself, calling him a bunch of foul names. As I watch him disappear over the hill, I shake my head, knowing Blake will rub a few blisters on his soft hands for nothing. Our property consists of fourteen acres of woods, fields, briars, bogs, and streams, not counting land leased to Mr. Cossantino for the vineyard and Mr. Carter for corn and vegetables. "Serves you right!" I say aloud.

I check C.B.'s desk and see that his papers have been fooled with. There isn't anything of value in the drawer so I close it and mentally re-check all our hidey-holes and feel confident they're too difficult to find. This makes me wonder if Blake might try force in order to find out where the money is. I don't care for this thought and rush into Mama's room. Blake's rifle is leaning against the bureau. I've never handled a Winchester, though Daddy owned a shotgun and rifle for hunting, both of which he took with him. All in all, guns frighten me, perhaps because I always thought my father would get liquored up one day and kill one or all of us.

I pick the Winchester up carefully, fearing it might go off, and withdraw four bullets from the magazine. I take them into my bedroom and slip them in a sock.

After cursing myself for literally being asleep while Blake made his stealthy house rounds, I consider driving the Buick to the police department. This idea goes against the grain so much that I just can't do it. There would be too much explaining to do, such as where Grandpa really is, why Blake is digging in the woods, and why I'm driving illegally. Those are for starters, and the more I think on all the questions Sheriff Shackrack would ask, the more I panic. I place the car keys in my pocket, however, so if I have to, I can make a run for it.

This gives me some courage. I risk a call to Eli. No one answers at the Houk house. They're probably out in the fields or in the barn. I decide to try him later but, in the meantime, to pretend everything is fine, to make coffee and breakfast like I do every morning, even if on this particular morning a side-winding snake of a cowboy is in residence. So far as I can figure, Blake doesn't strike me as the violent type, even for all his talk about fighting Daddy, which I suspect is a tall tale. His Romeo tendencies might be more difficult to handle.

A little after 9:30, Blake opens the kitchen door. He looks surprised to see me sipping coffee, but then gives me a big smile and says good morning. I notice his shirt sleeves are rolled up and damp. He probably washed the dirt off of his hands in a stream or in the lake.

"So what are you doing?" I ask him.

He pours himself a cup of coffee, adds four teaspoons of sugar, and draws back a chair. "Why, I thought I'd take a walk before it gets too hot. It's going to be a scorcher for sure."

"Yes, I think so." I plunk two slices of Wonder Bread in the toaster.

"Any word from your grandfather?"

"No, but that's like him. He's not much for using the phone.

I expect he'll come home without calling." I take the butter from the icebox. "Mama didn't telephone, either." I toss Blake a glance, but he's drinking coffee.

"Mmm. You make a mean cup of coffee, Charlie."

"That's how Grandpa likes it." I almost slip up and use the past tense.

"Your Grandpa sounds like quite a fellow. Tell me about his ministering."

Since it's Saturday, Blake will probably be around tomorrow. When Grandpa doesn't show up for chapel, Blake will be suspicious. "Well, we have a congregation of about forty or so people, depending. Sometimes I give the sermon. Grandpa thinks I have a gift for public speaking, and because I like to write, I guess the two go together." I butter the toast and put it on a plate for Blake. I watch as he slathers raspberry jam over both pieces. "I hope Grandpa is home tomorrow," I say, "but if he isn't, everyone will expect me to lead the service."

"Really?" He stares at me with eyes that now appear to be blue and licks a bit of jam from his full lips. "You have all kinds of talents, don't you?"

"Yes, I do." I hand him a paper napkin. "So, Blake, you never said how long you're staying or why you're here."

He considers this for a minute while he's munching toast. "I suppose it all depends on your mother. When she arrives. Or if your grandfather comes home and kicks me out." He gives me a small smile. "Of course, I doubt he'll do that."

I don't answer. The less said about Grandpa the better.

"If you don't mind, Charlie, I'd be pleased to sit in tomorrow. It's been awhile since I've attended church."

"Okay," I reply, wondering if one of our congregation will rescue me—maybe Mr. Simpson or Mr. Reid, both of whom are nice family men. But, then again, the same problems apply. I'd be placed in an orphanage. The image of one looms before my eyes: a damp, dark, house with locked rooms, rats, and gruel for supper. Grandpa always said I was blessed with imagination, but sometimes it's a curse.

I shake these thoughts from my mind, wash the dishes, noticing that Blake doesn't offer to help, and consider how to keep him out of the Hooch Shop and our liquor supply. I need to open for business soon because Saturday is a busy day.

"I might go into town for a bit," Blake says. "I like whiskey fine, but mostly I like beer."

"Okay. Say, can you can pick up a bottle of Chivas Regal? Grandpa is running low and probably has forgotten, with one thing and another." I hand him money, though it occurs to me I may never see it or Blake again.

As soon as he leaves the house, I phone Eli, but there's still no answer. I decide to write another check and cash it, this one for $75, because it's probably smart to get as much money out of the bank as I can. When I return from town, I go to the shed and open up shop.

- 17 -

Sales are good during the late morning. I even risk a daylight run to the house for more product. In between customers, I wonder what Blake is doing. It's possible he drove around by the lake to dig or else he's holed up at Bull's Butztown Bar & Grill, drowning his frustration. About four, I close shop and head into the kitchen to prepare a chicken dinner, though it irks me to cook for this thieving moocher. I could pretend I can't cook, but then I won't eat. An hour later, Blake rolls in and parks the Ford at an odd angle, and as he enters the front door at a similar tilt, he nearly knocks off his Stetson. He has a six-pack of beer under one arm and a bottle of Chivas in hand, which he lands on the bar with the studied care of a drunk.

"I have fulfilled my mission!" he announces grandly.

It appears that his primary mission was to get loaded. Blake aims himself at the kitchen, whacks his arm on the door frame, and curses. He stows the beer in the icebox then spies the bottle of hooch from last night. Clutching it against the roses embroidered on his shirt, he asks, "Mind if I have a little?"

I look into his bleary, red eyes and nod. From the freezer, Blake takes an ice-cube tray, swearing under his breath when it's cranky about yielding its cubes, and bangs it on the counter. As chips of ice flee the tray, he grabs a few pieces and plops them in a glass, then plops himself into a chair by the table.

"Well, gosh," he says, after a few long swallows, "I'm not being a gentleman." His words run together like slush. "It isn't polite to drink in front of a lady. No, siree. Not unless she's drinking, too." He gives me his mischievous grin, stands, empties my Coke in the sink, and pours me a hefty slug of hooch. "This'll warm you up."

The fact that it's eighty degrees or hotter in the kitchen, between the outside heat and the oven, makes me laugh.

Blake pats me on the back. "See, there? You're smiling already! Why, golly, you have the prettiest smile I ever saw!" He clinks his glass with mine.

I'm feeling resigned to his company. He laughs easily, as

drunks often do, and soon enough, despite my reservations about him and his morning archaeological pursuits, I'm laughing along with him. We move into the living room, and Blake tells me funny stories about various scrapes and exploits. Even though I wish he would leave, it's a relief to have company after all these weeks. And when all is said and done, he is a fine sight to look upon.

After checking the progress of the chicken, I open another jar of moonshine. I already feel a little high from the first drink, so to be cautious, I add more ice and a little water to my whiskey, though truth be told I'm like Grandpa on account of we don't care much for dilution. As I return to Grandpa's chair, Blake gives me an amused look. "Now, Charlie," he begins, "I don't buy this story about your Grandpa being in Syracuse."

"Well, it's the truth," I reply, realizing I've been too quick to answer. "He's probably on the way home this very minute."

He chuckles and shakes his head. "Ah, come on, Charlie, you can't kid a kidder. You're good but not that good. So where is he?"

I take a sip of hooch and can hardly swallow it. I set the glass on the table and stare at him, trying to gauge if I can trust this cowboy with my secret. His expression is unexpectedly kind, like maybe he cares a little, but he's a liar and a thief who brought a pick-axe and a shovel to steal Grandpa's money. Even so, it's been so long since I had someone to talk to, and with the whiskey working on loosening my emotions, I feel tears prick my eyes. I grit my teeth because I despise crying in general, and crying in front of a stranger is unthinkable. Inside, I'm yelling at myself to lie some more, but my heart has overthrown control of my brain.

"It's okay," Blake whispers. "You can tell me what happened."

I get the feeling he knows Grandpa has passed, but there's no way he can be certain, not unless I tell him. "It's a long story," I mutter, recalling that Blake said the same thing when asked how he met Mama.

"I'm listening," he replies, leaning forward a little.

A noose-like knot tightens my throat. "I think I better check on the chicken." I rise out of the chair and head toward the kitchen, but Blake grabs my arm.

"Hold on there, pardner. Something's wrong. Why don't you tell your Cousin Blake what it is."

I shut my eyes to keep the tears from falling and shake my head. I don't want him to know Grandpa isn't coming home because then Blake might stay, but do I really want him to leave?

"I can't."

He stands, still holding my arm. "Ah, Charlie," he says in a soothing voice, "You have to trust someone. Don't be scared of me."

"Why should I tell you anything? You'll be gone some morning when I wake up. I just know it."

For a second, Blake looks hurt, then sad. "Sugar, better to learn that everyone leaves sometime. That's the way life is. Why, I imagine you'll do your share of leaving people, too. Once you get a little older. And you already know about people going off." He moves closer. "But even with all that leaving, it's important to believe folks care when they say they do."

I smell smoke and whiskey. Grandpa's smell. Suddenly, I feel so tired and miserable. I desperately want Blake to be a rock, even for a little while until I can steady myself. I cave in and lean against him. His arms come up around me, and for a few minutes, I can't speak as tears slide down my cheeks. Finally, I whisper, "He's dead. Grandpa's dead. He died weeks ago. Before the end of school."

Blake pulls me tight against his shoulder, and as he does, the sadness and loneliness overpower my reserve. Although it was my firm intention not to tell Blake anything, I describe how Grandpa died in the Buick. I don't say where I buried him, but I'm so upset that I talk more freely than I should. When I stop, I'm shocked at how much I've revealed.

"And you've been on your own ever since?"

"Yes."

"My, my, you are something else. I don't know many girls who could handle a situation like this. Indeed I don't."

Although I know I should be careful with Blake, I feel safer than I have since Grandpa died. We stand together for a long while. When I quit sobbing, I reach in my pocket for Grandpa's blue handkerchief and blow my nose and dry my eyes, though more tears threaten. I clamp down hard, trying to get a grip because I've shown enough weakness for one night. Without a word, I leave Blake and walk into the kitchen, relieved he doesn't follow me. The smell of chicken is strong in the air so I pull it out of the oven. The skin is dark brown but not burned. The baked potatoes are done. After heating up a can of green beans, I place the food on plates and call Blake to dinner. He teeters slightly as he enters the room, but his expression is quiet and respectful. I hand him a beer. We sit and eat in silence.

When we finish dinner, I turn on the television in the living room for Blake, who wanders in looking worse for the alcohol. We're both embarrassed about what happened and avoid each other's eyes. I clean the dishes and go upstairs to read.

—

The next morning I rise early and creep into the bathroom. Although I'm afraid to take a shower with Blake nearby in Mama's bedroom, my hair needs to be washed so I look nice for the Sunday service. I step in the tub and rush through my scrubbing, thinking how smart I was to jot notes for the sermon earlier in the week because I'm exhausted. Instead of feeling relief after yesterday's emotional outpouring, more sadness has flooded in overnight. I always heard that crying refreshes the spirit, but after I turn off the water and swipe at the mirror with my towel, I don't see a face that looks refreshed, just red gritty eyes, flushed cheeks, and a forlorn expression. I try a smile, but it's absolutely unconvincing. As I'm staring at myself, it suddenly occurs to me what to tell my parishioners about Grandpa.

I sneak back to my room to dress, wondering what Blake will say at breakfast and how he'll behave during the service. I don't know which I'm more concerned about. Mostly, I want to hurry into my skirt and blouse in case he knocks on my door. Around my neck, I hook a little gold cross necklace Grandpa gave me, which he said I only needed to wear on Sundays for show. Truth be told, I always feel blasphemous when I put it on, although I can see the point of advertising my faith for the flock.

When I enter the kitchen, I'm surprised to see Blake flipping pancakes. He's wearing a tight white tee shirt, black slacks, and shiny black shoes.

"Good morning, Charlie," he says, giving me a cheerful smile. "Coffee's on." He points an elbow at the pot.

"Thanks," I reply and mean it.

"My pleasure." Blake piles pancakes on a plate and hands it to me.

After pouring coffee for us, I sit down, somewhat astonished at this turn of events. It's possible my impression of Blake is wrong, that in fact he's nicer than I think. He certainly was nice last night when I was wailing and sobbing all over him. And he didn't try anything funny, either, even though he'd been drinking. If he had plans of taking advantage of me, he could have done so then. Still, I harbor serious doubts about him, which makes me wonder if the bullets I hid in my sock drawer are the only ones Blake has.

"You're mighty quiet this morning," Blake says, after we finish eating.

"Sorry. I guess I'm kind of talked out from last night."

"Yeah, I can imagine. And you have your sermon today, too." He tries to hide his amusement.

"Yes, I do." I check my watch. "In fact, I only have twenty minutes until I open the doors. Are you coming?"

"Sure, Charlie. I'll clean up here and join you."

His offer to do the dishes is another surprise. If he wants to be agreeable and helpful, I'll let him. After bringing my plate and cup to the sink, I gather my notes and head into the chapel in order to pray to Grandpa for his divine guidance.

- 18 -

The usual crowd shows up. I greet my flock of worshippers at the door, my expression solemn, which requires no acting. After everyone sits, Blake hasn't entered the chapel. Instantly, my anxiety kicks in because this means he's alone in the house. I'm tempted to delay the service and see what he's doing, but just as I'm about to do so, he saunters into the room dressed in a black clerical shirt with a white collar and a black suit. His long hair is parted arrow-straight and flanks his face with cascading wings of gold; his hands are gathered in front of him, and he wears a pious expression so that he appears to be the very likeness of a cowboy-angel, or I might even go so far as to describe him as Christ reborn. In fact, the more I gaze upon him, the more I believe the Jesus-effect is what Blake is after. What else he's after, I have no idea.

As Blake takes a chair in the last row, all heads swivel in his direction and people begin whispering about who he is. Blake tips his head politely and gives me a quiet smile.

I move to the pulpit and clear my throat. All eyes aim forward, though Mrs. Croydon takes another gander at the handsome stranger.

"Folks, I must begin today's service with some very sad news, brought here by my second cousin, Mr. Blake William Cody."

Blake's expression transforms, like someone whose favorite dog has just this minute been run over. The congregation turns to give him another look, and a buzz ripples through the crowd as everyone puzzles over the complicated family relationship, the possibility that he's related to Buffalo Bill, and what the sad news is.

"Yes, Mr. Cody is the bearer of the worst news possible. I regret to inform you that my grandfather, Charles Barrett Whitestone, has suffered a heart attack. He died on Friday."

As I'm delivering this statement, I hear sudden intakes of breath across the room. Mouths fall open even on the faces of the most reserved parishioners.

Blake stands. "Excuse me, Charlene. May I add a word or two?"

This panics me because I don't know what he'll say and how it will jibe with my other fabrications, past and planned, but I nod.

He walks to the side of the congregation, his hands folded. "I know you all loved Charles Whitestone. He was a fine man, generous in heart and spirit, who has touched all of your lives as he has mine." Blake continues in this vein for some time, waxing poetic on Grandpa's many virtues, both real and imaginary, and explaining how Grandpa inspired Blake's own religious calling. "I was a lost and sinful teenager once, and C.B. came forward and showed me the light."

I try to keep my eyes down, but Blake is such a mesmerizing speaker and so beautiful that I can't help gawking at him.

After a few minutes of euphoric religious prattle, Blake reluctantly stops. "Folks, I'm sure you want to know what happened to C.B." He waits a beat for everyone to nod and murmur assent and then says, "Well, at his request, he and I drove to Syracuse. In hindsight—and believe me I regret this with all my heart—we should have gone someplace closer, but C.B. wanted to see this doctor and insisted we drive there." Blake shuffles his feet a little, like he's not used to addressing groups of people, sighs, and continues, "Anyway, we get to the doctor's office and C.B. explains that he's got a terrible pain in his chest. I shout for the doctor who comes running. By this time, C.B. is sitting on the sofa in the waiting room, breathing hard. His face is red at first, then goes absolutely white. The doctor listens to his heart and asks the receptionist to call an ambulance. Unfortunately, at that second, C.B. clutches his chest and whispers, 'Listen to me, Blake, and remember: Charlie's the one…the chosen one. Praise the Lord.'" Blake hangs his head, as if recounting this tragedy weighs on him, but also to give time for Grandpa's words to sink in. "After this, C.B. squeezes my hand and says, 'Tell them what I said, Blake.' And with that, he pitches forward and falls onto the floor. The doctor and I turn him over, but he's dead. It happened so fast that C.B. felt little pain except for a few minutes. There was nothing the doctor could do." Blake locks eyes with various parishioners in order to impress upon them the depth of his sorrow. "I know you all wanted to see C.B. these last weeks, but he preferred to keep to himself and not worry people. That was the kind of man he was."

Here, Blake pauses again for effect, his eyes tearing slightly. The tale he's spun is so theatrical that everyone can visualize the scene. He nearly makes me believe his story.

"Now, folks," he says, "I want you to remember that it took every bit of strength the good man had to express his dying words. 'Charlie's the one...the chosen one. Praise the Lord.' He wanted me to tell you what he said." He scans the quiet crowd. "And I believe each one of you knows what he meant. You've all witnessed Charlie's devotion and dedicated belief in God and how her character is straight and true..."

I'm feeling queasy as Blake continues down this thorny road, but I fasten my eyes on the red carpeting and act the role of God's servant, though I'm the biggest fraud who ever wore a little gold cross around her neck.

"Well, though she hasn't been to seminary, Charlene's had the finest teacher she could have in C. B. Whitestone."

Here, each person looks at his or her neighbor for agreement, and finding it, nods at Blake, who suddenly behaves like he's taking a straw poll.

"Okay," he says, "I see how you all feel, and though I understand you're heart-sore to lose your guiding light, I'm sure you want Charlene to carry on her grandfather's legacy, continuing with his charities and good works. After all, C.B. believed she was special, a chosen one. Maybe she was sent here by our good Lord, who, having recalled his servant, Charles Whitestone, left Charlene to replace him. As we all know, God operates in mysterious ways. In this case, folks, I think his intention is absolutely clear."

Some ladies are wiping tears from their eyes, and even several of the gentlemen are struggling. I'm praying that old Blake shuts up soon before he goes too far, which by my account he already has, but Blake has the bit between his teeth and is off on a gallop.

"Now, I know you're all curious as to who I am and thinking it's not proper for me to speak with you about such private and holy matters. All I can say is that I'm here to help Charlene in her time of pain and sorrow, as I'm sure you will. I come from the Western branch of the Whitestone family. That's why you haven't seen me around these parts before, though I visited C.B. and his daughter, Eileen, when I was beginning seminary. Charlie was just a little girl then, but I remember how extraordinary she was."

Blake gives me a sad smile, but I detect a flicker of humor in his pale eyes even though his forehead is creased with concern.

"I imagine, however, that you're more interested in hearing from Charlene herself." He raises a hand in my direction, ceding the stage.

For once, I don't know what to say. As I move behind the pulpit, everyone is staring at me expectantly, some with handkerchiefs hovering near their eyes in preparation for more waterworks. I think about how much money the chapel brings in each week and realize I might need the income, especially if Blake has decided to make my house his permanent roost. From what he just said, I suspect this is exactly the case. While I'm pondering, I ask Mamie Croydon to lead a few hymns. Everyone pitches in with honest and heartfelt fervor because their minister has been tragically taken from them. I wonder what Grandpa would think, hearing how sad they are. Would he see that he had imparted value and hope in spite of how he used his parishioners for profit; that while he was lining his pockets, he also did a lot of good?

When silence reigns, I read from the Bible: "And John said: 'I have no greater joy than to hear my children walk in truth.'" I let that sentence float over the congregation and add, "I only hope I can walk the same path my grandfather did. I know it was his greatest wish that I continue his work." I read a few Bible passages to buy more time. Finally, with conviction, I say, "Now, I know Grandpa loved you all and worried about your welfare. If one of you was sick, he was ever so concerned. He had great plans for the Glory Alleluia Chapel in the coming years, and though he isn't here to guide us, I hope we can carry on, God willing." I have to take a gulp after this because I'm on seriously thin ice. "Some of you may wish to go to other churches—and I'll certainly understand. But I'll be here every Sunday and will do my best to lead you in prayer and in song, just as C.B. did. This is a tall order for a girl my age, but Grandpa once said I was called to service, and Grandpa was a wise man. I hope you'll help me, because I'll need your help in order to continue." These last are the truest words I've spoken all morning.

I glance at Blake in the back row. He's beaming like a proud papa.

—

After I read a eulogy about Grandpa, it's difficult to usher everyone out the door because people are still weepy and also concerned for me. Blake stands to my right, one hand on my back, the other available for shaking. Everyone wants to utter condolences and ask about the funeral, which is something I haven't reckoned on. Blake explains that Grandpa wanted to be cremated so as to return to the earth he loved and that his memorial will be next

Sunday at the church service. He invites everyone to bring something to pass for a pot-luck luncheon afterward. As they leave, the parishioners scrutinize Blake, too impressed by the solemnity of the situation to ask whether he's Buffalo Bill's relative or where he came from, though by the way they stare at him, it's obvious curiosity is eating them like August mosquitoes.

After the congregation is gone and the outside doors are locked, Blake gives me a huge grin and throws his arms around my shoulders. "Jackpot!"

He wheels me in a little circle, as if we're dancing, and then steps back. "Oh, we're good, Charlie! We're fine!"

I'm still unsettled from everything that's happened. Part of me finds Blake's excitement contagious; the other part is mourning for Grandpa. Even though he's been dead for a while, my grief feels fresh and keen from the morning's announcement.

Noticing my expression, Blake's merriment fades and he apologizes. Although I'm already in his arms, he pulls me closer, which I want to last a lot longer, a desire he seems to share because he doesn't let go until I step away. I could be imagining his interest, but then again maybe I'm not. Something about his embrace reminds me of Eli's, and I wonder if I'm having special feelings for my fake second cousin. Somehow that seems like an incestuous reaction, or maybe it's because Blake and Mama are an item, at least they are according to Blake. With all the nonsense he's told me, however, that may be another lie. The safest course is to stop our relationship immediately.

In the morning, I'll tell him to saddle up his Ford and leave.

- 19 -

Blake and I turn out the lights in the chapel and head into the kitchen.

"So where did you find the clerical shirt and collar?" I ask him.

He pulls off his jacket and turns around. The back of the shirt is gathered in folds and crisscrossed with yellow masking tape. I can't help giggling.

"I hope it's okay that I borrowed one of your grandfather's shirts," he says. "It's a little large on me." He chuckles and runs a forefinger around the white collar. "And even though this is loose, golly, I don't know how anyone can stand to wear one of these damned things!"

"Grandpa fussed whenever he wore one. So how come you got dressed like this?"

"Well, I thought the best way for you to continue your chapel business was to have an adult by your side, and better yet, a man of faith. So, just this morning I have found the Lord!"

"That's about as quick as I found the Lord, too."

We have a laugh together, as I consider his point about having an adult pastor on the premises and how he's ingratiated himself with the congregation. Even so, I can't risk becoming more involved with him.

—

After Blake and I eat lunch, and I'm about to suggest he head for the hills, there's a knock at the front door. Blake catches my eye and runs into the living room. He returns and describes none other than Doc Fairchild, hat in hand.

"Tell him I'm grieving," I whisper. "And whatever you do, don't offer him any Chivas Regal or whiskey or else Doc will stay all afternoon, happy as a pig in mud. Got that?"

Blake nods and slips on his jacket as I rush upstairs to hide in my bedroom. I leave the door ajar so I can listen.

"Good afternoon. My name is Dr. Alistair Fairchild. I'm a friend of Charles Whitestone's and also, I might add, his personal physician."

"Oh, I see," Blake replies. "Very nice to meet you."

"And you are?"

"Blake William Cody. A relative of C.B.'s."

The doctor enters the living room. I imagine he's trying to work out whether Blake is related to Mr. Cody, and whether this and Blake's minister outfit elevates Blake nearer his own standing in society. It is well known in Butztown that Doc Fairchild is very conscious of what level someone is on and considers his status as physician as nigh on regal.

I'm hoping that Blake nips the visit in the bud, and, as if reading my mind, he quickly informs the good doctor that C.B. Whitestone has passed.

This doesn't surprise Doc. Although he doesn't attend the Glory Alleluia Chapel, the local grapevine is blistering fast when it comes to communications of a sensational order.

"So I've heard, young man. I was, of course, aware of his serious heart condition," Doc replies. "Please accept my profound condolences. C.B. was an outstanding member of our community and a dear, dear friend. I am very distressed and saddened by this great loss, both for myself personally and for his many friends."

He natters on, extolling C.B. until he finally runs dry or rather has worked up a thirst. I'm sure Doc has his eye on the Chivas bottle.

"You wouldn't wish to offer a friend a drink so that we might toast C.B.?" Doc asks.

"Well, sir, if this was my scotch, I'd be obliged to share, but since it isn't, I don't feel quite right pouring another man's liquor. Now, although we are honored by your visit, Dr. Fairchild, as you might imagine, we're not up to entertaining at the moment—"

"I quite understand," Doc interrupts. "If it wouldn't be too much trouble, however, could I have a word with Charlie?"

"I'm sorry. She's upstairs in her room. The service plumb tuckered her out. She's been through a lot the last few days."

"Hmm? Oh, yes," he says, as if his mind is elsewhere, such as on the insurance money. "Well, then, I suppose I'll leave you for now. When she is up to it, please have Charlie call me. I'll stop by in a day or so to check on her."

He talks for a few more minutes, hoping that I'll show my face or liquor will be offered, but Blake eventually whisks him out. As soon as I hear Doc's car door close, I rush downstairs.

"What a blowhard!" Blake exclaims.

"He is indeed."

Blake gives me a sharp look. "And unless I miss my guess, he wanted more than a glass of Chivas Regal."

His astuteness surprises me, but I don't say anything.

"Oh, come on, Charlie. What kind of scam was your grandfather pulling with that guy? I can tell he wanted a drink, but what else is going on?"

"I have no idea. Grandpa didn't tell me about all of his business dealings. He kept them mostly to himself. He always said that the less I knew the better."

Blake rubs his face, trying to assess my truthfulness. "You sure you don't know anything?"

"Nope. But it's possible the two of them were concocting some kind of scheme." I'm not certain Blake believes me. I'm rather inclined to think he doesn't, but unless Doc Fairchild blabs, which is unlikely, I can sit on the insurance money and use it for college tuition.

"Blake," I begin, "when is my mother really coming home? Or did you make that up?"

He tries a stunned expression, sees it doesn't fly, and guides me by the elbow to the sofa. "Charlie, it's entirely possible your mother is heading north. Entirely possible." He sighs and tucks up the side of his mouth as if he's reluctant to say more, then he glances at me and his eyes soften. "Look, if you want to know the truth—as much as it goes against my grain to tell it—your mother and I did shack up a few times, and, yes, I met your daddy, who is no account, pardon the expression. Your Mama told me all kinds of tales about you and your grandfather. I suppose they filled me with ideas about how nice it would be to meet both of you."

I shake my head and smile at him. "I bet those conversations put ideas in your head all right. But, really, Blake, do you think I'm some kind of dumb fool? That I didn't catch you hightailing it over the hill with a pick-axe and shovel? I know what you're after, but let me tell you this straight out, Grandpa spent most of his money. He lost a slew of it playing cards and gambling after my parents took off. He'd try his hand at anything—dog races, why even frog-hopping contests! If he has any cash hidden anywhere on the south side of the property, I can't find it, though I doubt there's anything left. Before he died, he was very concerned about having enough money to pay the bills."

I pause for a second as Blake digests this incorrect information; the money is, in fact, buried on the north side. "Mama didn't know about Grandpa's gambling, which was under control until she left, but when Grandpa and I were stuck here alone together, he changed. When he began to get sick, he confessed what stupid things he'd done and fretted about what I would do if something happened to him. Well, something has, and I don't know how I'll manage." I exhale from this long-winded lie. "Other than the chapel donations, I make a bit from the Hooch Shop, but when Grandpa knew he was ill, he destroyed the still because he thought it could cause me trouble with the sheriff or revenuers. I have a little money that won't last long, especially if you're here and I have to feed two of us."

Blake scrutinizes my face carefully. There is just enough emotional truth in what I say to make him believe me. "Charlie, I owe you an apology. I guess you're in a god-awful mess." He frowns. "I suppose it's not right for me to stay here with you under the circumstances." He raises an eyebrow, kind of hoping I'll relent. When I don't reply, he says, "Seems like we're both in a fix. I don't have a job, and you don't have anyone to look after you."

I start to protest, but Blake holds up his hands. "Now, listen here, you're smart as a whip and sassy as any gal I've ever met, but you're still young and you're female."

This raises my hackles. "I'm doing just fine!"

"Maybe for now, but it isn't right to leave you in this big house by yourself. Just isn't." Blake leans against the couch and considers for a minute. "Here's what I propose—and if you don't want any part of this, you speak up and I'll be gone in the morning." After crossing his legs and fiddling with a sock, he says, "Now, you run the service like you always do, for as long as those fools want to throw money on the plate. And when a more official presence is required, I'll step in. We do this for a while. Maybe expand the congregation and find a bigger place eventually."

"How are we going to do that? I'm not old enough, and I don't have any religious training at all except what Grandpa taught me."

"You do just fine, Charlie. And your Cousin Blake—I guess I'm your cousin now—might have an idea or two how to make this a more lucrative operation."

I don't like the sound of this and say so, but Blake steamrollers along.

"And once we sell all the moonshine, then we find something else to sell—like maybe your grandfather's car. By the way, he did have one, didn't he?"

I nod my head reluctantly. "Yeah, the Buick is up in the woods, but I'm not selling it. I'll need a car when I'm old enough to drive…although I already know how."

"Okay. We won't sell the car." He thinks for a minute. "I'm a first-class salesman…as I know you are. Together, we'll manage. I bet we'll make quite a team, in fact."

"I'm not sure, Blake. Once Sheriff Shackrack learns Grandpa's dead—which won't take long—I'm in serious trouble. Everyone knows my parents are away, so they'll send a social worker and all kinds of people to snoop around. Next thing, I'll be in some horrible orphanage and…" I start to choke up thinking of what will happen once word gets out that Grandpa is dead.

"Well, that's why you need me. I'll explain I'm your cousin and that I'll be responsible for your safety. A guardian. Yeah, that's what I'll be."

As I consider his proposition, I realize Blake might be the only solution to my dilemma. "I could create a document in which Grandpa leaves me in your care."

"Really?"

"Yes. I have a light box downstairs for forging signatures. And if I have to, I can get a lawyer to make it official. It'll cost us a little, but…"

Blake smiles and puts his arm around me. "Whatever needs to be done, we'll do it."

—

Monday morning rolls around, cloudy, with a fine case of drizzles that mirrors my mood. The thought of getting out of bed is not appealing, but then I hear Blake banging around downstairs. It seems he is an early riser—earlier than I am at least—which is of concern since he can search the house while I'm sleeping, although the only thing he could find is the hooch stored behind the coat closet and in the altar. When I walk into the kitchen, I notice his feet are bare, without the noisy boots. No wonder I didn't hear him pass down the hall. He's wearing a crimson-and-white cowboy shirt with a horse and cowboy riding the range on his left shoulder and longhorns grazing on the right.

After he cooks some over-easy eggs, Blake announces he intends to go grocery shopping. "I'll use the money from the collection plate, if that's okay."

I realize I'd forgotten to ask him for the cash yesterday, which he grabbed with quick fingers. "Well, I suppose. But I need to pay the electricity and telephone bills. So give me thirty dollars." I put out my hand.

Blake sighs and forks over the money, counting the bills carefully, as if he hates to part with one red cent. "You drive a hard bargain, Charlie. You know that?"

"I do and don't forget it."

"Okay." He folds the bills into his pocket and grins. "You sure are something."

We clean up the dishes. Then the telephone rings. Both of us are startled. We look at each other to decide who should answer it and I do. Immediately, I wish I hadn't.

- 20 -

The once-over-easy eggs flip-flop in my stomach, threatening to rise up my throat in one express reversal. I take a deep breath and swallow.

"Hello, Mrs. Livengood," I say in response to the caller. I didn't hear exactly what Mrs. Livengood's title is, but she's a social worker assigned to my case filed with the county by our dear and beloved Sheriff Shackrack. I'm sure he heard the news of Grandpa's death from H. L. Cyrus, who plays poker with him on Sunday nights after H.L. cleanses his soul at our chapel during the morning.

As I stare at Blake, who is wondering who the caller is, I realize Mrs. Livengood hasn't cottoned to who I am. Of course, other than 'hello,' I haven't had an opportunity to say much. I lower my voice. "Mrs. Livengood, this is Eileen Whitestone. I appreciate your concern for my daughter, Charlene, but I'm home now and will take care of her."

Blake sits down to listen, hand on his chin. His blue eyes are lit with amusement.

"Mmm, yes. I know you have to be thorough, but as you can imagine, Mrs. Livengood, with my father's death on Friday, I'm really not up to company."

Blake begins to chuckle, which is threatening to bloom into full-scale laughter, so I shoo him into the living room because he's making me giggle. Mrs. Livengood is running her mouth non-stop, whether I chip in a word or not. "I see," I say several times, although I don't have the faintest idea what she's talking about and am struggling not to laugh. When she asks again to visit, I reiterate that I'm unable to see her, but this woman is one stubborn, cussed mule.

"I shall be there tomorrow morning at 9:00 a.m." She apologizes about being so insistent and then hangs up.

Blake comes into the kitchen. "Well, is Mrs. Livengood going to be good for our livelihood?" He chuckles at this, but my sense of humor has flown the coop.

"I don't think so." I explain about her visit. "She thinks Mama is here, Blake. What are we going to do? I don't want to go to an orphanage!"

He stands there, staring at me. "Gosh, Charlie, we'll think of something."

"We better think of it darned fast."

Blake walks around the kitchen, considering possibilities. Finally, he stops his pacing and looks at me. "Don't worry. I have an idea."

—

I didn't sleep much all night, fretting about the appointment with Mrs. Livengood and having nightmares about bunking with Oliver Twist and the Artful Dodger in Fagin's den. When I arise and step out of my room, I see Blake down the hall in the bathroom. He's humming like a chipper blue jay and shaving around the left side of his mouth, twisting his lips to the right for better access.

When he sees me, he raises his eyebrows. "Good morning. And how are you this fine summer day?"

I'm not so sunny when I wake, so I give him a little scowl and don't answer.

"Well, it's a fine day, whether you agree or not." He rinses shaving cream off his face and briskly pats his skin with a towel. "Now, a question for you, Charlie. Can you sew?"

"Huh? No."

"Oh, come on. All girls can sew."

"Not this girl," I mutter.

"Hmm. Well, we need to do something about your grandfather's shirts."

"Hey, you're on your own."

Blake turns toward me. "Okay. I guess I can cut the backs and stitch them together tighter. Means I have to keep my jacket on all the time."

"Yes, it does," I agree, without much sympathy.

From a hanger on the bathroom door, he takes Grandpa's clerical shirt and slips into it. Then he adds the collar, cursing under his breath as it confines his throat.

"You're wearing that today?"

"Sure, why not? When Mrs. Livengood comes to the door... shoot, when she sees me, the virtue of this household will go up a gigantic notch. And besides, I'm supposed to be a minister."

I'm not altogether sure this dress-up scheme is a great idea.

I'm also worried about his involvement in my chapel fraud, but then if Blake is found out as a fake—either by the congregation or the sheriff or the social worker—everyone will blame him, the adult, and not me, if I play dumb. "Well, all right," I agree, "but as far as the chapel goes, I want most of the proceeds from the collection plate for food and the house. If you can figure out how to keep the services running, we'll discuss money if and when you succeed."

"If and when *we* succeed," he corrects me. Blake comes over and puts his hands on my arms. "You can trust me, Charlie. Absolutely."

"Grandpa always said that if a man insists he's trustworthy, he's not."

Blake smiles. "And you're Grandpa is right...but not in this case." He gives me a hug.

—

After breakfast, it's time for my transformation. I walk into Mama's room and pin my hair up in a bun. Mama never wore her hair like this, but Mrs. Livengood doesn't know that. Then I work on my make-up and slip into stockings, heels, and a sedate navy dress, which is roomy in the hips. The bust, however, is much closer to a fit than I expect, a fact which Blake notices when I open the door and walk out into the hall.

He whistles. "Wow, Charlie! You look just like your mother!" He walks around me, his hand circling my waist.

At first, I'm pleased by his compliment until I notice how he's ogling my legs, as if I am in fact Mama or another adult woman. I worry I've created a more serious problem than the one I'm trying to resolve with the social worker. When Blake's fingers drift down the back of the dress, I remove his hand.

He looks at me, stunned, but doesn't say a word. I hope his silence means he's aware of his inappropriate reaction. It also could mean he's startled by how he's feeling toward me.

"Now go downstairs, Blake," I tell him. "It's nearly nine o'clock."

He does as I ask, with one, quick backward glance.

A few minutes later, exactly on the hour, Mrs. Livengood raps on the front door. Blake lets her in, explains who he is, and offers her tea or coffee, which she refuses. Through the crack in my bedroom door, I watch as he shows her to the sofa. She takes the more upright Windsor chair instead, which faces me slightly.

The social worker is in her sixties, rail-thin, with gray hair tightly fastened by a black cat's head comb. Since cats give me the creeps, I take this as a bad omen along with her stiff posture and lack of make-up. In fact, from the downturn of her unsmiling mouth, I'd wager the chapel collection that Mrs. Livengood takes pride in not allowing a moment of fun or frivolity to enter her life. And if she has anything to say about mine, I've smiled for the last time.

After she's made herself comfortable, she glances at Grandpa's liquor collection, puckers her lips with disapproval, and gives Blake another examination. If I were him, I'd think she could see right through to the masking tape on the back of my shirt.

"Is Mrs. Whitestone present?" she asks in a flinty voice.

"Er, yes. She's upstairs, but I must tell you, Mrs. Livengood, that Eileen's really not herself this morning." He smiles at her sweetly, enjoying his little inside joke.

As he says this, I gasp, thinking he's sailing mighty close to the wind. Then I worry that I've overdone the make-up and lipstick and maybe should scrub some of it off. Both make me appear a lot older, however. I stare down at Mrs. Livengood, at her clunky tie shoes, pale gray shirtwaist dress with a hem falling well past her knees, a mess of brown age spots marching up her arms, and think I look too much like a jazz baby for this dowdy Puritan.

"I am sorry, Mr. Cody, or do you prefer Pastor Cody?" She doesn't pause to let him answer and revs up to high speed. "I really insist on speaking with Mrs. Whitestone. It is, I'm afraid, imperative. We have very strict rules to protect children, as you can well imagine." She rattles on about the safety and welfare of minors and launches into case histories to prove various points that only she—with her file-folder mind—can keep track of. Her favorite is about alcoholic parents who ditched a baby at a tavern. "Imagine that!"

Blake has clasped his hands together like he's the soul of humble attentiveness, which would be funny except this isn't a humorous matter. He nods and makes agreeing noises here and there, but these only serve to spur Mrs. Livengood on.

Finally, after about ten minutes of holding forth about protecting children, she again asks to see Mrs. Whitestone, at which point I decide to make an appearance. I press my handkerchief to my cheek and open the door. Blake and Mrs. Livengood look up at me.

"Good morning," I say in a low voice.

Mrs. Livengood stands and so does Blake.

"Ah, Mrs. Whitestone, there you are. Thank you for seeing me during your time of mourning."

I sniff a little and pat at my dry eyes. Because the stairs and hall are in shadow and at a good distance from the social worker, Mrs. Livengood can't tell that I'm not crying. "Well, it is very inconvenient," I reply, "especially when I don't understand what the trouble is. I'm home and taking care of my daughter."

"I see," she replies. Clearly, Mrs. Livengood is disappointed there will be no fresh fodder for the orphanage, although the proximity to grief seems to have invigorated her. Her eyes shine and a small smile threatens to upset the firm line of her mouth. "I am truly sorry to disturb you. As you might properly infer, I have much experience with matters of loss and do not wish to intrude more than is absolutely necessary." She pauses for a second before asking, "Though if I might, Mrs. Whitestone, may I speak to your daughter?"

"Oh, I believe she's down by the lake somewhere…reading or writing. We had a nice breakfast, and she asked to be alone for a while. She was very close to her grandfather and misses him terribly." I let my voice crack in order to communicate my emotional fragility. "I'm sorry. I really am not up to visitors. If there is nothing else…?"

Mrs. Livengood gives me a visual examination, but I seem to pass muster. Although she appears disappointed to have her outing terminated so quickly, she picks up her notebook and purse. "Thank you, Mrs. Whitestone. I regret it was necessary to bother you. Good day."

Blake takes her elbow and steers her to the door. As she is about to step over the threshold, she says to him, "Gracious, you are an extraordinary looking young man!"

"Why, Mrs. Livengood, thank you."

After her old flesh-colored Plymouth has negotiated the twisty, willow-edged driveway, Blake runs upstairs, laughing.

"Oh, Charlie," he cries, "I am an extraordinary looking young man!" He collapses on my bed and gives in to uproarious hilarity.

I'm less enthralled. "Well, it's fine for you to think this is funny. I bet she marches right over to Sheriff Shackrack and tells him Mrs. Whitestone is home and complains he wasted her valuable time. And that may bring the sheriff here, and if he comes, there's no way Shackrack will fall for me dressed as my mother."

Blake shrugs. "You worry too much."

"One of us has to."

He grabs my arm and pulls me to the edge of the bed. "Come on, cheer up!"

I don't feel comfortable with Blake on my bed, and I feel even less comfortable with both of us on it. I work out of his grasp and stand, moving away. "Look, we have a serious problem of how we're going to survive, especially with two of us."

"Aw, Charlie, we'll do just fine. You wait and see."

After lunch, Blake announces he has some errands to run. When I ask him what they are, he gives me a mischievous grin and refuses to say.

—

With Blake out of the house, I don Mama's blue hat and run up the hill to Grandpa's Buick, figuring it's a good opportunity to collect pyramid money from the post office boxes. It's sorely tempting to lower the convertible top, but I can't risk the visibility that Grandpa prized. I crank the windows half open instead, since it's hotter than a fox in springtime, as he used to say, and take off down the hill.

"I do love driving! I do, indeed!" In fact, if I had more money with me, I envision traveling to Florida to see the Everglades and the crocodiles and pink flamingoes. I picture Eli driving with me and how much fun we'd have, but then I reject this daydream. Even so, it revives a feeling of wistfulness so I detour past Eli's house, hoping I'll see him. The front door is closed and no one is around.

I continue down the road, switching my thoughts to Blake and what kind of scheme he has up his sleeve, or rather Grandpa's shirtsleeve. As I visit the post offices and pocket five-dollar bills, I realize Blake has been on my mind more than Eli. This makes sense because he's living in my house, but there's more to my feelings than that. I return to the car determined to stifle any romantic leanings I might have toward him and equally determined to forget about Eli.

Once home, I park the Buick in front of the house because I don't have to hide it any longer. Upstairs, I place $45 from the pyramid money in my bedroom closet's secret compartment and keep $15. Then I change into jeans and a tee shirt, feeling fairly pleased considering the mess I'm in. Or at least I do until Blake rolls in two hours later.

- 21 -

He's drunk, blasting beery breath all over me. Even though he's concentrating hard to sort out his feet, Blake is grinning ear to ear.

"Charlie, I'm one brilliant son of a gun!"

"What have you done, Blake?" I ask him like a stern mother.

He drops on the sofa and crosses his legs. "Well, I've had a conversation with the local radio station."

"Why?"

He treats me to a devilish smile. "We have an interview next Sunday morning—"

"What? But we have service!"

Blake holds up his hands. "Yes, we do. You're right, but a Mr. George M. Sheridan from Rochester is coming to listen to the Reverend Cody and C. B. Whitestone—"

"Blake! There is no C. B. Whitestone!"

"Oh, yes there is." He points to me and chuckles.

I regard him with amazement that scurries along into full-fledged anxiety. "You didn't say we're both ministers, did you?"

"No, I didn't. But I told Mr. Sheridan that you have wondrous powers." His hands flutter toward the heavens.

"Oh, my! You didn't tell him that, did you?"

Blake nods, his bloodshot eyes bright with excitement.

I begin walking the floor in front of Grandpa's chair, my arms crossed. "I can't believe you! Why did you do that?"

"Because you and me are going to make a heap of money, sugar. A heap."

I stop my pacing and stare at him. "How in God's name are we going to do that?"

"Just as you said...in God's name!"

"Blake! Will you quit talking in circles and answer me?" My temper has now chased away the anxiety.

He gives me a hurt look. "Gosh, I thought you'd be pleased. Mr. Sheridan is going to listen to our sermon—"

"*Our* sermon?"

"Of course. Our sermon. You need a bona fide minister to help you run things. Least until you go to seminary yourself." Blake twists his mouth into a little sideways grin.

"I have no intention of ever going to seminary!" I shout. "And you know absolutely nothing about preaching." I realize I don't know much myself, but I've absorbed a great deal from Grandpa, who, admittedly, conjured most of his sermons from thin air and from a few church services he attended as a child.

"Now, don't get all riled, Charlie."

"Why not? It isn't your grandfather who's dead! It isn't your mother who's run off or your daddy! You don't understand what kind of situation I'm in."

"Yes, I do."

Blake stands and tries to comfort me, but I back away from him, in no mood for coddling, and retreat to my bedroom.

—

The week passes quietly. I have good business selling product and even a Bible, both to Mr. Wasser. He seems to be doing a similar trick as H. L. Cyrus, who prays then gambles and drinks. Mr. Wasser, on the other hand, says he drinks and then prays, which makes more sense to me. If you have to pray, it's best to be liquored up so everything goes down easier. At any rate, shortly after Mr. Wasser left, H.L. himself came to buy a jar of moonshine. He's the only one of our flock who partakes of Grandpa's product, which is fine because the fewer of our parishioners know about our other businesses the better. However, Mr. Cyrus, like most everyone, thinks Daddy is responsible for the still and that I'm just doing my father's bidding. I constantly remind our customers to be careful who they talk to, and, for the most part, they are silent as tombs, not wanting word to get out to the wrong ears and thus deprive themselves of an inexpensive and convenient source of liquor. In H.L.'s case, he has an additional reason to keep his mouth shut because Mrs. H. L. Cyrus is a devout teetotaler and a strident opponent of gambling. She has been known to fly into a rage on the occasions her husband goes wayward on either count, and because he usually commits both sins at the same time, he gets both barrels from her. Even so, I made H.L. promise on the life of his prized pig that he won't tell a soul about where he gets the hooch. We shot the breeze for a bit, though he was curious about Blake and what bough of the family tree he was perched on and where my mother was. I was vague on both subjects, especially since H.L. and Sheriff Shackrack are thick as thieves. That might not even be a metaphor.

And now it is Saturday. Blake drove to Brockport and then spent hours in the chapel with the doors locked. I knocked. He told me he was busy. I tried to see through the outside windows, but they're placed high so no one can observe the worshippers during service. As a result, I couldn't tell what fakery my fraudulent cousin was concocting.

When he emerges at long last and sits at the kitchen table, he looks happy.

I ladle Campbell's baked beans over two hot dogs. "So, what are you doing in there?"

Blake tucks a napkin in his shirt and starts to eat. "All in good time."

"You're mighty infuriating, do you know that?"

"Yeah." He tosses me a self-satisfied smile.

I try a few other tacks, but he won't budge. We eat lunch in silence, me trying to figure out what's going on, and Blake trying to figure out how to do what he's planning.

—

About 3:30, Blake scares the bejesus out of me. I'm down in Worm Heaven in the Hooch Shop when he thumps on the locked door. I rush up the ladder and yell at him, but he's so pleased with himself he doesn't notice, though he takes a long look at the underground supplies, making a mental note for future forays.

"Don't you think you can go down there and help yourself," I tell him. "I keep track of every jar, whether it's pickled onions or whiskey."

"Okay," he replies, "but Charlie, you have to come see."

"I can't right now," I say, "I have afternoon customers, and Mr. Carter is bringing some corn like he does every Saturday."

A hurt look settles across his face. "Please?"

I feel a flash of remorse. "Well, just for a few minutes."

After I slide the hatch in place, lay the rug, and stack some Bibles on top, Blake grabs my hand and hauls me to the chapel lickety-split. Inside, a fan is whirring and sticks of jasmine incense are flowering the air with sweetness.

As I'm trying to analyze the strange smells in the room, Blake switches on the lights. "Now, check this out."

Ten feet past the pulpit, Blake has attached a gold cross on a

136

square of white cloth, which hangs from a dowel rod decorated with gilded flowers.

"Very nice," I say, "but how is this going to impress your Mr. Sheridan?"

"Look behind it."

Blake lifts the material away. On the wall is a strange sight.

"What the hell is that?" I ask him.

"Pretty clever, huh? Look closer."

I do and am amazed. "Well, I guess we're not related at all."

"How's that?"

"Because no one in my family has any artistic talent."

He grins at this. Then his creation gives me an idea. "Blake, follow me."

—

When I wake the next morning, I feel like I'm starring in a school pageant or a Christmas play. I also have a serious case of the guilties on account of how my charlatan ways are about to increase in depravity. At breakfast, I try to save the last remnant of my soul, such as it is.

"Blake, I've changed my mind. I don't want to do this."

He pours my coffee with a flourish. He's all bounce and lightness and sunshine. "Oh, come on, Charlie, this'll be fun. And profitable, too. You have to look at the big picture. Where we want to be in a few years."

"Where I want to be is at a good college studying, not in a jail cell." I'm now persuaded that my evil deeds will reap more stringent punishment than being incarcerated in an orphanage. I have shifted from Fagin's pickpocket stage to Bill Sykes' robber and murder stage, or so it seems. Thinking this as I spread raspberry jam on my toast, I decide to swear off Mr. Charles Dickens for a while because reality and fiction are sliding together in my mind.

"I know, I know. But in the meantime, we have to make a living," Blake says.

"*We* don't have to make a living. *You* do. I can manage off the moonshine sales and the chapel collection."

"But you need money for college. And once you run out of moonshine, then what?"

He has me there. I can't fess up and say how much buried treasure is lying around on the property. While I sincerely doubt he'd do me violence, I'm not altogether positive that Blake can keep his greed under control if he knows how much money is hidden. And if I'm the only impediment to his having it? I think about the Winchester in his room and consider why Blake brought it into the house. Even though I've removed the bullets, he might have more somewhere. I sigh and agree that I have no choice but to participate.

"That's the spirit, Charlie!" he says, patting me on the back.

After doing the dishes, we hurry upstairs to dress for the production.

—

When our congregation arrives with flowers, casseroles, soda, and cookies, we're ready. White candles are blazing and a framed photograph of Grandpa resides in a place of honor by the pulpit. In the rear of the chapel, card tables are set with forks, napkins, and paper plates. Everything appears dignified and yet festive, as C.B. would have liked. I muse on this for a second and wish he would guide me from on high, or on low, wherever he is, anywhere except the whiskey still, moldering away, an image that fills me with horror.

Blake is decked out in his religious finery, wearing Grandpa's most ostentatious cross, one given to C.B. by a nutcase old woman who has long since passed. I tell Blake the cross is gaudy, with its fake rubies and emeralds, but Blake explains he was born Catholic and Catholics are staunch believers in flamboyance of every conceivable kind. He also says the Catholic Church owns a quarter of New York City and a slew of other cities, and if they're as rich as that, then their practices must be successful. I allow as how he's right, though Grandpa believed in a more conservative approach. Blake agrees to behave, but I think the Catholic way of thinking is embedded in him deep, because if someone believes he's born as something, then sure enough that religion has hooked the poor fellow before he's had an opportunity to think for himself.

About ten minutes prior to the start of service, a strange man arrives, straw hat in hand. This must be Mr. George M. Sheridan of radio renown. He's wearing a pink shirt, red tie, and blue-and-white seersucker suit with a navy handkerchief sprouting from his breast pocket. If I didn't know better, I'd say he's all ready for the Fourth of July or else is running for political office. Mr. Sheridan's hair is a wooly gray-blond and still bears the impression of his hatband. On his large nose are silver spectacles whose thick glass enlarges his eyes to the size of fat blueberries. With his florid cheeks, it's likely Mr. Sheridan has done some imbibing in his time.

Blake rushes over to greet him and pumps Mr. Sheridan's hand, but I hesitate because I don't wish to appear eager about meeting our visiting celebrity. I am, after all, supposed to be a teenager grieving for her grandfather.

After exchanging a few words, Mr. Sheridan exposes a set of prominent teeth that reminds me of Mr. Cossantino's old horse, Hilda, who has a habit of exposing her choppers while she's chewing. At least Mr. Sheridan's teeth aren't covered with grass stains, though they do appear yellow from cigarette smoke. At any rate, Mr. Sheridan takes a seat near the door, presumably for a fast getaway, and crosses his arms like he's defending against any attempts we might make to delude him.

Blake joins me in the front to give a general welcome and then sidles off to the back of the room near the door to the main house, leaving me in charge. I read from the Bible and ask Mrs. Croydon to lead a hymn, at which point Blake disappears while everyone is focused on hitting the notes, more or less. It always amuses me to see how those with better voices try to ensure their talents are properly appreciated. Some—especially some of the gentlemen—are louder than they are good and often receive glares from their wives, who are more sensitive to pitch, tone, and the refinements of singing. Once I notice Blake slipping into the room again, I take off my Timex and lay it in front of me. I have eleven minutes until the chicanery starts.

- 22 -

I begin the memorial service with a biography of Grandpa, one embellished with ornate epiphanies and visions of Jesus coming to him in all sorts of places, such as the moment he met his future wife and the Lord told him she was the one for him. Of course the only epiphanies I recall Grandpa having are moments of sudden clarity as to how to foist off a con, and these usually entered his head via the facility of Chivas or his aged moonshine.

I keep these mental asides to myself as I rumble on about Grandpa's beliefs and good works in the community and for his parishioners. Everyone is nodding and hanging on every word. After nine minutes have elapsed, I wrap up with how much Grandpa loved them and wanted to make his Glory Alleluia Chapel a place for all to come and share their sorrows and joys. When I ask for a moment of prayer, Blake stands beside me.

The place is quiet except for breathing and some foot shuffling. Then, from beyond, comes Grandpa's voice: "My friends, you have the ultimate privilege this morning. My granddaughter, Charlene, has seen the light and the light is now within her."

Every head jerks up, eyes wide and startled. I have to chew on the inside of my mouth to keep from laughing because everyone is wearing an identical expression. Even Mr. Sheridan's mouth is agape.

"Yes, it is true," Grandpa continues, "Charlene witnessed our Lord, Jesus Christ, while she was standing on the shores of Lake Ontario, gazing out at the magnificent waters, the clouds scurrying past. He came to her and said she must carry on his work, that she should be prepared in the event something should happen to me and I am called to him."

These last sentences were on Grandpa's practice tape, the one he made for my debut at the Glory Alleluia Chapel months ago. I hadn't heard this version until I remembered his collection of recorded sermons and shared them with Blake. Because Grandpa didn't utter these particular words at the service, perhaps to avoid alarming anyone about his health, when his parishioners hear the speech now, it's for the first time.

"If this occurs, my friends, please listen to my granddaughter and heed her, for she has been chosen."

The silence is stunning. The tape slithers to an end, though no one can hear this happen. Blake and I erased twelve minutes of other practice sermons before the message and 30 seconds after, cutting the tape to keep additional material in case further revelations from heaven are necessary. I wait a beat or two after Grandpa finishes and perform a perfectly timed swoon into Blake's arms. Even though my eyes are closed, I feel people rushing to the pulpit.

"Stand back, please," Blake says.

On cue, I flutter my lashes and come to, raise a limp wrist to my cheek, and gaze at Blake with growing amazement. Seeing his beautiful blue eyes this close makes it a snap to create an astonished expression.

"Charlene, are you all right?" he asks.

I stand upright with his assistance. The parishioners are communing with their neighbors and glancing at me with concern.

"Yes," I reply, blinking. "I think so. What happened?"

Blake still has his arm around my shoulders. "You fainted."

"I did?" I shake my head as if confused. "But I heard Grandpa and...then another voice."

"Who was it?" asks Mamie Croydon, who has edged in close.

I act dazed. "I'm not sure." I stare up at the ceiling and sigh. "The voice said I was called...that I must obey and be faithful... to spread the word." I utter this as if I'm waking from a long sleep.

Mrs. Croydon raises a white-gloved hand to cover her mouth. "Oh, my goodness! The Lord is speaking to us through Charlene!"

Mr. H. L. Cyrus moves nearer, a look of wonderment on his face. "Mamie, I think you're right!"

"Charlene? What else did he say?" Blake prompts.

"I'm not sure." I squint as if this will help me remember. "Something about...no, the rest is gone. I'm sorry."

I gaze at the congregation like I'm still weak, acting all drifty and out to lunch. Then Blake takes over. He clears his throat and raises his left hand. In his right, he holds the tacky cross and kisses it like it's his first love. This strikes me as funny so I stare at the floor to maintain a solemn expression.

"Ladies and gentlemen, dear friends, and fellow worshippers," he begins, "we have heard something extraordinary this morning...a message from beyond the grave." Blake pauses for effect and scans the audience, making eye contact with everyone, especially Mr. George M. Sheridan, who is listening attentively. "I believe the Reverend Whitestone felt so passionate about his belief in the powers of his granddaughter, Charlene, that he mustered the energy to return, to impress upon us that we must heed his admonition."

Blake stumbles on the word *admonition* because his vocabulary isn't as large as mine. I wrote his speech without realizing he prefers smaller words.

"We must listen and respect his wishes," he continues. "And then there is the second message...perhaps coming directly from God. Only time will tell whether Charlene heard our Lord. We pray that she has...that he has selected our small chapel as a sacred place and Charlene as his voice here on Earth."

At this point, we're supposed to hit the crowd with our second barrage of magic, but Blake decides to save it for another service because this first act has been so successful. While he watches me with a concerned expression, I slowly snap out of my fog and pull myself together, thanking everyone for their many kindnesses toward Grandpa and their support of his efforts. The collection plate is passed, and I see the flash of five-dollar bills, which for farm folk is a lot of money. Blake spots this, too, and gives my elbow a little squeeze from behind.

After the service, everyone gathers by the food and soda, chattering away about Reverend Whitestone's amazing message and the possibility they've witnessed a miracle. Mr. George M. Sheridan introduces himself, laying a heavy paw on my shoulder.

"You are quite the public speaker, young lady," he says.

I don't answer because my public-speaking ability is supposed to be God-given, and thus I can't take credit for it.

Blake steps forward. "She is indeed, Mr. Sheridan. I don't think Charlene is aware of her effect on people. In fact, I'd go as far as to say she's innocent of her own powers."

"That so? Well, I don't think it'll be long before that changes." He gives me an appreciative look.

Blake and I both stare at him, acting puzzled, which we're not in the least. Mr. Sheridan is so busy conjuring ideas that he doesn't notice our theatrical expressions and that they are formed in perfect unison.

"Yes, Miss Whitestone, Mr. Cody, I believe you have captured my imagination, and when I am captured," he chuckles, "I am the very epitome of creative thinking."

"I don't quite understand," Blake says, his brow slightly furrowed.

Mr. Sheridan chuckles again and nods. "I don't want to say more at this time. No, but I will return next Sunday to visit, to see if my first impressions are correct." He treats us to his Hilda-the-horse smile. "And now, it appears we have many delectable things to eat."

After lunch, no one rushes off until they see I'm okay. People touch my hand or my arm as they might a religious object or a horseshoe—there isn't any difference between religion and superstition, one being the same as the other as far as I can tell. At any rate, the collection plate is piled high—eighty-eight dollars—plus we have leftovers to last us most of the week.

—

"Sheridan's hooked," Blake exclaims, as we turn off the chapel lights.

"You think so?"

"Yeah. He has that greedy look in his eyes."

Since I am staring at Blake and seeing that same expression, I know what he means. "I'm glad we didn't use our second trick."

"Me, too. You were right. We needed to do the Grandpa miracle first." Blake fingers the cash from the collection plate, but I snatch it out of his hand.

"You get twenty dollars and that's it." I give him the money.

"Gee, that doesn't seem right, especially when we don't need to buy food."

"Sorry, but I have bills to pay."

He hangs his head but accepts my decision. We then carry Grandpa's Wollensak reel-to-reel tape player to the basement, in case anyone comes snooping, and by that I mean Sheriff Shackrack, who will no doubt learn of the appearance of Grandpa's grand presence from either H. L. Cyrus or another bubbling wellspring of information.

After we've tidied up and changed clothes, Blake pours me a tot of scotch and grabs a beer for himself. We go sit in the living room. Blake is now comfortable in his black cowboy boots, jeans, and two-toned white and black shirt, which he washes and irons himself on account of I informed him that I'm not his laundrywoman.

"So, do you think Sheridan will wait a week or come to us sooner?" Blake asks.

"I don't know," I reply, sipping my drink and wondering what kind of craziness is about to befall me.

—

That night I ponder my situation. Even though I'm flush with money, the $5,000 life insurance policy is out there waiting. The problem is I can't file a claim without a body, and I can't show anyone where Grandpa is. My story has an additional tangle because I told everyone Grandpa died at a doctor's office. If this happened for real, the doctor would probably fill out papers for the authorities so I could hit up the life insurance company. If this is how it works, I have to get the documents faked, and in order to do that, I have to find a doctor, and I only know one of those, more or less.

This line of reasoning splits into two thorny twigs. First, how do I collect the insurance money without Blake getting his grubbies on it, and second, how do I get Doc Fairchild to cooperate when he wants his share of the insurance payouts from Dory Blinkenhausen and Gregory Elkhorn. All in all, I am in a pickle, but the longer I delay on applying for the insurance, the more suspicious everyone will be. I think on this so hard my head is pounding. Then, at last, I have the answer.

—

Because I sleep in, Blake is off before I venture downstairs, no doubt prospecting for buried treasure. This suits me fine. I quickly help myself to toast and orange juice, then jump on my bike wearing old clothes that I've outgrown so that I look a bit pitiful, though my guess is that pity is not an emotion that stirs in the good doctor's heart. I know what does, however, and though I intend on appealing to his kindness, I also plan to appeal to his greediness.

Doc's office is attached to his house, which is a rambly old thing that's been painted a million times. Unfortunately, the lazy cuss who did the painting wasn't partial to scraping so that the overall effect of the siding is bright and white but splintery. On the office door is a brass plaque with "Alistair Fairchild, MD" engraved in fancy script, kept polished by Daisy Mossbacher, Doc's housekeeper, receptionist, and secretary. I heard tell Daisy, when she's feeling sprightly, has allowed Doc other attentions but not on a regular basis, either because he doesn't pay enough or because he's just too old.

It's 10:40 and the office is open. I go inside but Daisy is else-where so I sit on a red leather bench and do the vocabulary quiz in *Reader's Digest*, which is a snap. Business is pretty well dead in the water so far as I can tell. By and by, Fairchild comes out. He's wearing a white doctor's coat and has a stethoscope dangling around his neck. When he sees me, he blinks twice, as his mind gets its gears engaged.

I stand and say good morning, shaking his hand like the sweet little kid I'm not.

"Hello, Charlie," he says. "You're up bright and early."

"Yes, sir."

"Your, er, cousin, Mr. Cody, did he give you my message?"

"He did indeed, sir. That's why I'm here."

Doc nods and works his shaggy eyebrows, trying to create a kindly expression, and suggests we go into his private office.

I follow him meek as a lamb, figuring the more he thinks he's in charge, the better things will go. He walks around a huge ma-hogany desk and sits in a high-backed chair whose brown leather is surrounded by brass studs. I take one of the two guest chairs and notice both are lower than his in order to emphasize his el-evated station.

"Now, Charlie," he begins, "do you know why I wanted to talk to you?"

"I'm sure it was to express your condolences, sir."

"Ah, yes, of course." He tells me what a splendid fellow C.B. was, what a fine friendship they had, and a lot of long-winded hooey that makes it difficult for me to keep focused. Finally, Doc runs out of conversation, probably because it isn't what he wants to talk about. After inquiring if I'm okay—to which I reply in the affirmative—he narrows his eyes so I won't see too much of what's going on in his mind.

"Now, Charlie, I hate to ask you at a time like this, but I be-lieve your grandfather had some money he owed me."

"Yes, sir. I know that."

Doc can't hide a smile though he tries hard. "Ah, good, good!"

"Well, yes and no, Dr. Fairchild. You see I have a big problem and it seems like you have one, too. Maybe we can solve both of our problems together, if you're willing to help me...and good-ness knows, I need someone who has experience and is respected in the community."

Although Doc loves a compliment more than most, he's eager to get on with things so he waves his hand to keep me talking.

"Here's the situation," I explain. "My cousin Blake took Grandpa to Syracuse to see a doctor. Why Grandpa wanted to go there, I have no idea, especially when he already had a fine physician." I nod at Doc, who acknowledges the tribute. "Anyhow, as soon as Grandpa got to this office, he collapsed and died. Blake was so upset that he ran outside and took off in Grandpa's car." I give a long sigh here. "Blake's never been to Syracuse and immediately got lost. When he tried to return to the doctor's office, he couldn't remember how to find it on account of Grandpa drove there, even though Grandpa was feeling poorly, and he couldn't recall the doctor's name to ask directions. It took him hours to find his way home."

"I see," Doc Fairchild says, fiddling with a fancy black fountain pen. "So where is your grandfather's body now?"

I hang my head and think of C.B. in the whiskey still. Two tears slide down my cheeks. "Oh, Doc, I don't know where he is!" I muster my most mournful expression. "And Blake has no idea, either. So you see, I can't even bury Grandpa. I feel so bad!" I'm crying now, which is probably having no effect on Doc Fairchild, but theatrics are nevertheless required.

"Hmm," says Doc in an absentminded way because he is most likely contemplating the problem of the life insurance money. "There has to be a death certificate issued, Charlie. Perhaps the doctor made one out using information in C.B.'s wallet."

"I don't think so," I reply, wiping at my face with my fingers. "Grandpa gave Blake his wallet and keys because he didn't want to leave them around when he went in to undress for the examination."

"In other words, some unknown doctor at an unknown office in Syracuse has a man die in his waiting room and he doesn't ask for identification? Well, surely C.B. made an appointment and the doctor knew who he was."

"No, sir. Grandpa had heard about this doctor and went there because he was feeling so bad. He and Blake just showed up." Tears are falling fast. It doesn't take much to get me going these days. "He didn't have time to give his name to the receptionist before he took ill."

"That's an incredible story." Doc's eyes are sharp on mine. "I find it quite unbelievable."

"Oh, Doc, it's the truth! I know it sounds crazy, but I'm so scared because without having that death certificate I can't get to Grandpa's checking account or have his will read."

Doc is trafficking on the same lane as I am. "And was C.B. in the habit of depositing all his money in this checking account?"

"I think so, sir. But I am not absolutely positive. Awhile back, he mentioned something about putting a large amount in the bank. Whether he did or not, I can't say." I shrug after having delivered this information. "Now, Doc, I know I shouldn't have been listening, but a few months ago I overheard you two talking about life insurance policies for two of your patients."

Doc sits up straight and leans forward. "Charlie, you probably misunderstood what we were discussing. Especially if you were eavesdropping."

"You might be right, but either I heard what I heard, in which case the two of you were up to something a bit shady, or else you weren't, in which case I don't think Grandpa has any money of yours, unless he owes you for a doctor visit or something."

Doc sighs, seeing that the trap has sprung from all sides. He's quiet for a long time. I pluck a Kleenex tissue from a wooden holder on his desk and blow my nose.

"So what should we do?" I ask him.

He sighs again. Sitting on the horns of his dilemma is painful. "I suppose you need me to write a death certificate, don't you?"

"That would surely be a big help."

"And I guess I can assist you with the authorities, too."

"That would also be a big help."

Doc glances at me to see if I'm being sassy, but I maintain a serious demeanor.

"We don't want Sheriff Shackrack in on things, or so I imagine," I say.

He shakes his head and says a little too quickly, "No, we don't."

I have him and he knows it. "Well, sir, since you're being so kind, I think I should offer you something in return."

"Oh?" he says, his eyes brighten.

"Yes. Because you and Grandpa had an arrangement," I pause here and stare at him so he knows I'm aware of the illegal nature of the arrangement, "The fair thing would be to divide half of what is in Grandpa's checking account with you. Now, I don't have any idea of how much is in there because Grandpa didn't bother balancing his checkbook. He always said he had all his information in his head. That might have been okay when his head was still alive and working, but now it isn't. Of course this leaves me kind of high and dry."

Doc takes this in and pretends he's concerned about my welfare, which doesn't interest him at all. "Isn't your mother return- ing soon? I'm sure she will when she hears about C.B."

I'm relieved he hasn't been talking to the sheriff, who probably thinks my mother has already arrived—if Mrs. Livengood reported to him—but like Grandpa, Doc stays clear of the sheriff for the same reasons. And Doc wouldn't have heard any tales from Mrs. Livengood, who comes from the social welfare office over at the county seat.

"Yes, Mama will be home eventually," I agree, "but even when she comes, she probably won't have any money." I replace my stare with a sad look, gradually, however, so as not to appear like I've just fallen out of a 1930s movie.

Doc sighs for the third time, which is obviously a trait he has acquired in the pursuit of the helping profession. "I think under the circumstances there will be enough in C.B.'s checking account to satisfy us both."

I give him a doubtful look. "I hope so, Doc. I really do. For both our sakes, but like I said, I can't make any promises about what's in there."

"I understand, my dear. Well, though I am not altogether positive I believe this story about a doctor in Syracuse, it appears you need my help. In addition to a death certificate, there is the problem of the body…where it is and how it will be properly dis- posed of."

"Cremation, sir. That's what Grandpa wanted."

"Oh? Yes, that's very sensible under the circumstances. But Charlie, how do we cremate a body that's missing?"

He has a point. "I suppose we could just assume it's been done already," I suggest.

Doc gives me a shrewd look. "Hmm. I see. So the Syracuse story is pure fabrication?"

I refuse to validate my dishonesty, so I shrug. He shakes his head in dismay, but because I have him dead to rights on insur- ance fraud and other unseemly behavior such as selling fake med- icine, Doc wisely decides to let things pass.

"I believe Farrell's Funeral Parlor might be willing to handle matters," he says, clearing his throat. "They've done other favors for me from time to time."

I wonder what those favors are and shudder at the thoughts that spring to mind, such as the disposal of bodies that Doc Fairchild has brought to an early demise through professional—or should I say unprofessional—incompetence.

"That would be very helpful," I agree, "and no service is necessary. We did one at the chapel." I'm hoping that I won't have to give the Farrells a bribe, but because Doc doesn't suggest one, either he's so eager to get his paws on the insurance money that he's willing to pay them himself or else he's running a bill with the funeral parlor to cover errors he needs to shove under the carpet, in which case a little body-less paperwork is a small request.

He takes a sheet of paper out of his desk and uncaps his fountain pen. "Now, Charlie, can you give me the particulars on C.B.?"

Without additional prompting, I slide over Grandpa's Social Security card, driver's license, and birth certificate and tell him the date and time of Grandpa's death—or at least the one that matches the Syracuse story.

- 23 -

I'm feeling bold and brilliant as I pedal home. That is until I see Sheriff Shackrack's police car cooling its muffler by the Hooch Shop. I stop dead in my tracks. Should I disappear into the woods and leave the sheriff to his investigations? Then I spot Blake standing by the door and decide I better support my newfound cousin.

"Ah, here's Charlie," Billy Shackrack says to Blake. The policeman is leaning against the building like he owns it. One leg is cocked at an angle so that the polish on his high black boot reflects sunlight.

As I approach, the sheriff straightens and checks me up and down, slowly, in that wolfish way of his. Blake notices this and immediately comes to stand beside me.

"The sheriff wants to see your mother," Blake says.

I ignore this and lace my arm through Blake's. "And how are you, Sheriff?"

"I'm fine," he says, his eyes tight to mine. "Been off fishing this last week."

"Catch anything?"

He gives me a sly smile. "Yes, as a matter of fact, I did."

Since he isn't supplying more information, I nod. "Good. Glad to hear it. Fishing has been only so-so around here. Caught a big brown trout not long ago, however."

Sheriff Shackrack snorts in recognition of this do-si-do we're doing. "Charlie, I understand your grandfather is dead."

This is blunt, even for him. "Yes, sir, that's right."

"Sorry to hear it."

Not a whit is he sorry to hear it. "Thanks," I reply. "It happened suddenly. In Syracuse. Blake was with him when he died."

Sheriff Shackrack's lips compress, then twitch as he stares hard at Blake's cowboy attire. "You don't say," he replies, like he doesn't believe anything either one of us says.

"Dr. Fairchild is working on the death certificate today," I tell the policeman. "He's handling it as a favor to the Syracuse doctor because that man never even met Grandpa until he keeled over in his office. I'm sure all the forms will be finished pretty soon."

Blake listens, not showing the slightest surprise.

"Well, that's fine, I guess," Shackrack says.

He takes a step forward so he can tower over both of us. It seems like the shadow of his wide-brimmed hat has extinguished the sun. I tighten my grip on Blake's arm, though Blake has shrunk mightily compared to Shackrack.

"Now, I also hear your mother has returned. Where is Eileen?"

"Er, I am not altogether sure," I reply. "Blake, have you seen Mama?"

Blake shrugs. "Like I told the sheriff, I haven't set eyes on her since breakfast, but then again I was off by the lake."

"And I went to see Dr. Fairchild," I explain. "A bit of a sore throat." I rub the ailing part of my anatomy. "That's how I know he's doing Grandpa's paperwork."

"How come it seems that whoever I want to see is never here?" Shackrack isn't pleased.

"Bad timing," I answer.

Shackrack shakes his head and glares at me. "Eileen couldn't go far unless she has her own car."

"No, she doesn't," I say because I don't want the sheriff to keep an eye out for a car that is never in the driveway.

"And I see your grandfather's Buick is still here. I assume that Ford is yours, Mr. Cody?"

"It is," Blake agrees. "Sheriff, I don't know where Eileen has wandered off to, but perhaps she could call you?"

Shackrack's eyes glint with animosity as he stares at Blake. "Make sure she does," he says in a curt voice. "I need to know if Eileen's in residence because of Charlie being a minor. I trust I make myself clear?"

"Yes, sir," I reply. "I'll have her telephone you."

The sheriff hitches his mouth to the side, like he's working on something unpleasant stuck in his teeth, then heads to his car.

After he leaves, Blake turns to me. "I don't cotton to policemen much. Especially him."

"Me, either. And now I have to transform into my mother again."

—

Just before dinner, I call the police station, hoping the sheriff is away at supper. Deputy Gary Rees answers, which is a stroke of luck because he's dumb as an ox. In my mother's voice, I announce who I am. He says Shackrack is off duty.

"Please tell the sheriff that I'm home and perfectly able to take care of my daughter, Charlene. And furthermore, I request that he does not come round the house scaring her. I don't approve of his behavior," I say with a firmness I don't feel.

"Yes, ma'am," says Gary. "I'll give him the message."

Relieved, I hang up.

"Why is Shackrack so interested in your family?" Blake asks.

"Beats me."

"I think he kind of likes you...in a funny way."

I ponder this, wondering if Blake is teasing me or making an observation. "Well, I don't care for him one bit."

"And I don't like the way he stares at you, Charlie. That guy has ideas."

"You think?"

Blake nods. "You better steer clear of him."

I consider this protective streak in Blake and realize he's fond of me. Maybe he even feels more strongly than that. I'm not sure if I'm safer with him than the sheriff, but it seems so. "Thanks," I tell him.

—

The next morning I'm still feeling good about my cowboy visitor. I hand him fifty dollars and tell him to go buy a new suit. "Nothing flamboyant, Blake." I point to his cowboy boots. "And those have to go, at least when you're out in public."

He gives me a hug. "Thanks, Charlie."

"No stopping in at the bar, either. Bring back the change."

After he leaves, I regret my generosity, but Blake has a role to play and needs to look the part, which, in the long run, will help me, too, although I'm not positive I want to be helped in the direction we're going.

I drive to the post offices and fetch five-dollar bills in envelopes, recouping what I gave Blake and then some. I consider cashing another check on Grandpa's account, but I decide it's too risky because the bank will be notified of the date of his death, and it would look suspicious if money is withdrawn after that. Since I'll legitimately inherit everything, I'll get the cash at that point. Of course I promised Doc Fairchild to split whatever is in the checking account, which I better do. He's going to be powerfully upset when he learns the insurance money isn't there, but I'll deal with that problem later.

When I get home, there's a postcard of Saint Bartholomeus

Cathedral in Frankfurt, Germany, from my cousins Buck and Corey. They're stationed nearby and say they miss Grandpa and me, especially because they didn't visit after boot camp or during their military leaves. At the bottom of the card, they printed their address so I sit and write them a letter explaining about Grandpa and telling them not to worry, though I know they will.

—

Blake is disappointed that Mr. Sheridan hasn't called or come by. "I swear, Charlie, I was sure he had the hook in his mouth."

I don't answer because I have no idea. Mr. Sheridan seemed curious but cautious.

"And one more thing. How're we going to explain why your mother isn't at the service?"

"No problem. She never did attend and everyone knows that."

When Sunday rolls around, however, Mr. George M. Sheridan presents himself at the chapel door, eager to expose his enormous front teeth and announce his presence in a booming voice. Blake is pleased to see Mr. Sheridan, whereas I'm concerned we're heading for big-time trouble. I don't lack aspirations, but Blake's dreams aren't mine. I think back to the argument I had with Grandpa about participating in his schemes and realize I was right to refuse then and should refuse now. But if I do, Blake will leave and I'll be alone again, neither of which I want.

I deliver a sermon about being kind to the elderly, babies, children, dogs, cats, and the deluded and hope when I'm exposed as a fraud that someone will remember this speech and take pity on me. I go on for some while, citing lines from the Bible, which forced me to read more from that book than I like. Anyhow, we sing for a bit, and then Blake steps forward, bows his head, says a few words of praise for Jesus Christ, God, and calls on every saint he can think of—probably a Catholic habit—to watch over the congregation. As I observe him holding forth, I'm impressed with his transformation into a holy man and have to credit his acting ability.

After he's gone on for ten minutes, Blake scans the crowd and a small frown settles on his face. "Folks," he begins, "I planned to talk with you last Sunday about something that's just happened, but we were so surprised by the sound of Reverend Whitestone's voice and in awe of what occurred that I decided to wait until today."

Everyone is attending to Blake, as is Mr. Sheridan. Blake knows he has everyone's curiosity riled up and is milking it for all it's worth.

"The morning after C.B. died, Charlene came into the chapel to ask the Lord why he had taken her grandfather and to pray for guidance. She faced this painting of Jesus." Here, Blake turns and gestures at a fake Titian that Grandpa scrounged at a Chinese auction. "She prayed hard and long. Because I was worried about her, I came into the chapel…concerned she might need some comfort in her time of great distress. Well, as I walked toward her—she's kneeling, her eyes closed—all of a sudden I see it."

Like a good storyteller, Blake pauses to build the dramatic effect. I glance over at Mr. Sheridan and note he's as intent as the rest of the audience.

"Then, because I didn't want to upset her, I led Charlene into the house and locked the chapel doors. I made this banner so she wouldn't see what I will now show you."

After a tiny hesitation, Blake walks to the wall and turns to the parishioners as if he is reluctant to divulge anything more. This makes them even more curious, so much so that I swear Mrs. Croydon and Mr. Wasser are about to fall off their folding chairs.

"I trust this will remain the secret of our Glory Alleluia Chapel," he continues, knowing full well it won't. "Because I believe it is meant for us alone." With this, he reaches for the gilded dowel rod and slowly lifts the white cloth away from the wall. As he does so, all eyes and mouths open in amazement.

There, painted in dark brownish-red on the white wall, is a profiled silhouette of a woman, hands clasped together. The woman looks a little like me, especially the reproduction of the shape of the head and hair. Because the figure is a solid mass, no features are visible, however. Toward the bottom and off the elbows are dried drips, as if the person was bleeding, which is exactly the effect Blake was after.

I look appropriately shocked and lean against the pulpit for support. Mrs. Croydon bolts to her feet as do several others. Throwing their usual reserve to the wind, they creep closer to the strange creation. Blake steps aside so they can crowd around the "miracle," which is the word people are whispering.

Mr. Sheridan comes forward to examine the image, wets his forefinger, and applies it to the painting. Before we can stop him, he licks his finger.

"Oh, my God!" he whispers. "It's the real thing! It's blood!"

I hear "oh!" and "ah!" and "my God!" around me. Even I gasp because I thought Blake had used paint. And not to be outdone, my fake cousin appears equally amazed.

And then, as if synchronized, the parishioners retreat in awe of the mysterious red figure.

Mr. Sheridan stares at me and at the painting. "It's Charlene!"

Everyone looks at me and at the wall. In a second, they're all talking at once, pointing at parts of the painting that indicate a likeness to yours truly, a likeness nicely captured by Blake from a photograph of me taken by Grandpa. I let this chatter continue for a few minutes as Blake advised during our rehearsals. Then Blake parts the crowd and steps toward the red version of me. He falls to his knees as if felled by the heavy hand of God. Palms pressed together, he bows his head and prays. Sure enough, just as Blake said, the group follows suit, each man, woman, and child dropping to the floor. I'm so astonished by the accuracy of his prediction that I'm left speechless. I start to kneel but realize I shouldn't because everyone is praying to my image, and it would be unseemly for me to pray to myself. I glance at Blake for direction, but he's now calling out, "Hallelujah! God be praised! Come to us, Lord!" and phrases of this ilk, all sliding together in long strings. Pretty soon his voice rises and becomes contagious as a chorus of parishioners join him, crooning like a pack of bloodhounds.

"Glory be! Praise the Lord!" he says.

"Glory be! Praise the Lord!" everyone repeats.

This goes on until Blake has run out of religious jargon to toss to the heavens. I stand there surprised he remembers most of the stuff I wrote for him yesterday. Even though Blake's vocabulary is impoverished, his memory is first class.

In the silence, I step forward and touch Blake's shoulder. He stands, turns, and looks at me with a smile that warms like the sun.

"Charlene," he says in a gentle voice, "God has written a message on this wall. Do you see it?"

I nod in a dreamy way. "Yes."

"Perhaps you should sit down."

I sway a bit to give the impression of unsteadiness, as if buffeted by the obligation of my task. Blake takes my arm and leads me to a chair in the first row. I sink into it and everyone gathers round.

"Do you know what you must do?" Blake asks.

I allow a fleeting expression of incomprehension to cross my face and am momentarily silent. "I think so."

Blake turns to the audience. "We need to give Charlene time to recover from the shock. As I said, she didn't know about this message from God." He ushers people to the side by the chapel doors, picks up the collection plate, and begins to pass it. In no time it's overflowing.

"Thank you," he tells each person as they leave, though most people are reluctant to be separated from the miracle painting and my exalted personage.

I sit still and close my eyes as if exhausted from hosting our savior or God or whomever I'm supposed to be a vessel for. To my right, I hear Mr. Sheridan telling Blake that he wants us to do a radio show next Saturday evening and that he'll call on Tuesday to make arrangements. Listening to this, I try not to frown, but I can't help it.

—

"Ninety-seven dollars!" Blake crows.

"That's the best take we've ever done so far as I can remember." When I tell Blake this, he beams with excitement. I also tell him there were five new parishioners who attended.

"That's nothing, Charlie. Wait until next week after Saturday's radio show. You'll be the talk of the town. People will be lining up outside to hear you."

Being the talk of Butztown isn't saying much. "I don't know, Blake. I'm not sure I want to be on the radio." This isn't altogether true. Like my fake cousin, I have a bit of ham in me. However, I'm terrified of being exposed as a fraud and say so.

"Oh, you'll do fine!" he exclaims, "and I'll be right beside you. Don't worry about a thing."

This reminds me of Grandpa's adage about not trusting people who insist they're trustworthy. Telling me not to worry makes me darned sure I should worry. All in all, there isn't much I can do because if I don't show up at the radio station and the congregation hears about it, they'll think I'm afraid or, even worse, not filled with the Lord's light. I feel like the noose is tightening around my neck.

"Well, I do worry, Blake. I can't help it."

Blake is in residence on Cloud Nine and doesn't hear me. "Did you like the bit about using real blood?"

"Where did you get it?"

He grins. "A butcher outside of Rochester. He collected a jar of pig's blood for me. Had to work fast 'cause the stuff dries lickety-split."

I make a face. Blake laughs and says, "Yeah, it was disgusting, but I wanted the painting to look authentic."

"But what if someone tests it?"

"Hell, not in this hick town. Everyone is too damned gullible."

I'm not so sure. If the sheriff gets wind of what's happening at the Glory Alleluia Chapel, he might be quick to take a sample. I express this concern to Blake, but he waves it away.

"Won't happen," he says.

"But why did you use blood in the first place?"

"I had to use blood to get the right color...to create a stigmata."

"What's that?"

He looks pleased. "Spontaneous bleeding like from Christ's wounds. I heard about it in Sunday School class. And at some point we might have you bleed a little at your wrists or—"

"Hold on there! I'm not cutting my wrists to make a few bucks. No, sir!"

"We wouldn't really cut you...just cover your hands with gauze bandages dipped in beef blood or whatever we can find."

I sit down in Grandpa's chair and shake my head. "No, Blake," I tell him, but somehow I know this isn't the end of the idea, especially because we'll need fresh material soon.

—

Sure enough, Mr. George M. Sheridan telephones Tuesday, at nine in the morning. It's a good thing he calls early because Blake is half crazy from four cups of Maxwell House coffee and a gigantic bout with anticipation. After he hangs up, Blake announces we're supposed to be at the radio station at six o'clock, an hour before we go on the air.

"But what am I going to say?"

"Well, I'll start with what happened with your grandfather's voice—Mr. Sheridan will ask us about that. Then I'll explain about the painting. You can chime in with some Goody-Two-Shoes stuff and some Bible verses. Like you do in your sermons."

"Won't Mr. Sheridan ask where my parents are? Or how old I am?"

"If he asks your age, give it. That'll make you sound innocent. And I'll tell him your mother is sick and couldn't come."

I sigh, feeling pretty sick myself.

"And just think! We're getting paid fifty dollars!" Blake exclaims. "Which is nothing. Once we get going, why, the sky's the limit!"

I stare at him like he's nuts. "Blake, I don't want to do this."

"Oh, Charlie. It'll be a piece of cake."

I recall eating an entire chocolate cake on my fourth birthday. It was sitting on the counter out of my reach, or so Mama thought. I threw the whole thing up an hour later. Whenever I hear the phrase "piece of cake," I think of that. And considering how nervous I'll be on Saturday, I better not eat a bite of dinner before.

I cross my arms across my chest. "You heard me. Going on the radio will be like poking a stick at a beehive. When the sheriff hears about it—and he will—he'll get even more suspicious. He might even come to a Sunday service, although he is not a churchgoing man, which is one of his only attributes as far as I can tell. And if he comes, he'll realize we're fakes and close us down. Plus he'll cotton on to the fact Mama isn't here and that will be even worse."

"I know you're worried, Charlie," Blake tells me in a calm voice. "But if things get hot, we'll take off."

"You mean you'll take off."

This takes the wind out of Blake's sails for a minute. Then his eyes soften and he hugs me. "I won't leave you. I promise."

His embrace feels good. I don't know what he means by it, whether he's trying to manipulate me into doing what he wants or whether he really cares. And if he does care, what kind of caring is it? I want to ask him, but I'm afraid. I don't want to hear him lie.

"Just give it a try," he urges.

I feel his lips near my neck. He doesn't kiss me, but I get a little buzz all the same.

"I'll do the show once," I tell him. "And that's it."

He pulls away and smiles. There's something behind the smile, but I'm not sure what. I remind myself that Blake is fifteen years older and too old for a kid like me.

—

On Wednesday, in anticipation of a packed house on Sunday, Blake and I drive to the lumber store to purchase wood for four benches so we can seat twelve more people in the chapel in addition to five chairs that we plan to bring from the kitchen and

Grandpa's room. As we aim the Ford into the diagonal parking slot, Blake insists we should begin two services every Sunday, one at 8:30 and one at 10:00.

"You're crazy," I reply. "Not that many people will show up."

We buy hardware and stain for our construction project and head outside to load everything in the flatbed. After we finish, I see Eli standing a few feet away, staring at me. When our eyes meet, he walks over, switches his gaze to Blake and examines him with what appears to be hostility. Blake is in jeans and a navy tee shirt, with his cowboy boots hidden under his pants, so that he looks like everyone else, but to Eli, he's a stranger, and a stranger who is with me.

"Hey, Charlene," Eli says.

"Hi."

Blake tosses his yellow leather gloves through the open window of the truck and comes around to be introduced. As he stands there, I see the same expression on his face as Eli's, like they're two dogs trying to decide who's boss. Eli takes his hands out of his pockets, but Blake, after surmising Eli is no threat or because he doesn't want to shake hands, jams his in his jeans.

"Blake, this is Eli," I explain. "He's in some of my classes at school."

Blake hesitates a second before saying hello.

"Blake is my second cousin," I explain.

Eli narrows his eyes but nods a greeting.

"Blake's been helping out since my grandfather died," I add.

Eli regards Blake with suspicion, then glances at me. "Oh, yeah. I'm really sorry to hear about him."

"Thanks."

"And is your mother around yet?" He says this to show Blake that he has intimate knowledge of my family and, presumably, of me.

"Charlie's mother arrived awhile ago," Blake counters.

Blake sounds protective, as he was when Sheriff Shackrack visited. For some reason, this feels good, because I'm still annoyed with Eli, especially at the moment when he seems more interested in me as his territorial possession. I stand closer to Blake, who gives me a smile.

"Well, we have work to do, don't we, sugar?" Blake asks.

I touch him on the arm and agree.

As I'm climbing in the truck, Eli walks over to my window.

"You sure you're okay? I mean, if you need anything I'm

around. We were away for a while helping my uncle on his farm, but I'm home until school starts."

"Okay, thanks."

"Maybe I'll see you sometime?"

A month ago this half-baked invitation would have revived my interest in Eli. Now, in comparison to Blake, who has slid onto the front seat beside me, Eli seems like a kid and one who didn't treat me very nicely. I tell him that I'll see him in school.

Down the road a piece, Blake clears his throat. "So, that's your boyfriend?"

It sounds a little like Blake is making fun of Eli and of me. "He *was* my boyfriend. We broke up a while ago."

Blake glances at me. "Oh?"

"I've decided I'm not interested in boys. At least not right now." Blake is quiet so I add, "I thought I was. Now I have other things to attend to."

"That's a fact," Blake replies. "But don't give up on us poor souls forever."

I look at him and see he's teasing me. I can't tell if his smile is friendly or flirtatious. That's the way Blake is, half of both.

"I won't."

On the ride home, I consider how strange it is that a few months ago I was mooning over Eli and allowing him to take liberties. Eli was once attractive to me but no longer. Maybe this is because my attentions have shifted to Blake. Thinking about him, I jam up inside. In many ways, he is shifty; in other ways I believe he cares for me. And if I were older or we were closer in age? I shouldn't be having these thoughts, I tell myself. Blake isn't interested and I'm not interested in him.

- 25 -

Mr. Sheridan greets us in the front office of the radio station. He's wearing a green paisley bowtie and a long-sleeve pinstripe shirt even though it's a broiling hot summer evening. Blake is suffering since he can't remove his suit jacket because of the masking tape on the back of his shirt. I'm in a sleeveless white blouse and navy skirt, but I'm still sweating up a storm.

After introducing the crew, Mr. Sheridan brings us into his office. The smell of cigarette smoke permeates the air, and masses of papers and recording tapes crowd the desk and bookcases. A minute later, a woman carries in three bottles of Coke. I drink mine fast, glad to have something to wrap my hands around so they don't shake. Mr. Sheridan sucks on a cigarette with big inhalations, displaying little smoke clouds in his partly open mouth.

He reviews the questions he intends to ask, though he says he might ask others, depending on how we answer. I don't like surprises and say so. He frowns at this, but since it's time to go into the studio, he doesn't fuss. Inside the recording area, cold air blasts from two air-conditioning units built into the wall. Mr. Sheridan dons a one-eared headphone and parks his cigarette on the ledge of an overfilled ashtray. A microphone sits on the table in front of him and another sits two feet from us, which Blake and I are supposed to share.

Once the countdown hits "One" and the "On Air" sign goes on, Mr. Sheridan begins a short introduction. Blake is asked whether he's related to Wild Bill, and he puts on his best aw-shucks act as if he's embarrassed to be singled out for his heritage, then admits to it. This false humility sticks throughout his performance, as does the return of his Western-Southern accent, which has nearly disappeared in recent weeks. Blake recounts the amazing goings-on at the Glory Alleluia Chapel and how extraordinary my powers are. Mr. Sheridan and he are working in tandem like they've been practicing for months.

Once Mr. Sheridan has ascertained my age, he asks about my first religious experience. I give him the song and dance about God appearing as I stood near Lake Ontario, keeping the saga simple so it sounds modest, and giving Blake opportunities to embellish. I try to act amazed as I talk, like I'm still stunned by what happened. Mr. Sheridan is baring his yellow teeth and nodding, signaling how pleased he is. I add a few details about Grandpa and how he knew I was chosen. As I say this, I almost gag on a big waft of cigarette smoke, but I manage. Mr. Sheridan explains about tasting the blood and asks us if we really believe it's the blood of Christ.

"I do think it is, sir," Blake replies in an earnest voice. "It's the only explanation."

Of course, the most obvious explanation is that my fake cousin loves to paint with fresh blood from a butcher shop.

"No one was in the chapel all week," I tell Mr. Sheridan, "and the outside and inside doors were locked. The painting just appeared."

"It seems to be a miracle…or rather two miracles because your grandfather's voice came to us the week before." Mr. Sheridan stubs out his cigarette and lights another.

"I can't tell you what all this means," Blake says, "but I believe Charlene has been called specially. Even though she's young, our Lord has selected her for his work. What the future will bring to her, Mr. Sheridan, well, we'll have to wait and see."

We finish up with a few stupid questions such as will I go to seminary—I say probably—and whether I have a boyfriend—which annoys me because I'm supposed to be a holy woman.

"I don't think I'm meant for that kind of thing," I explain. "I did have a boyfriend once, for a little while, but when I had the vision, I knew I was supposed to devote myself to people, not to one person." This sounds good, though I can't resist a peek at Blake to see if I'm doing okay. He doesn't notice because he's so distracted by his newfound celebrity.

Once the program ends, Mr. Sheridan gives Blake fifty dollars. They shake hands and agree to a series of Saturday night interviews, to be scheduled once every two weeks if the reports from tonight come back favorably. I stand there feeling mad as a hornet because no one is asking me whether I want to participate, plus I'm fuming because Blake was paid the money.

Outside, by Blake's blue Ford, I let him have it. He looks at me like I'm crazy, but I keep at him as we get into the truck until he agrees to split the money with me. I tell him that's fine and dandy, but after this, no more radio shows.

"Well, let's just see how it goes, okay? I mean, you can't look a gift horse in the mouth."

"I can!"

—

The benches take us so long to build that we don't have time to stain them. Blake then wants me to make up some pamphlets to sell, or rather to place on a table next to a box labeled "Suggested Donation: Fifty Cents." After I finish writing two one-page sermons, I show him the printing press and the California type cases in the basement. Grandpa has a complete font of ten-point Baskerville with larger sizes for display and some Caslon leaf ornaments. For official documents, we use Gothic Blackletter and Snell Roundhand, which is a pretty italic.

Blake acts surprised to see this equipment, but because he explored the house from top to bottom whenever I was out selling hooch or sleeping late, he shouldn't be, a fact I point out to him. He gives me a nervous laugh and doesn't respond.

Although I still have to pick through the type case to find a few letters, I set up the lines on the composing stick, insert them on the tray, and surround the type with wood blocks that Grandpa called furniture. After everything is square, I tie string around the assembly to hold it together, ink the type, place a sheet of paper over it, and run the press.

After printing fifty of each, Blake and I go upstairs while they're drying. We have lunch and then I escape to my room to work on a short story. By and by, I hear some noises outside my window. When I look down, I see Ed and Noreen Krychek pulling weeds and planting flowers by the chapel entrance. Their hyperbouncy, seven-year-old daughter Carlotta is playing hopscotch in the dirt driveway. I walk downstairs and through the chapel.

"Good afternoon," I say.

They both look a little embarrassed.

"We thought maybe a garden would be nice," Mrs. Krychek explains, waving at the pile of pulled crabgrass next to boxes of pink, white, yellow, and red zinnias awaiting new homes. Mrs. Krychek is short and round, the opposite of her tall, rawboned husband.

"That's very kind of you."

Mr. Krychek takes off his gloves and wipes his brow. "Sure is hot."

This is the most I've heard Mr. Krychek utter in years. To be polite, I offer them iced tea.

"No, thanks, but you know what would please us the most?" Mrs. Krychek says.

"What?"

"We'd love to show our little girl the miracle. She wasn't with us on Sunday."

I'm not happy with this request, but because the Krycheks are planting a garden, I can't refuse. I welcome them inside, including Carlotta, who is usually left at home on Sundays because she can't sit still and interrupts sermons. I turn on the lights and unveil the painting.

The Krycheks look suitably awestruck, but Carlotta comes near the wall and shakes her head so vigorously that her black curls rocket in all directions. "Somebody painted that thing!"

"Hush," Mrs. Krychek tells her daughter. "It's a miracle."

"I don't think it's a miracle." She folds her arms across her chest. "I think it's stupid!"

"Oh, dear," Mrs. Krychek says to me as she corrals her daughter. "I'm so sorry! Carlotta can be difficult."

I'm thinking Carlotta is the only bright one in Butztown, or at least of those individuals who have seen the painting, but instead I say, "Why, Mrs. Krychek, I just believe she's a little young to understand, that's all."

Mr. Krychek nods his head, then escorts his wife and forthright offspring outside.

—

In search of a seamstress, Blake and I drive toward Rochester to avoid being recognized in local establishments and find one at a dry cleaning store. Blake gives her three of Grandpa's shirts to alter and then she takes my measurements for a linen gown that Blake has envisioned, one with a red cross on the chest, floppy long sleeves embroidered with small purple crosses, and a tapered collar. Needless to say, I'm not keen on the idea of wearing religious clothing, but Blake says it's necessary and that bit by bit we'll add fancy stoles and other things.

After the seamstress, we drive to a fabric store and buy a red silk cord for use as a cincture, or at least that's what Blake calls it. He seems to know a fair amount about religious fashion and allows as how the best part of religion is the show itself, which is designed to impress and humble the masses. I insist that I'm not in the business of humbling or impressing anyone much less the masses. Blake says I have a responsibility to my new calling.

That night, we transport more moonshine into the Hooch Shop. I notice we're running out of product faster than usual, but then again Blake has been helping himself on a frequent basis. I tell him he's got to buy his own liquor and quit stealing. He looks at me with those big eyes and says he has never taken one ounce that wasn't offered.

"I don't believe you for a second, Blake."

—

Mr. Sheridan telephones. Blake takes the receiver and agrees to some kind of an offer, which makes me blistering mad because I told him I wasn't going to do any more shows.

"Charlie, the radio station doubled their number of calls during our program," Blake whispers, covering the phone. "He'll pay us seventy-five dollars for the next one!"

"I don't care."

Blake tells Mr. Sheridan we'll be there on Saturday and hangs up.

Just as he's about to pull his usual huggy act in order to coerce me, the phone rings again. This time I answer it. It's a Mr. Robert O'Rourke from the *Butztown News*. He wants to interview us tomorrow morning. I start to say no, but Blake perceives it's a reporter and snatches the receiver. Before I can stop him, Blake invites Mr. O'Rourke for a ten o'clock appointment.

Over breakfast, I threaten a full-scale rebellion. Blake is busy folding our pamphlets while he's drinking coffee and doesn't really listen to my tirade. I keep at him, saying I won't participate any longer, but finally I give up. And despite all I said earlier, an hour later Blake again suggests the bleeding wrist option for Sunday.

"No!" I shout.

"Come on, Charlie…"

I shake my head. Blake sighs and mentions his second idea: a visit from God.

—

During the interview with Mr. O'Rourke, we use the same material as on the radio, though Mr. O'Rourke asks a few tough questions.

"Excuse me for sounding impertinent, Miss Whitestone," he says, "but do you feel a little odd preaching sermons to adults?"

When Blake starts to answer, I interrupt. "No, sir, I don't. Maybe because I feel like the words aren't coming from me. Yes, I'm speaking them, but I lose myself when I stand at the pulpit... as if Charlene doesn't exist. I can't explain it very well because I don't understand what happens." I deliver these last lines with gauzy-eyed puzzlement.

Mr. O'Rourke writes all this nonsense down as well as biographical information about Grandpa and the Glory Alleluia Chapel. I'm tempted to name some charities we help—in West Virginia, for example—but decide it's best to have fewer lies in print in case someone researches these places and finds out they don't exist. Keep your lying simple, as Grandpa always said.

After Mr. O'Rourke snaps a few photographs of Blake and yours truly in the chapel, he wants to take a picture of the miracle on the wall. We tell him he can't because it's unseemly. He's not happy about this restriction, but we allow him to see the painting.

"Interesting" is all he says as he examines it.

Blake and I exchange glances behind his back, worried that he'll expose the painting as a fake and us as shams. Before Blake covers the silhouette, Mr. O'Rourke makes a quick visual comparison to me. He scribbles in his notebook and thanks us for our time.

Once he's left, Blake and I fret about the article, but we have other pressing matters to attend to, namely a trip to see Mr. Lambeau Hastings, attorney-at-law.

- 26 -

Mr. Lambeau Hastings is a skinny weasel of a man with slick, black hair parted dead center on his bony skull. He greets us with little bows intended to make him appear subservient when in fact he is first and foremost high on old Number One. Unfortunately, Mr. Hastings is as smart as a whip and is therefore a devious customer to reckon with.

In the attorney's office, Blake looks more like a country cowboy than a preacher, even though he's wearing clerical garb. Something about the lawyer discombobulates Blake, perhaps because he senses the man is sharper than he is. I catch a break on account of my age and female status and thus can fly under the radar, whereas Blake can't. I see that right off and take charge.

"Mr. Hastings, this is my second cousin, Blake."

The two shake hands.

I continue, "As you know, Grandpa is dead." I give the lawyer the package that arrived from the county. "Here are the papers."

"Thank you, Miss Whitestone," the attorney says. He dons a pair of black-framed glasses.

Below the level of the desk, Blake takes my hand for a second, more to reassure himself than me. I give him a nod of confidence, though I'm worried that all my preparations in the basement won't pass scrutiny.

"I believe you have Grandpa's will?" I ask, once Lambeau Hastings sets the papers aside.

"I do indeed, Miss Whitestone. Shall we open it?"

As I already know from reading Grandpa's copy, he left everything to me except for what he deposited in my mother's checking account.

"Hmm," Mr. Hastings says, straightening his already-perfect maroon bowtie. "Everything appears to be in order. The only difficulty is that you need your mother or father...or a guardian to represent you."

"I can sign any papers myself."

"Because you are under legal age, you must have a parent present."

"I'm her guardian until her mother returns," Blake says, though to my sensitive ears he sounds less than persuasive.

"Oh, yes, sir. That's right." I open my satchel and produce a typed, signed letter from Grandpa to Mr. Hastings instructing his cousin, Blakewell James Benko, to act as the guardian of Charlene Beth Whitestone until she comes of age or until her mother or father returns to resume parental responsibility. It is witnessed by Harley Garfoyle and Lorna Hartnette, who were delighted to endorse the document in exchange for jars of moonshine. I've also affixed a notary seal, which Grandpa kept for legal occasions, and forged the signature of the fictitious notary.

When I read the letter aloud, Blake's face pales when I use his real name, but he doesn't say anything. I used it because Mr. Hastings might request identification, and because Blakewell James Benko is on his automobile registration, it's probably on his driver's license. Sure enough, Mr. Hastings asks for proof of identity. Blake pulls out his wallet and shows his license. While Mr. Hastings is jotting notes as to Blake's address and name, Blake shoots me a glance that I return with a cheerful smile.

"This is all somewhat irregular," Mr. Hastings tells us.

"I realize that, sir, but on account of my parents being away for some time, Grandpa was concerned that I might be left alone if he became ill or worse. You see, he understood his heart wasn't strong—Dr. Fairchild told him so. He wrote this up a few days before he died, at a time when he was quite sick, though he was in his right mind. As luck would have it, Mr. William Lawson, the notary, just happened by to purchase some pickled onions when Mrs. Hartnette and Mr. Garfoyle were visiting."

"Yes, but why didn't he come to me to draw up proper papers?" The attorney is observing us with skepticism.

I shrug. "I can't say what was in his mind. You know C.B. He did things his own way."

Lambeau Hastings knows this quite well but is most likely miffed that Grandpa skipped the cost of writing the document, thus depriving him of income. "You're correct about that," he agrees. "Your grandfather didn't always follow the rules. In fact, far from it." He examines the notary seal carefully. "Well, it appears this document is legal."

"Yes, sir, it is."

He scratches his neck as if he's reluctant to believe it. "Miss Whitestone, you're absolutely positive your parents can't be reached by telephone or mail?"

"No, they can't. Blake is the only family I have except for my cousins Buck and Corey, both of whom are off in Germany somewhere. They won't be back for months and then only for a short time. They're in the army, you know."

"Yes, I heard something to that effect," Mr. Hastings says.

"I'd like to stay home with Blake until my parents return. I can pay the bills. I've been keeping Grandpa's accounts and know how to do it. If you can get the bank to let me."

"We can establish an estate checking account and transfer funds into that. This account is for the sole purpose of paying expenses incurred before your grandfather's death and for burial costs—"

"He was already cremated," I cut in. "Blake paid for it."

"Well, yes, that's very thoughtful of Mr. Benko. But there are legal and filing fees, that sort of thing. I'm also concerned about this arrangement because of your age." Here he scrutinizes Blake, who obviously doesn't meet the standard of a proper guardian according to the lawyer. Even so, Mr. Hastings can't find an excuse to refuse.

"Perhaps you could speak to Mr. Dryfuss at the Butztown First Farmer's Bank," I suggest. "He's the manager and knows me."

"And I'd be happy to co-sign any checks with Charlene," Blake says.

Mr. Hastings strokes his pointy chin, sniffs, and resets his glasses on the thin bridge of his nose. "Thank you, Mr. Benko. Yes, you would need to co-sign checks and documents." The lawyer stares at Blake with distrust, probably wondering what part of the family Blake belongs to, and whether he is prone to the same kind of fraudulent behavior as Grandpa. Because I'm a girl, the probability that I'm of my grandfather's crooked persuasion may not have crossed his mind.

I sense the attorney's growing mistrust of Blake, so I play my last card. "Mr. Hastings, I am much obliged for any help you can give. Grandpa always said it was prudent to pay for professional services." I place an envelope on Mr. Hastings' desk. "Like I said, I need access to Grandpa's checking account and would greatly appreciate your help."

Mr. Hastings hesitates, then reaches for the envelope and flips it open to see the contents. His eyes flicker for a second before he slides the envelope into his desk drawer. When it dawns on him that I've bought his allegiance, that I am, indeed, a chip off

Grandpa's block, his lips compress, a giveaway that he knows he's been had. "You're very generous."

I withdraw Grandpa's checkbook and last month's bank statement from the satchel and pass it over to Mr. Hastings. "There's enough money in Grandpa's account and from rental properties to pay for the house and for me until Mama returns," I explain. "When she does, she can come see you and we can cancel Blake as my guardian."

He examines the bank statement and unsnaps the checkbook.

"You'll see Grandpa's handwriting in January," I tell him, "but I've been handling his account and paying bills ever since. Of course, he signed the checks."

Mr. Hastings nods. "Well, we're not talking about a lot of money, Miss Whitestone." On a yellow legal pad, he notes the last withdrawals and deposits in neat columns, the final amount in the account, and promises to contact Mr. Dryfuss. "As for the house and its contents, everything appears to be yours. Since there is no mortgage on the house as I recall—"

"And no loans on anything else," I add. "But Grandpa did have a life-insurance policy." I place the document on his desk. "Five-thousand dollars, I believe."

Mr. Hastings unfolds the multi-page policy and reads it. "I see. Yes, you are correct."

Blake edges forward in his seat, interested in this news.

The attorney continues, "It will take some time before the insurance company sends you a check. Probably about as long as it will take to settle the estate. To begin, we must post notice of your grandfather's death in the newspaper to be sure he has no outstanding debts. I will contact you and Mr. Benko regarding the property transfers and any other matters. The estate account, however, can be created in a day or so, unless there is a problem."

"I'm sure there won't be," I tell him. "And can you call my school to tell them Blake is acting as my guardian?"

Mr. Lambeau Hastings agrees, though his perpetual frown has deepened.

———

Once we're outside, Blake exhales, "I hate lawyers! They scare me to death."

"About as much as the police?"

He gives me a sharp look. "Yeah. Say, how much did you give that creep?"

"A hundred dollars."

"Wow! No wonder he didn't fuss. And, by the way, how'd you know my real name?"

I laugh. "Same as you knew about Grandpa's printing press and a bunch of other things."

"And where'd you get the paper signed by your grandfather?"

"I thought it might come in handy," I reply, enjoying myself. "I always plan ahead."

"Damn! You're full of tricks, Charlie. I swear we must be cousins."

I grin at him. "Well, we are now or at least until Mama comes back. And just you remember that even though you have guardianship of me, you don't have any rights other than co-signing checks and keeping me out of the orphanage. Got that?"

"Got it." Blake gives me a phony-looking smile.

I think of the six-hundred dollars in the account and realize I better be sure to grab the estate checkbook before my new guardian does. Likewise the insurance check.

—

On our next radio show, Mr. Sheridan invites listeners to call and talk with us. I don't care for this approach one whit, but unlike in Mr. Lambeau Hastings' office, Blake takes to this situation like a duck to water. We're asked all sorts of stupid questions from skeptics and believers alike. Blake hands off the believers to me and deals with the disbelievers himself. When one caller insists we're frauds, Blake turns to Mr. Sheridan.

"Now you've been an impartial witness," Blake says. "What do you think happened?"

"I challenge this man to come to the Glory Alleluia Chapel to see for himself. Personally, I was very impressed," Mr. Sheridan replies with conviction.

This seems like a silly thing to do, to invite trouble through our doors, but Blake piles on more claptrap about God's mysteries and says to the listener, "Sir, please attend our service with an open mind and heart. We don't know why we were chosen and are trying our best to understand. This is a special time to be treasured and honored." This onslaught of sweetness silences the man and he hangs up. Blake smiles at me and says in the microphone, "Folks, I extend my invitation to all of you." He gives details as to time and place.

After the show, the manager reports that the radio station was flooded with calls, more than the switchboard could handle. The man is grinning like a baboon and gives Blake seventy-five dollars and promises more in two weeks. He then hands me a shoebox of letters sent from listeners and encourages us to answer them. I leaf through the envelopes and see over thirty.

We drive home in silence. In the kitchen, Blake pours us some Chivas and shakes his head. "Charlie, this is really big. I mean, really big!" He drinks his scotch and pours another. "Unless I'm wrong, we're going to fill the chapel even with two services."

"Blake, there aren't that many people in Butztown."

"No, but the radio audience extends to Rochester and for miles in every direction. Just you wait."

- 27 -

The chapel is packed on Sunday morning, in part because of the sensational article written by Mr. O'Rourke. Some of the regular parishioners aren't thrilled to see so many strangers and are casting chilly glances at the interlopers, but they also seem proud their chapel has become so famous. We even have a girl arrive in a wheelchair. She's skinny and pale, nervous, with long, curly black hair. Probably a few years younger than I am. Her father and mother place her in the front row, on the end by the door.

My hands are shaking as I stand before the congregation. Outfitted in my cream-colored long gown with the embroidered sleeves and a big red cross on my chest, I half expect a bolt of lightning to come shooting through the window and hit the cross like a bull's eye.

I welcome everyone and start the sermon. "From Jeremiah: 'Ah, Lord God! behold, I cannot speak: for I am a child. But the Lord said unto me, Say not, I am a child: for thou shalt go to all that I shall send thee, and whosoever I command thee thou shalt speak. Be not afraid of their faces: for I am with thee to deliver thee, saith the Lord.'"

I look at the sixty people crammed on chairs and benches and almost believe I really am chosen. Perhaps it's the effect of sunlight pouring through the window on my face and Blake's, but suddenly I understand how people are persuaded that little white, winged creatures exist because Blake and I appear so angelic. Observing the rapt attention of my parishioners, I talk on, realizing these people have entrusted their faith to me even though I'm as false as their god.

"Friends, neighbors, and first-time guests, I cannot say with any certainty that God has selected this chapel to exhibit his wondrous miracles. I cannot say I am empowered, though something very amazing has happened to me, something that has changed my life."

This, at least, is not a lie. I pause, watching my Timex that lies next to the Bible. "I think of my grandfather and what he would have wished for me. I will try to honor him as I ask you to pray in silence, remembering the special people who have passed into the kingdom of the Lord."

As I bow my head and wait as we rehearsed, half a minute later, a deep voice comes drifting down from on high or, more accurately, from Mama's closet. "Children of mine, believe and have faith." There is a small gap at which point everyone stares at me. Then the voice continues, "You must all go from this holy place and do good work. Be charitable to your neighbors and to those who have less than you. Remember, I ask you to be kind and loving every morning, every afternoon, every evening, and to have faith in my son, Jesus Christ."

The voice is, of course, Blake's, placed down a few notches and bleached of his accent. The words are mine. Most of the writing I'm doing these days is for the business.

After a short break, the speaker says, "Throw off your worries, cares, sadness, and physical pain. Do not be burdened by your life but find joy in it. Feel my love and be light and happy. Rise up and celebrate!"

"Oh! I will! I will!"

All eyes turn to the girl in the wheelchair. She is gazing upward, an expression of rapturous delight on her face. Her lips part, she smiles and nods as if someone is hovering near the ceiling. I rush over to her and, without thinking, touch her shoulder, which startles her. She looks at me with such intensity that I step back.

"Thank you!" she cries. "Thank you!" She grips the arms of her chair with bony hands and struggles to her feet. Her knees shake with effort, but she doesn't seem to notice.

"Lydia!" her mother screams.

Lydia lets go of the wheelchair and reaches out. Her father jumps from his seat, takes her arm, and encircles her waist, worried she'll fall.

"It's a miracle!" exclaims one woman.

"God's work!" says another.

"She's walking!" Mamie Croydon points to Lydia as the girl steps away from the chair, her father by her side, steadying her.

I stand next to Lydia as her parents rejoice. Then I glance at Blake, thinking he paid these people to fake the whole scene, but he appears to be genuinely surprised. I can't believe what's happening is legitimate, yet the congregation thinks so. Everyone is gabbing and whispering and drawing near Lydia, who is still on her feet. Tears of happiness stream down her cheeks, which are now pink with excitement.

After the girl tires, she refuses to return to her wheelchair and instead sits on a folding chair. I risk a glance at the spot where Lydia is staring, see a soft light, and shiver, in spite of the fact that I know this is a reflection from the windows. What would Grandpa make of this, I wonder? I turn toward Blake, who shakes his head in bewilderment.

Finally, the crowd settles. I ask Mrs. Croydon to sing "Holy, Holy, Holy" followed by "Amazing Grace."

—

Blake's impersonation of God is overshadowed by the excitement of "The Healing," as everyone calls it. We net eighty-three dollars in the first service and ninety-four dollars in the second one, which is even more crowded on account of people love to sleep in on Sunday mornings. If they can get their religion fix and still have time for pancakes, they're happy. Of course, I have to usher everyone out from the early service so they don't hear the tape again and am relieved that no reporters are present. In between shows, Blake runs upstairs to rewind God's speech. My sermon is rushed because we're slow to start, but everything works fine. Two reporters visit during the late show and stay to ask questions. I make them wait until the congregation leaves before posing for photographs with Blake. One of the reporters works for the news department of a local television station and wants to run a feature. Blake accepts on the spot, although not without negotiating a hundred-dollar fee. He explains the money is a donation for the poor families in Florida who lost work due to a factory fire and another charity that takes care of little homeless children in Baton Rouge. By the time everyone is gone, I'm exhausted but burning up with curiosity about the wheelchair girl, Lydia.

"Blake, did you hire those people?"

He shakes his head. "Nope. I never saw them before."

I believe him. I sit down at the kitchen table and rest my head on my hand. "Well, wasn't that the darndest thing?"

"It surely was," he agrees, sitting across from me. "Maybe it was for real. Do you think so?"

I stare at him. "You mean God came down and healed her?"

"Well, it's possible," he says slowly. "Or you did."

I laugh. "Oh, come on!" But then I see he's half serious. "I can't make someone shoot up out of a wheelchair. That's ridiculous!"

Blake searches my face. "I don't know, Charlie. How else can you explain it?"

"She's some crazy kid, that's all."

"Might be," he says reluctantly.

"Oh, hogwash!" Although I sound emphatic, a tiny doubt creeps in. I know I don't have any healing powers, but I'd be a lot happier if Blake had bought the services of this family and my religious disbeliefs could remain intact.

We make sandwiches. Blake doesn't say more about our unplanned miracle. He is, however, exhilarated with our success and says he's going to stain the benches and build more.

"You know what, Charlie?"

"What?"

"I bet we'll have to rent a big hall one of these days."

—

Business is excellent for the next few weeks at the chapel. I make Blake promise not to promote "healing" of any kind, but a few infirm people arrive, having heard about Lydia, who has returned to Niagara Falls—one of our parishioners said her family lived near there. Nothing happens to improve the lot of these sick folk, though they seem more cheerful and uplifted after attending. In a way, I'm relieved I don't have a special touch because it would have been a talent that would require serious reversals in my philosophy. Blake still regards the Lydia event as a possible miracle, which surprises me since I thought he's as skeptical as I am. He now seems even more enthusiastic about our venture, and, at his urging, I agree to add a third service at one o'clock on Sunday to accommodate the hordes of people coming from Rochester and Buffalo. Blake and I do three radio programs and two television interviews and make fists of money, though I'm struggling to keep abreast of writing the sermons and Blake's speeches as well as answering the barrage of letters and cards. We even have to clear more space in the driveway to park cars. All in all, we're raking in over four-hundred dollars a week.

This activity makes me wonder where Sheriff Shackrack is and why he hasn't come round on a Sunday morning to investigate, especially with all the publicity. I figure his absence is due to the fear most folks have about messing with religion and religionists, though the politicians and the believers don't exhibit much anxiety about trampling on the rights of any other kinds of groups so far as I have observed. Grandpa always said that people in this country are supposed to be free to practice or not practice as they please, that there's a wall between church and state, but he also allowed that the wall was pretty darned flimsy. The sheriff doesn't seem like he'd worry about stepping on anyone, however, so when Harley Garfoyle stops in for his weekly purchase, I ask him what's up with Shackrack. He says the sheriff was vacationing in Florida for two weeks and came home to find that Mayor Bigby embezzled money and ran off with some woman of less than savory reputation.

"He had to go after him," Harley explains, "'cause some were saying the mayor bribed Shackrack to leave town while the stealing was going on." Harley spits in the weeds. "Don't know when the sheriff will be back, but it's always a good thing when the law is elsewhere." He chuckles at this and shoves a Mason jar in an old army knapsack.

I agree yet secretly worry that one of these days Shackrack will have his boots on my doorstep again.

—

Finally, school starts—my junior year. I'm taking math and chemistry on grade but senior history, French, and English—Mrs. Kimbell teaches this in addition to the junior class. I'm looking forward to seeing her, but first I have to get through the day, which has not started well. Apparently, word has spread about my oracular talents and the miracles at Glory Alleluia Chapel. Instead of asking questions and being friendly, my classmates make a point of looking away from me. Although I've never been popular, this really hurts. I can understand why kids who don't go to church might not like me because of my new religious reputation, but what have I done to make everyone else hate me? I wander through classes and lunch without one exchange of greeting or one person asking how my summer was. I even become aware that some of the teachers are uncomfortable, glancing at me as if I might fly up and out the window or start pulsing with golden light like some kind of heavenly firefly. The one exception to this ostracism is Mrs. Kimbell. After class, when all the other students have left, I walk up to her, and she gives me a huge smile.

"Charlene, welcome back!"

"Thanks, Mrs. Kimbell."

She catches my somber mood but makes no comment. Instead, she says, "I think you'll be very happy to hear some news. Remember the stories I submitted for you last spring?"

I nod, suddenly excited.

"One was accepted for publication in the *Erie Journal*. In fact, it won first place."

"What?"

Mrs. Kimbell smiles. "The galley proofs arrived two days ago." She opens the tall cabinet where she keeps her raincoat. "Here they are."

When I see my story, "Tennessee Spring," in print, I can't help grinning.

"I thought you'd be pleased." She hands me a letter with the journal's letterhead on top. "The editor made a few suggestions—all of which seem reasonable, though it's your decision as to what you change. He describes your style as a young New York-state Mark Twain."

"Really?"

"Yes. And in addition to publication, there's this." She hands me an envelope containing an award for best story submitted by a high school student and a check for $100. "That will look very good on your college application, and I'm sure you'll put the money to good use." Mrs. Kimbell is as delighted as I am. "I also heard that 'Grandpa Goes Fishing' is under serious consideration at *Lake Huron Literary Review*. Remember I told you they were running a special submission period for writers under the age of eighteen?"

"Yes," I reply, feeling overwhelmed.

She gives me their letter, which I'm too dazed to read.

"I think they'll accept it," Mrs. Kimbell says.

After all the rejections during the day, this news makes my head spin. I think of Grandpa and our vocabulary and grammar lessons and how much joy this would bring him. Tears work at the edges of my eyes. Mrs. Kimbell sees this and puts an arm around my shoulder. Suddenly, it is all too much and I lean into her flowered dress and cry.

—

After depositing the check in my personal account, I ride home feeling strung out between the misery of the day and the validation of my talent as a writer. Blake sees my red eyes and asks what's wrong. When he hears about my stories, he says, "Well, gosh, Charlie! What are you crying about? That's great!"

I want to explain how important my writing is, how the religion sham is making me sick at heart, how I was shunned by my classmates, but all of these conflicting thoughts and feelings are too tangled to explain. "Yeah, that part is."

He looks confused. "I don't get it."

I shake my head. "I'm tired of all this stuff, Blake."

"What stuff? Everything's okay."

"No, it isn't. I can't do it all. I just want to be a kid. To have friends…a family."

Blake sees that I'm about to start crying again and pulls me to him. "Come on, Charlie. I know you miss your grandfather and all, but we'll manage."

I want to believe him but I don't. I bite my lip and force down tears. Blake holds me, but it's not like Mrs. Kimbell's hug, which felt comforting and kind. Blake's is more big-brotherish at first, but when it lasts too long, I sense we're drifting into taboo territory so I pull away and head into the kitchen. Blake follows me, but the phone rings and he answers it. I try to set my mind to dinner, yet when I glance at Blake, I see tension on his face. I suspect the caller is Lambeau Hastings, a supposition that proves correct when he hands me the receiver.

"Miss Whitestone, the estate account is ready. You and Mr. Benko will need to go to the bank to sign a few papers. They'll give you a limited number of checks to pay bills that came due while your grandfather was still alive. When the estate is finally settled, you'll inherit the amount left, which may not be much, perhaps nothing. Let me know if the bills exceed your inheritance, and we'll discuss solutions, such as a loan based on your Grandfather's life insurance policy."

"That won't be necessary. I have other income," I remind him of the land rental fees, "and Mama will be back soon."

"All right. My secretary will set an appointment to change the house deed and car title."

After I hang up, Blake takes me to visit Mr. Dryfuss at the bank.

—

The next day, during study hall, I go to the librarian and ask to review the college catalogues. She leads me to a small cubicle in the back of the room that smells of paper, floor wax, and dust. I research the schools Mrs. Kimbell suggested, settling on the one where her sister works, which appears to be the most expensive and one of the most competitive in terms of the ratio of applications to acceptances. I write down all the information about Cavendish Falls College in Burlington, Vermont, a women's liberal arts school that offers a bachelor's degree in creative writing. I note they want results from a Scholastic Aptitude Test, but so far as I know, our school doesn't give them.

I ask the librarian permission to visit the guidance counselor, Mrs. Roche, who is a nice woman, a bit overly helpful and chatty because she doesn't get many voluntary customers—most Butztown students won't apply to college and her other visitors are sent to her for causing problems in class. She's well aware of my scholastic record and often refers to my high IQ with pride, regarding me as the smartest student in school, which is always embarrassing.

I sit down at her desk. It's cluttered with files and papers, knickknacks like a tiny plastic palm tree from Sanibel Island, and photos of her children, husband, and dog. She asks how she can help and I explain my plans.

"Charlene, you're still a junior," she reminds me.

"I know," I agree, "but you said it might be possible for me to graduate early. I'm taking mostly senior classes right now."

She checks my grades. "And you're doing extremely well. Even so, you're already a year younger than your classmates." Mrs. Roche looks at me. "Perhaps we can discuss this again at the end of the marking period?"

I'm disappointed. Seeing this, Mrs. Roche sighs. "Well, I suppose we can schedule your SAT tests at least." She picks up the phone, and after speaking to two people, arranges for me to take the exams in Brockport.

"And I'll help you with the application to Cavendish," she says, although we'll have to wait to submit it." Then she points out how expensive the tuition at Cavendish is. I explain that I've inherited money from my grandfather. Since the woman knows he's dead, having received notification of Blake's guardianship, she doesn't question my ability to pay. I also tell her that Mr. Brookman, my freshman English teacher, and Mrs. Kimbell have offered to write recommendations and that Mrs. Kimbell has asked her sister, who teaches at Cavendish Falls College, to put in a good word.

Mrs. Roche listens attentively and promises she'll take care of everything.

When I arrive home, I don't mention my afternoon investigations to Blake, who has finished the benches and is tapping down the lid on the can of stain.

"Charlie, I have something fantastic to tell you! I got a call this afternoon from a television producer. This guy wants to meet on Friday to discuss a weekly half-hour show…to be broadcast every Sunday morning."

"But what about our services?"

"Don't worry, we'll still do them. The show will be taped during the week."

I want to protest, but Blake is too wound up. All I say is, "I don't know," before he rattles on. "They want me to interview a different minister or a priest every week. You know, chat with him about his religious experiences and let him gab for ten minutes. Then we'll take questions from the audience, who will be carefully selected so we don't have any nuts in the crowd."

"I thought that's who would come to something like this." I'm partly serious and partly teasing him.

"Well, they'll screen the crowd as best they can," he replies, not paying attention to what I said. "Anyhow, we'll need you for the first show and to reappear every few weeks."

"But I have school!"

He stares at me in surprise. Clearly he's forgotten this detail. "Oh, yeah." He thinks on this for a minute. "Heck, I'm your guardian, right? So if I want to take you out of school for a few hours, I can."

"I don't want to get behind in class, Blake! Why don't you do the show by yourself?"

"Oh, come on, Charlie! I need you. Please? We're building on the success of the Glory Alleluia Chapel…your success. The producer wants to call the show 'The Oracle.'"

"And I'm an oracle? You're crazy!"

In response, Blake grins at me.

—

I receive special permission from the principal to go to the television studio so we can record our half-hour program. I feel like a first-class fool sitting in front of the huge camera. Blake, however, has swallowed Hollywood lock, stock, and barrel. He's glib and smooth and sweet. His eyes glow with excitement, and he looks as handsome as a movie star, especially because he's cut his hair shorter and looks less like Wild Bill Cody.

When we're finished with the television ordeal, I can't wait to get out of the building and am upset that I must return in two weeks for a repeat performance. As much as I hate all this, the money is impressive. Week by week as our income steadily increases, I've hidden cash in the secret recesses of my bedroom closet. Yesterday, when Blake was at the store purchasing new shoes and a suit, I walked out to my willow tree and hid five-hundred dollars in the Russian Imperial Tea Cookie box, as well as the Buick's title and house deed that I brought to Lambeau Hastings earlier in the afternoon for the official switch of ownership. I sprinkled leaves and dried grass over the burial and erased my footprints, although I was careful to step on logs, rocks, and firm tufts of grass as I walked near the burial spot. It's highly doubtful Blake possesses any cowboy scouting skills, but there's no point in taking any chances.

- 28 -

I slave away on religious sermons and on my homework, determined to keep my grades perfect, and make Blake do the shopping and cooking and his own laundry. He still has time to invent new miracles and other staged shenanigans such as bringing a poor hobo kid to a service. He found Lucy wandering around town, footsore and filthy, and hauled her in front of the congregation so they could see how their weekly donations were rescuing poor unfortunate children. During the service, Lucy went upstairs to bathe and get dressed in new clothes and shoes that Blake had purchased. When she returned, everyone was ecstatic with the new, scrubbed-clean, pretty child. She then had to get dirty again and dress in her rags for Shows II and III. Afterward, Blake wanted to drop her at the bus station with $20, but I was already upset about his callous behavior and insisted she was too young and mentally slow to be on the street. He took her to the orphanage instead, but I refused to go near the place and felt like a gigantic hypocrite. Lucy didn't seem to care one way or the other.

On Monday, when I return from school, Blake's truck is in the driveway, but as I come around the stand of willow trees by the Hooch Shop, I see six or seven people hunkered on lawn chairs and blankets in the middle of Mr. and Mrs. Krychek's zinnias.

I sneak around and enter through the kitchen door. Blake isn't in the house. Presumably, because he can't get the hang of my school schedule, he's out with pick and shovel on a treasure hunt. He hasn't given up the search for Grandpa's fortune. Fresh mud has been on his boots several times, which I now find more amusing than upsetting.

I walk into the chapel and peek out the door. None of the squatters is known to me, though it's possible some attended one of the services yesterday. I decide the damage is already done to the garden and go upstairs to await Blake's return. When he shows up, I make him dress in collar and clerical shirt so he can look authoritative as he shoos them away.

"They wanted to see the miracles," he explains to me later.

"I don't like this, Blake. Not one bit."

He is deep in thought and doesn't answer at first. "Well, maybe we can get some mileage out of their interest," he says, half to himself. "Hmm. We could open the chapel a few afternoons a week. After you're home from school."

"Oh, no! I have assignments to do and moonshine to sell. And I don't want a bunch of weird people traipsing in and out of the chapel. No, Blake. No afternoon openings."

I might as well talk to the wall. Green dollar signs are shining in his blue eyes.

"Come on, Charlie. I'll take care of everything."

"No, you won't. I'll get stuck with this somehow."

"Let's just try it next week. We'll announce visiting hours on Tuesday and Thursday."

I give him a frosty look and fold my arms across my chest. "No."

All through dinner, Blake cajoles and wheedles, suggesting a slide bolt on the interior door in addition to the regular lock in order to protect the house, and to split the take with me even if I don't participate. The latter is a whopper fib because we both know he'll pocket most of the money.

Worn out, I finally give up. "Okay, but I'm not lifting one finger to help. And you can call Mrs. Krychek and tell her what happened to her garden."

"But Charlie—"

"That's the deal."

———

After the success of our half-hour television show, the radio broadcasts, the newspaper articles, and the neighbor-to-neighbor transmission of information, we're overrun on Sunday, even with three services. People are left standing outside so I open the chapel doors to let them hear. The Tuesday and Thursday openings are also packed with curiosity-seekers and rabid religionists arriving from more than fifty miles away, some carrying crosses to lean against the chapel, others sporting Jesus pins and hats. I hadn't realized the power and scope of radio and television until I witnessed the astonishing results of Blake's publicity program. And despite my stand about participating on weekdays, between the noise and the clamor for my presence, I usually make a brief appearance so people can stare at me and touch my hand. As soon as I'm able, I retreat to the Hooch Shop, but all this religious activity has an adverse effect on the moonshine business because our regulars are unable to make stealthy purchases with the hullabaloo nearby. I begin selling liquor after dinner, but this taxes my studying time and my courage since I don't enjoy going into Worm Heaven in the dark or walking out to the shed, which is partly surrounded by thick woods. Plus, from time to time, strange people are wandering about whenever their fervor or drunkenness is at such a pitch as to prompt a visit to the newfound shrine. The only advantage is that I'm selling Bibles as fast as I can order them, though you'd think everyone around these parts would already have one. What is most unbelievable is that some folks want me to autograph their Bibles as if I were the author.

Blake thinks all of this is funny. Sometimes, I see the ironic humor of a devout non-believer making a fortune at this religion business; other times I don't. I keep telling myself that the money will buy my freedom, a college education, and a new life, but mostly I feel terrible about what I'm doing and not particularly charitable toward those foolish enough to think I've been sent from the big guy in the sky. All in all, I'm so crazy busy that when Mr. Cossantino invites me to stomp the grapes, I refuse because I don't have time and it's no longer a proper activity.

—

In early October, I drive to Brockport for my college exams. I'm nervous as an aspen leaf twittering in a stiff gale. This is the most important test I've ever taken, and I'm also afraid of being caught in the Buick. It's necessary to drive myself, however, so that Blake doesn't know what I'm doing. Luckily, because it's Saturday morning, he's busy with miracle-creating, and I slip out, enjoying the crisp autumn air. Farm stands are piled high with red and yellow apples, orange pumpkins, and tan corn stalks. In some fields, the last crop of corn is being harvested; in others, the soil is being overturned for next year. The trees are wild with gold, orange, and red colors. Goldenrod is flourishing along the road's edge along with blue chicory.

The exams are hard, especially the math. After I finish and put my pencils in my pocketbook, my usual confidence is absent. I watch as the other students are picked up by their parents, everyone talking excitedly, hugging and kissing. Finally, I climb into the Buick and feel the weight of my future pressing down. I've done my best, but it may not be good enough.

Because I'm halfway to Rochester and I've outgrown everything we bought last spring, I drive into the city to buy clothes: more socks, shoes, skirts, blouses, jeans, and three bras because I've filled the old ones and then some. While I'm standing at the cash register, I see Mrs. Rees, the deputy's wife, in the sweater aisle. I finish paying the salesgirl and hightail it out the fire exit. Outside, I run to the car, thankful that I've escaped detection.

At a filling station, I get gas and a road map of New England so I can locate Cavendish Falls College. Then, I drive home on back roads, hoping no one will see me. As I carry my bags of clothes upstairs, I do so quickly so Blake won't know I've been on a spending spree.

—

My birthday arrives on Saturday, October 22, 1960. I'm fifteen years old and feel much older. It's hard to believe a year has passed since I've seen my parents and harder to understand why Mama has been gone so long without writing me or coming home. I spend an hour working on a short story but am too sad to concentrate. Mid-morning, I walk to the lake's edge and stand there, compiling a list of wishes and trying to figure out how to make them come true. My life is up to me, I tell myself. I can't rely on anyone else.

After I return to the house, Blake is off gallivanting. In the mail, I find a small magazine wrapped in brown paper. The *Erie Journal* and my first published story! After a quick glance at the contents, I flip to my page. Little shudders of excitement travel through me when I see my name in print. What a perfect birthday present! But how sad that Grandpa isn't here to see the journal and to share this moment! And how disappointing that Mama isn't, either. I sit down in the living room and read, feeling elated and dejected at the same time.

When I've read through my piece, I lean back in Grandpa's chair to savor the experience. A minute later, I smell fresh cigar smoke. Maybe he's with me after all? I dismiss this thought as wishful, sigh, tuck the journal under my arm, and continue to sort through the house bills, finding another happy surprise: the five-thousand dollar life insurance check made out to me. I'm rich!

My first impulse is to deposit the money in my checking account, but Blake, as my legal guardian, might withdraw it by forging my signature. I could open another account at a different bank, somewhere out of town, but I'm not sure this is possible without Blake. I stew on this conundrum for a bit and decide it's safest to hide the check underground in the cookie tin and keep my checkbook in the secret compartment of my closet.

When Blake rolls in, I tell him the life insurance check arrived and that I rode my bike into town and deposited it in my checking account. This lie might stymie him from demanding the check outright and give me an opportunity to see if he tries to steal the money, which will give me a better notion how trustworthy Blake is. As I report the deposit, his brow furrows for a brief second, then he catches himself and proclaims this is exciting news and congratulates me. Because he doesn't know the ins and outs of the banking regulations regarding minors and their accounts any better than I do, I hope he won't try to withdraw money without my checkbook or account number or without me being present. If he does, Mr. Dryfuss would sense something was fishy; if Blake requested a large amount that wasn't there, Mr. Dryfuss would probably call the sheriff, especially because Blake is a stranger.

"How about we go to dinner to celebrate your birthday and the arrival of the life insurance money?" Blake asks.

I hesitate to tell him about the story because the pleasure feels private, and Blake had no connection to its creation or my writing. But there is no one else except him and Mrs. Kimbell who will care.

"And my first real publication," I reply.

"What?"

I go to my room, return with the *Erie Journal*, and hand it to him.

"Gosh, Charlie! You wrote this? Why, my goodness! I'm so very proud of you!" He reads the opening paragraph and looks up. "I bet your grandfather would be busting his buttons over this."

I nod and feel sad again.

"Well, shucks, we'll go out and have a fine old time!" Blake says, giving me a hug.

I offer to pay for our meal, but he insists that I should be treated on such a special day. Then he suggests I dress in Mama's clothes so that people are less likely to recognize me. Wherever we go in Butztown, people come up to talk, even laying hands on me if they need a holy fix. Blake also says if I appear older, I can have a cocktail or a glass of wine with dinner. We go upstairs and he begins to rummage around Mama's closet. Most of her clothes are tailored and sedate, but this is because she took the flamboyant ones with her, including some hats whose feathers were bright as a parrot's.

After flipping through the hangers, Blake hands me a black dress. I agree with his choice and carry it to my room. Because I've grown to nearly five-foot-eight inches, I'm now taller than Mama, and the hem rides above my knee, which Blake observes immediately when I step into the hall to show him the dress.

"You sure look fine, Charlie!" he says.

—

I direct Blake to Delmondo's Grill on the western outskirts of Rochester, a nice restaurant where my parents brought me six years ago when I received my first straight-A report card. After that, they became adjusted to my perfect grades and didn't bother, or something else took top billing, which frequently happened as Mama became obsessed with increasingly lunatic projects.

The interior of the restaurant is dark, with drippy candles in green wine bottles, red-and-white checked tablecloths, and high-backed booths that enclose us in a wooden embrace. The dining room smells of charcoal from the grill and cigarette smoke and beer. Blake orders a bottle of Pleasant Valley champagne. The waitress hesitates, giving me the once-over.

"Dear, I hope champagne is what you prefer," Blake says, leaning toward me as if we were a courting couple.

"Yes, I think so," I reply, "to start."

This charade amuses us and convinces the waitress that I'm a legitimate drinker. After she goes off with our order for wine, two grilled T-bone steaks medium rare, baked potatoes, and salads with Russian dressing, we start to laugh as we watch her hip-swinging departure. When she returns with rolls and the champagne, we're more or less under control, but just barely.

The waitress pours some bubbly. Blake clinks my wine glass. "Happy birthday and congratulations on your story!"

"Thanks," I say, enjoying the champagne. "Having the stories published means more to me than anything." I explain how I want to concentrate on my writing, but after a few minutes, Blake's attention wanders. Although he compliments me on my success, he says my short stories and sermons are equally good, as if they're the same thing. To me, they're as different as lovemaking is to prostitution.

"Charlie," he says, when his enthusiasm for our "business" surges past his politeness, "we're going to be famous. Why, heck, I think we already are!" He takes a drink.

"Why don't you do all of the television and radio shows by yourself?" I tell him.

"Because you're the star." His soft lips form a smile.

I shake my head and disagree. "You're the handsome guy they want to see."

He gives me a searching look, in part agreeing with what I've said, then his expression slides into a close examination of my face. "I don't think you know how pretty you are."

I take a large swallow of champagne, my second glass. He's right. I don't know and to me it doesn't matter. I grew up with my mother absorbing the limelight, mostly because of her crazy behavior but also because she could be radiant if she wasn't down in the coal pits of hell.

"When you're all got up like this," he continues, "you look like a million bucks."

His pale eyes glitter with an intensity similar to when we discussed the television and radio shows. Now, they seem afire because of me. I'm not prepared for this switch and don't know what to say.

"Charlie, I wish you were older." He sighs and looks off into space, as if he's frustrated.

When his gaze moves away, the room goes cold. "Blake, what do you mean?" This slips out before I can stop it.

His eyes are on me again. "You know what I mean. You feel it, too."

I'm rescued by the arrival of dinner: silver platters with steaks that hang over triangles of toast, slices of red tomatoes tucked beside potatoes. Blake orders another bottle of champagne. He's had a bit more than I've had, but I'm feeling a little high and decide to slow down.

He pours bubbly in our glasses, drinks half of his, and refills. "Sometimes I think we should just say the hell with things. What does age mean anyway?"

This is rhetorical so I get busy cutting my steak. Blake lets his sit because he's so intent on the point he's trying to make. "Why can't we do what we want? Who's around to find out?"

I'm surprised. He's staring at me, waiting for a response. "No one, I guess." This was not what I meant to say.

He grins. "Well, then. I take that as a maybe?"

I chew on my steak and think I might choke. Here's this beautiful guy who says he's attracted to me. Any girl in her right mind would swoon and shout "yes." But I'm not any girl, and whether my mind is right is a matter of some debate. As we lock eyes, I feel the heat of his gaze and don't trust myself to answer. My face feels hot and red.

Blake sees my reaction, smiles like he's just pulled a con, and picks up his knife and fork.

- 29 -

Blake keeps drinking and giving me winks and private smiles so that by the time dessert rolls around, he's drunk and heated up. When the waitress clears the dinner plates, he takes my hand in his and traces the lines on my palm like he's not just seeing my future but intending on creating it. As always, I veer back and forth between two islands of thought: besides the fact that he's blindingly gorgeous, I owe Blake a lot, but he's probably using me, and, if I allow myself to fall in love, he could use me in the sexual department also. There's no doubt I'm attracted to him, but I was attracted to Eli and that was a disaster.

When Blake's apple pie à la mode and my chocolate sundae arrive, I'm relieved to have my hand back, though he returns it with reluctance. He pours himself the last of the champagne, which he swallows quickly, as he has most of the second bottle. I've been drinking water for some time, figuring one of us better stay more or less sober.

The chocolate sundae is too much after the heavy dinner. Blake doesn't finish his pie, either, and after I talk him out of a brandy, he pays the bill. Even without the brandy, when he stands, he's in no condition to operate an automobile.

As we walk to the parking lot, Blake embraces me. I tell him I'd like to drive.

"Hey, you don't even have a learner's permit," he says.

"I know how. Just give me the keys."

He laughs happily like this is a great lark and roots around in his pocket until he finds them in his jacket. "Here you go. I guess if you're old enough for one thing," he gives me a kiss that smells of after-dinner mints from the restaurant, "then you're old enough to take us home."

I'm relieved he's so agreeable until I realize he'll have two hands free while mine will be busy with the driving. He holds the door and I slide into his truck, scooting the seat forward. As he approaches the passenger side, he stumbles and steadies himself on the fender. After he gets in, I start the ignition. I'm not used to the clutch and shift on the Ford, so I begin cautiously. Pretty soon

I have the hang of the gears and am enjoying myself. Once Blake sees that I'm okay, he comes closer and encircles my neck with his hand. I glance at him, which he takes as permission to stroke my skin. Goosebumps rise but I force my attention on the road. Then he leans over and kisses me below the ear. My arms go weak and I can't think straight.

"Blake," I whisper, "wait until we get home." This sounds like I'm promising something. Mostly, I'm trying to stall until I can sort things out.

He continues kissing me until he remembers I'm an inexperienced driver or else—as I hope—that he has come to his senses.

Forty minutes later, I turn into the drive, past the willows that appear almost white in the moonlight as does the pile of leaves skirting their trunks. I park the Ford in front of the house and immediately Blake pulls me to him, his mouth on mine. His lips are incredibly soft, and despite the alcohol, he is gentle. We kiss and touch, but eventually the stick shift gets in the way, and he steps out of the car. I'm dizzy with fear and excitement as he takes my hand. We walk toward the house, our fingers entwined. At the foot of the porch steps, Blake stops and we begin kissing again. He pulls me tight to him, slides his hand down my back, and begins to hitch up my dress. I try to back away, but his arms are strong.

"Come on, Charlie," he whispers. "I've thought about this for so long. You have, too."

"No, I haven't," I say, though I'm not telling the truth.

He laughs. "I don't believe you."

I press my hands against his chest. "Please, Blake, we can't." Even though I'm protesting, I want him all the same and he knows it. He continues lifting my dress. The cool air makes me shiver. I feel my body respond to his, but my mind is screaming this is wrong. "Blake, no!"

Just then, the front door opens and the screen slaps loudly in the quiet night.

A man's deep voice says, "What the hell are you doing?"

Blake releases me and together we stare as a rifle barrel emerges from the darkness. At first, I think it's the sheriff. Then I realize the man is my father, and he's holding Blake's Winchester.

"Oh, my God!" I cry.

Blake drifts away from me, retreating down the path, his hands held up in front of him. "I didn't mean anything."

"Yeah. You did, you bastard!" my father shouts. He's slurring his words, staggering as he comes forward onto the porch.

"Blake, the gun isn't loaded," I tell him.

"Shit! Yes, it is! I put more bullets in."

My father raises the gun to his shoulder. "Eileen, get over here!"

Suddenly, I realize my father thinks I'm Mama because I'm wearing her clothes and have grown so much since he's seen me. Blake figures this out, too, turns, and sprints for the woods.

"No!" My scream is obliterated by the retort of the rifle. The first bullet wings into the trees as does the second. I dive to the ground as my father fires again, this time hitting Blake in the back. A fourth shot slams into his body, pitching him forward into the bushes. The Winchester carries four bullets in its magazine unless one was in the chamber. I hold my breath, praying that he's out of bullets and that in his drunken fury my father doesn't turn the gun on me. Still aiming at Blake, my father pulls the trigger again and nothing happens so he tosses the gun on the porch and starts to descend the stairs, missing the top step. He tumbles downward until he lies a few feet from me.

"Oh!" he cries. "Eileen, help!"

Slowly, I come to my feet. My legs shake as I stare at my father, who is face up and furious, spitting epithets through clenched teeth and holding his right elbow.

"Jesus Christ! Get over here, woman!"

Ignoring him, I run to the edge of the forest where Blake lies on the snapped stalks of two young sassafras trees, whose orange scent is faint on the air. I can't see blood on his black jacket, but he isn't moving. I've seen this kind of stillness before and am terrified.

"Blake?" I whisper.

No answer. I step to the right of his body and pull on his arm until he faces the sky. When his coat falls away, there is a large crimson stain on his white shirt.

"Blake?" A moan rises from somewhere inside me and un-coils into a strange sound. I feel like the bullets pierced my chest. I press my hand against myself, but the pain doesn't stop. Above, the dark trees seem to spin like a sudden squall has arisen, but then I realize I'm the one who is spinning. Feeling like I might fall, I kneel on the ground, inhale and swallow hard against the dizzi-ness, the shock. My mind freezes. I can't think.

By the house, my father yells, "Charlie? Is that you?"

I don't answer. All I can do is stare at Blake, at his beautiful face. I lean down and touch his lips, his cheeks; note the expression in his pale eyes, eyes that don't see me. I memorize each feature so I won't forget. Tears sting and spill. A deep sob shudders my body. I grip the lapels of Blake's jacket, trying desperately to hold on to him.

"Blake, don't leave me. Please!" I whisper that I love him and have since the first time I saw him. But he can't hear the words, words I should have said earlier while we were kissing in the truck. If I hadn't been such a coward, he would have died knowing how I felt. I can only hope he understood because I can't imagine dying without someone loving you. I take his hand and fold his cold fingers around mine, but it's too late to give or receive comfort.

I stay beside him until I sense he is truly gone, until his lifelessness is unbearable. Then I rise unsteadily, lifting my eyes to observe the dark forest and the jagged pieces of night sky that shift between the branches. As if from a great distance, I become aware of my father's moans. I hesitate, wanting to preserve the last connection between Blake and myself, but my father's ugly curses intrude. I turn toward him. He's twisting in pain, demanding help. All I can think is that he is a murderer, that he killed Blake, that I hate this cruel man who is shouting at me.

In an instant, my grief fires into rage. My fists clench. I want to pound my father into the earth.

As I come nearer, he struggles to focus on me. "Charlie?"

"Why? Why did you kill him?"

He stops swearing, sensing my anger. "Hell, I don't know. Thought you was Eileen," he mutters, "but I forgot...that dumb broad's in the loony bin. Goddamn her...useless piece of—"

"You bastard!" I kick him in the chest as hard as I can. His head snaps back and he flattens against the ground. Again and again, I kick his body—especially his broken arm—and then lean over and punch his face—a blow for all the times he hit me as a child, for the bullets he fired at Blake.

Finally, his muscles go limp. When I realize he's unconscious, I stop, though I yearn to hurt him more. Gulping air, I stand over my father, fury crackling like lightning through every nerve. My head feels like it's exploding. I'm shaking, tears are flying down my cheeks. I run into the house and slam the door, lean against it until I catch my breath, terrified my father will come after me. As I try to turn the door lock, I see its broken. Probably my father jimmied it because he lost his keys or couldn't find them in his drunken stupor. I slide the brass bolt instead, and after a few minutes of listening, I run upstairs to my mother's room and remove her clothes, touching the dress, wishing she would suddenly, miraculously inhabit it. What would Mama feel about Blake's death and about what Daddy did? I may never know because I may never see her again.

This realization fills me with panic. I want to escape, to find my mother, but I have no idea where she is. I rush out of the room and into the hall, desperate for help, for someone to take charge. I shout for Grandpa, for Blake, and for my mother. The silence is intolerable and loud. I stand there, whirling and disoriented, and consider calling Billy Shackrack. I hurry into my room and throw on a sweatshirt and jeans, but my resolve evaporates as I begin crying again. I plunge into bed, pulling the covers tightly over me, wanting to disappear into the darkness.

It is night when I awake, but the crows are beginning to chatter and the sky is lighter. Frightened, I jump out of bed and run downstairs to look through the window. My father is still sprawled on the walk below the porch. Blake's body lies out of sight in the bushes. I go into the kitchen and scrub my face and hands, noting the vivid bruises discoloring my knuckles. Taking a deep breath, I call the police.

—

The patrol car tears down the driveway, wailing its siren so loud that it scares off the crows and wakes my father, whom I'm watching through the living room window. I unbolt the door and stand on the porch as Sheriff Shackrack strides up the path. My father raises himself, gingerly holding his arm and wincing with pain. His face is caked with dried blood which has dripped onto his pale blue shirt. He rolls a tongue around in his mouth and scowls at the approaching policeman, who is accompanied by Herbert Hiller, one of Shackrack's deputies. A second police car is racing past the Hooch Shop with an ambulance in its wake.

My father turns to look at me with red eyes, shakes his head as if he can't remember what happened. "I just came home to wish you a happy birthday, Charlie," he says in a weak voice that almost sounds wistful.

I stare at him in disbelief, though for a split second I'm startled that he remembered my birthday. Then all of his other atrocities extinguish this glimmer of parental caring. I want to kick him into unconsciousness again.

My father glances at Shackrack and says, "It was an accident.

All I saw was that guy Blake kissing my wife." He turns to me. "I thought you were Eileen. I was drunk." When I don't answer, his head falls on his chest. "Once he run off and left Eileen, she went over the edge. It just finished her." A flicker of anger lights his eyes and his unshaved, gaunt face tightens. "It's all that guy's fault, Charlie. He's a bad one, he is. He had it coming. I'm glad I shot him."

My face burns. I want to scream a thousand things at him, to protest his beatings, drunkenness, desertion, and every rotten thing he ever said. I step down off the porch to the sidewalk. In an icy voice, I say, "She's not your wife, and I'm no longer your daughter." My hands tighten into fists.

Seeing that I'm about to explode, Shackrack comes over to me. "Take it easy, Charlie."

I look up at the tall policeman and hate him, too. Then I realize he's on my side. He even gives me a small smile. "Your father just confessed to murder. He won't bother you any more."

I stand there in silence, glaring at my father. Sheriff Shackrack spies the Winchester and checks that it's empty. He squints at my father, concentrating revulsion in his glance. "You always were a useless son-of-a-bitch, Jack." He hands the rifle to Hiller, who takes it to the patrol car.

My father bristles at Shackrack's words but is in too much discomfort to fight. Shackrack snorts at him and looks at me. "Charlie? Where's the body?"

I point to the bushes. The sheriff nods and tells the two other policemen to escort my father to the car. Just before they walk him away, my father steps toward me.

"Charlie, please, I'm sorry. I've always loved you."

I've never heard my father say he loves me. I've also never heard him apologize. Momentarily, I'm stunned by both statements but am unable to react.

My father waits for a response, and when none comes, he allows himself to be led toward the patrol car.

Sheriff Shackrack pats me on the shoulder. Then he crosses the driveway into the edge of the forest, hunkers down, parts the foliage so he can see better, and examines Blake before calling for the ambulance personnel. After Blake's body is placed on a stretcher and covered with a dark blue blanket, Sheriff Shackrack returns and suggests we go into the house so he can take a statement in addition to what I've told him on the telephone.

Once in the living room, I excuse myself to post a sign on the outside chapel doors: "The Glory Alleluia Chapel Services Are Cancelled Today and Forever." I regard this notice with sad satisfaction before returning to the sheriff, who is sitting on the sofa. I take a seat in Grandpa's chair and am assailed by the memories of an earlier visit by Shackrack and how frightened I was. I look at him with his bristly hair and massive body and don't feel the same fear as I did then.

"Sheriff, thanks for your help," I begin. This sounds formal so I add, "I was pretty scared."

The policeman nods. "A lot has happened to you."

"Yes, sir, it has."

He allows a few minutes of silence, then says, "Now, tell the truth. Is Eileen home for real this time? Did she return with your father?"

I recall that I told him Mama was home already. Another lie probably won't fly, but I'm so afraid of what Shackrack will do if he thinks I'm alone that I can't think of an alternative. "No, Sheriff, she didn't. But she'll be here tomorrow afternoon."

Shackrack studies me carefully. "Eileen's been gone for a long while. She's really coming back?"

I picture Mama in an asylum, locked up forever. The enormity of this loss chokes me up. I swallow hard. "That's what she said on the phone."

"Well, I'm glad to hear the news. I'm sure you're looking forward to seeing her."

The sheriff has misinterpreted my emotional response. I also note a hopeful glint in his eyes. This reaction perplexes me until I realize that with my father in jail my mother will be on her own and available. Billy Shackrack always had a sweet spot for Mama.

"Yes, sir," I reply, fighting the urge to tell the sheriff the truth and asking him to find my mother in Arkansas or wherever she is. Even though the sheriff is being nice, I have too much at risk to trust him. "I can manage here overnight until Mama arrives."

He's still contemplating private thoughts. When he takes in what I've said, he replies, "I know you're very capable, Charlie, but I can't allow that. You being a minor and all."

"I know, but I'll be fine. I have food and everything. And I'd like to straighten up the house for my mother...you know, change the sheets because Blake has been sleeping in her room. If I have a problem, I promise to call you right away."

"I'm sorry, but I don't have any choice."

"I'll call Mr. Carter who rents from us. He'll come by or I can go stay with him overnight."

The sheriff hesitates. Then his walkie-talkie starts sputtering. He stands and goes into the kitchen, listens, gives some instructions. "Yeah, fine. I'll be there in about half an hour." He signs off and returns to the living room.

"Okay, Charlie, give me your account of last night." He takes a pen from his pocket and clicks it. "Start from the beginning."

We review what happened in detail. I even explain that I locked the door and was too much in shock to call the police for several hours. It's a huge relief not to tell any more falsehoods except omitting that I drove Blake's truck home and drank champagne at the restaurant. I was also a little vague about who Blake was, though I did volunteer that he was Mama's boyfriend at one point, which is why my father shot him.

When I finish and Shackrack has asked all of his questions, he tells me he has to go to the station. "My guys will be leaving soon because this is a pretty clear case with a confession," he says. "But you know I can't leave you here. I'll drive you over to the Carter place."

"No, that's okay. I'll ride my bike."

He shakes his head. "I'm not comfortable with that, Charlie."

"Sheriff, I'll call if I need anything."

He sighs. "You promise to go to the Carters' house?"

"Yes, sir, I will."

"Well, all right. Mr. Carter can take you to school in the morning. I'll stop by tomorrow afternoon to check that Eileen is here. And you call me if you need anything." He squeezes my arm and smiles.

When Sheriff Shackrack walks out the front door, the house is horribly quiet. Through the window, I watch as the wind whisks brown leaves off the oak trees. I feel like I'm floating in the breeze myself, untethered to anything or anyone. Even though I've just recounted my story to the sheriff, I go over what happened again, recalling every moment of my dinner with Blake, the kisses, the emotion, the gunshots, and my father saying that Mama was in an institution. I'm not surprised at this because she was becoming crazier with each passing year, with fewer normal periods. Perhaps this is why she left—so I wouldn't see how sick she was or because she didn't want to hurt me more than she already had. The news of her hospitalization means that it might be a long time before she's well, and that for the near future, probably until I'm an adult, there's no one who will ride in and rescue me. As terrible as this thought is, I've been hovering on the edge of this abyss ever since Grandpa died.

I go into the kitchen and drink a lot of orange juice and eat two pieces of toast to sop up the aftereffects of the champagne. My eyes feel red and gritty from alcohol and crying. I also don't like how I behaved with Blake last night, how the liquor weakened my determination to the point that I could have succumbed to his advances, and how his behavior changed under the influence, causing him to act in a manner he would have regretted.

Alcohol certainly didn't help my father, either. Through the years with him, whenever he had a bottle in his hand, all hell broke loose as the liquor fueled his abusiveness. It also sapped his ambition and kindness, what little there was. We had a few happy times, but not many, and those were when he was sober.

Grandpa was a heavy drinker, too, but he was never violent or mean. Even so, the alcohol might have watered down his scruples so that he could ignore the harm he was doing. As for myself, drinking is no better for me and can only lead to serious trouble. I don't want to be driven by a thirst that only gets increased by drinking more. On the spot, I pledge to quit my scotch-nipping and wine-sipping ways. I don't want to turn out like Daddy, with his blind rages and shiftless life. And after my physical attack on him last night, I worry that alcohol works on me like it does on him. I also don't want to continue the schemes and frauds instigated by Grandpa and carried on by Blake. I am not like them, I say to myself over and over. I am not.

I go upstairs. From my window, I see parishioners arriving for the services so I stand behind the curtain. When they notice the sign, they begin to talk among themselves and then finally leave. I run a hot shower and stand in it for a long time, trying to scour away what happened. Then I get dressed and pull two big Pullman suitcases from the closet.

- 30 -

On Monday morning, I visit Mrs. Roche, the guidance counselor. She's surprised to see me because I called earlier to explain why I wouldn't be in school and that my mother was returning in a few hours. I ask her for my completed Cavendish Falls College application as well as copies of my grades, tests, and the letters of recommendation written by my two English teachers.

"But why do you need everything right now?" she asks.

The question requires almost more energy to answer than I have. I force myself to sit straight in my chair and say, "Because I'm going with my mother to Vermont to see my guardian's family...for the funeral. Then we're visiting the college, and I'll give them my application in person." This lie is not one of my finest, but I'm too tired to improve on it.

Mrs. Roche appears to doubt my story. If I were her, I would, too, because she's heard all sorts of tales about my parents, grandfather, and guardian. She sits behind her desk, trim in a white starched blouse and charcoal suit, frowning slightly. I worry she'll refuse, but then she stands, walks over to the sand-colored filing cabinets and pulls my folder. Without a word, she goes into the secretarial office next door to copy my papers on the new Haloid Xerox machine.

When she returns, Mrs. Roche smiles and hands me a complete set of my files in a manila folder printed with the school's name and address. "There you are."

"Thank you," I reply. "And could you send them my SAT results when they come in?"

"Well, yes, I could...but aren't you rushing things a little? It's fine if you want to visit the school because you have an opportunity, but usually students don't interview until the summer before their senior year." Mrs. Roche scrutinizes me. "You wouldn't be considering early graduation, would you?" She folds her hands on top of her desk, as if she intends on blocking such a move.

I remain silent. We stare at each other for a long minute.

" I just want to see the campus," I tell her, trying to arrange a pleasant look on my face.

Mrs. Roche narrows her eyes but sees that I'm determined. "I guess we can discuss matters when you return, Charlene. I assume you'll be absent from school this week?"

"Yes. I'll be back next Monday. Thanks."

I leave her office, go to my hall locker, empty it, and walk to Mrs. Kimbell's office to wait for the end of her class. By the time the bell rings, I'm feeling lightheaded and teary again, yet resolved not to cry.

Like Mrs. Roche, my English teacher isn't expecting me, but she takes my arm, leads me into her room, and closes the door.

"Charlene, we heard what happened. Are you all right?"

"Yes, sort of." Seeing her, I feel the creep of tears and swallow hard. "Mrs. Kimbell, you've done so much...I don't want to ask for anything else, but there's no one else who can help." I concentrate on a gold rose pin on her lapel, hoping I can hold myself together.

Mrs. Kimbell removes some books from a chair. "Why don't you sit down and explain what's going on?"

We both take seats.

"Well, I was wondering if you could telephone your sister and tell her I'm coming to Vermont. I want to apply to Cavendish."

She looks at me, puzzled. "What? You have more than a year to graduation."

"Yes, ma'am, I do." I repeat what I told Mrs. Roche about the interview.

Mrs. Kimbell knows me better. "Charlene, I said Cavendish Falls was a unique and very independent school, but I seriously doubt they'd consider you without a diploma...if that's what you have in mind."

"No, I don't suppose they would," I agree, though that's exactly what I was hoping they would do. "But maybe they'll see me? I have my school files from Mrs. Roche."

"She gave them to you?" Mrs. Kimbell is mildly surprised.

"Yes, ma'am."

She considers this. "And I told you the place is very expensive, didn't I?"

I nod. "I've inherited money from my grandfather."

"It sounds like you've been thinking a lot about this," she says. "So how do you plan to get to Cavendish? Your father's in jail, isn't he? And your guardian is dead."

"I'll take a bus...this afternoon. One of my neighbors will drive me into Rochester."

"Are you going by yourself?"

I shrug. "I could call your sister when I arrive. I mean, if that would be okay?"

I can see that a lot of questions are crowding Mrs. Kimbell's mind. "I can't let you take a trip like that without an adult."

"I'll be fine. Don't worry."

"What about your mother?"

I could spin a version of the story I told the sheriff and Mrs. Roche, but another outright lie is too much to manage. "Daddy said she was still in Arkansas. I hope she'll return when she hears what happened."

"So you're all by yourself?"

I feel the pressure welling up inside. "I've always been alone. One way or the other." I exhale slowly. "I'll be okay. When I get back, I'll go to Sheriff Shackrack. He'll put me in some kind of foster home or orphanage, but..." I turn to stare at the blackboard, at the perfectly slanted strokes of Mrs. Kimbell's handwriting, trying not to cry.

Mrs. Kimbell places her hand on top of mine. "Don't you have some family?"

I shake my head.

"Oh, Charlene, I'm so sorry! I wish there was something I could do."

She is silent, then stands and walks to the window. I set my jaw and brush away a tear that sneaks down my cheek. When Mrs. Kimbell returns to her chair, I hazard a look at her. She sees the track of the tear and looks sad.

"You've been through so much, dear. I can't imagine how you've withstood it all." She sighs. "Against my better judgment, this is what I'll do." She removes her purse from a desk drawer and takes out a small address book. She writes her sister's name, address, and telephone number and then her own information on a sheet of paper and hands it to me. "I'll make arrangements for you to stay with Ella—that's my sister's name. You call and tell her what bus you're taking and she'll meet you. And when you return, Charlene, you come see me and we'll deal with everything together. Maybe Mrs. Roche and I can work out an arrangement of some kind so you can finish school next spring."

"Really?"

"Yes. I can't guarantee anything, but I'll give it my best shot." She gives me the kindest smile I've ever seen.

I don't know what to say. I realize she could get in all kinds of trouble by letting me go off on my own, especially because she's a teacher.

As if reading my thoughts, Mrs. Kimbell says, "I shouldn't be doing this. It's irresponsible and wrong. That said, you are the stubbornest child I've ever known and the smartest. I'm sure you would figure out a way to get to Cavendish whether I help you or not."

I'm so relieved that all I can do is grin at her.

"Now, you must promise to agree by these rules, or else we're going to the principal right now."

"I promise."

Students are milling around outside, waiting for the door to be opened for class. Mrs. Kimbell stands and gives me a kiss on the forehead and a hug.

"You take care of yourself, Charlene," she says. "And good luck at Cavendish. I'll see you in a few days."

—

Back at the house, I transport my suitcases to the Buick and most of my cash, the insurance check, my reference books, typewriter, pictures of Mama and Grandpa, the red-handled trowel, and the light box, which, though I've sworn off schemes, I might need to forge a signature or two, such as Blake's from his guardian papers. I also take Blake's tan Stetson and his black cowboy boots. Both are too big, but I want to have them with me.

I have no idea if I can produce a miracle at Cavendish Falls College or whether I'll be back within a week, but I want to be prepared to stay there. I think about Mrs. Kimbell's offer of help and figure that either way things will be okay.

After the car is crammed, I telephone to stop utility and phone services, lock the Hooch Shop and the house, leaving a note for Mama on the kitchen table and a note for the sheriff on the screen door, telling him I'll see him when I return. Although I hate doing it, I write a check to Doc Fairchild for half the money in Grandpa's estate account. Then I sit, watching the sunlight stream through the willow trees. The house feels like I've already left, like no one has cooked a meal in the kitchen or slept in a bed upstairs for months. Though I'm sad to leave because I'll lose the slender thread to Grandpa and Mama and Blake, it's time to go.

On the way out, I deposit the insurance check and visit Grandpa's various post offices to gather the last envelopes from the pyramid scheme, returning box keys to the postmasters. Then

I spread the map on the seat beside me and start the long journey east to Vermont.

Photo by Vicki DeVico

ABOUT THE AUTHOR

Laury A. Egan is the author of *Jenny Kidd*, a psychological suspense novel, and *Fog and Other Stories*, which was short-listed for a UK Saboteur Award. In addition to writing fiction, two full-length poetry collections, *Snow, Shadow, a Stranger* and *Beneath the Lion's Paw*, were issued by FootHills Publishing as well as a chapbook, *The Sea & Beyond*. Her work has appeared in over 35 literary journals and anthologies and has been nominated for two Pushcart Prizes, Best of the Web, and Best of the Net; a story was a finalist for the Glass Woman Prize. She lives on the coast of New Jersey.

why western NY?

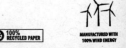